RISE

RISE

ELLEN GOODLETT

LITTLE, BROWN AND COMPANY
New York Boston

Little, Brown and Company
Hachette Book Group
1290 Avenue of the Americas, New York, NY 10104
Visit us at LBYR.com

Little, Brown and Company is a division of Hachette Book Group, Inc. The Little, Brown name and logo are trademarks of Hachette Book Group, Inc.

The publisher is not responsible for websites (or their content) that are not owned by the publisher.

First Edition: June 2019

Produced by Alloy Entertainment
1325 Avenue of the Americas
New York, NY 10019

Book design by Marcie Lawrence

Library of Congress Cataloging-in-Publication Data
Names: Goodlett, Ellen, author.
Title: Rise / Ellen Goodlett.
Description: First edition. | New York ; Boston : Little, Brown and Company, 2019. | Summary: "Sisters Akeylah, Ren, and Zofi are all a step closer to their dying father's throne, but their pasts continue to haunt them as their blackmailer threatens everyone and everything they hold dear"— Provided by publisher.
Identifiers: LCCN 2018038115| ISBN 9780316515351 (hardcover) | ISBN 9780316563635 (library ebook edition) | ISBN 9780316515344 (ebook edition)
Subjects: | CYAC: Inheritance and succession—Fiction. | Sisters—Fiction. | Kings, queens, rulers—Fiction. | Secrets—Fiction. | Extortion—Fiction. | Fantasy.
Classification: LCC PZ7.1.G6538 Ris 2019 | DDC [Fic]—dc23
LC record available at https://lccn.loc.gov/2018038115

ISBNs: 978-0-316-51535-1 (hardcover), 978-0-316-51534-4 (ebook)

Printed in the United States of America

LSC-C

10 9 8 7 6 5 4 3 2 1

✳

For Mom, my first editor, my role model, my biggest fan. I just want to say...I'm sorry for that cliffhanger. Hope this makes up for it.

✳

1

Akeylah

*U*nderstand *what I do to my enemies. You're one of them now.*
The words of the blackmailer's latest threat rang through Akeylah's mind, over and over, while she and Queen Rozalind hurried through Ilian Keep.

We were wrong about our aunt. Yasmin, King Andros's overbearing twin sister, wasn't the blackmailer. The countess, Sun accept her soul, never blackmailed or threatened Akeylah and her sisters. All Yasmin did was use the Vulgar Arts to forge a mental bond with her brother, the king.

Akeylah learned that when she suffered another vision. Another threat from the blackmailer, who was still out there. Still stalking this Keep.

She needed to find her sisters. At her side, Queen Rozalind

paused to catch her breath, and flashed Akeylah a look. "Are you going to tell me what any of this is about?"

"Not yet." Akeylah steered toward the nearest staircase as she mentally debated whether to make for Ren's or Zofi's suite first.

The mental bond Yasmin and Andros created meant Yasmin couldn't have known about the girls' treasonous secrets. Otherwise King Andros would know, too. And if her father the king ever learned what Akeylah did—that *she* was the source of the curse burning through his bloodstream, killing him from the inside out—he'd have her executed without a second thought.

The king's condition had only worsened since Countess Yasmin's death. He'd been bedridden since her funeral. Akeylah and her sisters told the Keep he was in mourning, but that excuse would only hold up for so long. Soon people would find out that more than his sister's death was ailing him. Soon the curse Akeylah planted in his veins would take his life.

And then Yasmin's murder wouldn't be the only one within this Keep.

Murder.

Up until a few moments ago, Akeylah had been certain Yasmin leaped from the sky gardens of her own accord. She assumed the countess couldn't live with the guilt of Andros learning she'd hidden his daughters' secrets from him, or how she'd blackmailed his heirs.

But now, Yasmin's fall from the towers looked a lot more sinister.

Did the blackmailer push her?

A shiver ran through Akeylah's body at the memory of the blackmailer's latest vision. They'd forced an image of Akeylah's abusive stepfather into her mind, used him to threaten her. But threats were one thing. Could the blackmailer have escalated? Were they willing to kill someone as powerful as Yasmin?

If so, who would they turn their sights on next?

I have to talk to my sisters.

"Akeylah." Rozalind panted behind her. Only then did Akeylah realize she'd been practically sprinting, her feet guiding her toward Ren's chambers on autopilot. Ren, the put-together sister. Ren, the one who had the most experience with the vipers that infested this Keep. She'd know what to do. "If you don't want to tell me what's happening, at least tell me how I can help," Rozalind said through labored breaths.

Akeylah paused halfway up the ash tower steps to consider. "Can you go to Zofi's chambers and fetch her? Ask her to meet me in Ren's rooms. We need to talk."

Rozalind climbed close enough to reach for Akeylah's hand, and Akeylah caught the queen's, with only the barest glance at the empty stairwell around them. Rozalind squeezed her fingertips gently. "Are you certain you're all right?" the queen asked, voice pitched low. "One moment you were on the floor convulsing, the next you're sprinting out of the library, yelling that you need to find your sisters. I'm worried about you, Akeylah. You won't tell me what's going on." Roz's gaze bored into hers, a gaze that would be so easy, so simple to get lost in.

Akeylah's heart wilted. She moved down a stair, onto the same step as Rozalind. With the queen in heels, she stood a few inches taller than Akeylah. But it was Rozalind who seemed smaller now, shrunken with worry. Akeylah cupped her cheek. Leaned in to press a single, lingering kiss to her mouth. "I promise I'll explain everything soon," she whispered. Then, conscious of the open halls around them, she disentangled her hand from Rozalind's.

Akeylah resumed her climb, hurrying toward Ren's rooms. It wasn't until she reached the top step and turned down a side corridor that she heard the answering clack of Rozalind's heels beginning to descend the stairs in the other direction.

Unease churned in her stomach. She wanted to reassure the queen that everything would be all right. But how could she say that, when she didn't believe it herself?

Understand what I do to my enemies. You're one of them now. The blackmailer had sounded different this time. Angry enough to kill, perhaps the same way they'd felt when they murdered Yasmin...

She drew up outside of Florencia's door and banged on it. "Ren!" She pressed an ear to the wood. Listened for sounds of life inside. She heard a rustling, a soft inhalation, like a gasp. Worried, Akeylah grasped the doorknob. It turned easily in her hand, and she threw the door open, just as a figure sat straight up in bed, hair a mess.

For a split second, Akeylah thought it was Ren. Her hair was the same color, and she had that oh-so-Kolonyan regal nose. But then Akeylah noticed this girl's wider face, higher brow, wider-set eyes. Not to mention her clothes, the kind of gown serving maids wore.

Akeylah's face flushed. "I'm sorry, I didn't mean to interrupt."

The girl, for her part, looked even more horrified and embarrassed than Akeylah. She flung herself out of the bed, straightening her gown, grabbing the covers. "No, *I'm* sorry, ah, my lady. I didn't...I mean, I wasn't..." Between her bleary eyes and the bags underneath, not to mention the mussed bed she was now hurriedly remaking, Akeylah could guess what the maid had been doing. It must be exhausting to serve ladies in this Keep. She'd need to sneak in rest where she could.

"It's all right, really." Akeylah spread her hands, palms up, to put the girl at ease. "I was just looking for my sister Florencia."

The girl's hands stilled. "Ren?"

The use of the nickname stirred Akeylah's memory. Of course. Ren had served downstairs, must have friends among the maids.

Meanwhile, the girl's gaze darted past Akeylah, toward the windows. The sun outside cast a long shadow across Ren's hardwood floor. "She told me I could rest here while she went to the baths. I must have dozed off...But she ought to be back soon. That was only half an hour ago at most."

"Where are the baths?" Akeylah asked, tone sharper than she intended.

The girl tilted her head. Considered Akeylah for a moment. "I'll walk you down there," she said finally. "It's a bit tricky to find on the first go."

They strolled out of the chamber together. After a moment's silence, the girl spoke up again. "I'd, um...I'd appreciate it if you didn't mention to anyone about me lying down on the job. It's just, Ren and I have an understanding, and—"

5

"No need to explain yourself to me. Honestly," Akeylah added when the girl flashed her a doubtful glance. "I'm Akeylah, by the way. Did you work with Ren? I mean... before all this."

"Audrina." She bowed, shrinking in on herself in a way Akeylah recognized all too well. "And yes. Ren and I worked together as ladies' maids, before she found out about her heritage."

"Well, it's lovely to meet you, Audrina. And I completely understand why you'd need a break; I had a difficult enough time serving my own family back at home. I can't imagine what it's like to serve so many noblewomen here, especially given how... ah..."

"Finicky they can be?" Audrina supplied with a shy smile.

Akeylah returned it. "I was going to say spoiled."

"If they look spoiled to *you*, my lady, imagine how they seem to us lowly maids." Audrina hesitated, eyes wide again. "Begging your pardon, my lady, if I speak out of turn."

"Of course not." Akeylah winced. "You're right, I can't fathom what it must be like for you here. I can only say I sympathize. My father... Well, he treated me like something even worse than a servant. Like an abomination."

Audrina flashed her a curious look. "Mine too," she finally replied. Then she reached for a door. "The baths are through here, my lady."

Akeylah tailed her into the narrow room. At first, it took a moment for the scene within to make sense. All she saw was billowing steam, thick and humid in the blindingly white room. Then enough steam cleared for her to see, and her heart dropped.

Two figures resolved through the mist. One at the edge of the bath, prone, and the other in the midst of tugging the first from the water.

"Well, don't just stand there!" the second figure barked, and Akeylah recognized the girl Ren was always feuding with in the dining hall. Sarella.

"Do something," Sarella snapped, and only then did Akeylah truly process what was happening.

Only then did she see her sister, clad in nothing but a strip of modesty cloth, spiky short hair plastered to her inert face.

Ren.

"Call the menders," Akeylah ordered to Audrina, whose jaw had gone slack with shock. The shout seemed to rouse her, and Audrina dashed toward the bells that hung along the far wall, like they did in every room of the Keep, there for nobles to summon their maids or to call for help in an emergency.

At the same time, Akeylah dashed toward Ren.

"I came in for a bath." Sarella was panting. "My damned private tub has sprung a leak, so I'm forced down here like some commoner—"

"What happened?" Akeylah dropped to her knees beside her sister. Her skirts immediately soaked through with the water puddled around Ren's body.

"I found her floating on her stomach. I managed to pull her out, but..." Sarella gestured helplessly.

Akeylah bent to hold her cheek next to Ren's mouth while her fingers groped under Ren's chin. No breath. A pulse, but soft and fading fast.

Akeylah tilted her sister's head up and back.

"What are you doing?" Sarella asked.

Akeylah had never done this before, but she'd watched sailors perform it enough times. Life in a seaside town with frequent storms meant she'd seen more than her fair share of unlucky trawlers fished out of the port and onto the docks, half-drowned and unresponsive.

Ignoring Sarella's question, Akeylah pinched her sister's nose and inhaled. Then she planted her mouth over Ren's parted lips and blew.

She sat back. Watched. Waited.

Somewhere in the background, she heard the bells clang on and on, Audrina hanging on the bellpull. If they couldn't revive her now, Akeylah knew it would be too late by the time trained menders arrived.

"Should something be happening?" Sarella tried to elbow closer.

"Give me space." Akeylah bent over Ren again. Breathed into her sister's lungs once more. Sat back on her heels to count to three. Fear and anger warred in her veins.

Come back, Ren. We need you.

I won't let our enemy take you.

She inhaled. Exhaled into Ren's mouth.

"I don't think it's working." Sarella pursed her lips.

Akeylah's heart clenched. *No.* She couldn't lose Ren. Not now.

One more try. She leaned down. Breathed into her sister as hard as she could, and at the same time, offered up a prayer. *Mother Ocean, please don't let her die.*

This time, a spurt of water rose up in response. Ren gurgled, then spat in Akeylah's face.

Akeylah fell back on her heels with a cry of relief. Ren coughed, sputtered, spat again. Began to choke, and Akeylah rolled her onto her side and patted her back. Kept doing that until Ren had forced what seemed like at least half the baths out of her throat.

Next to them, Sarella cursed as Ren's coughs spattered across her knees. The noblewoman leaped up and away, and a near-hysterical laugh threatened to bubble out of Akeylah's mouth.

Only then did Akeylah realize she had tears streaming down her own face. Tears of fear or joy, she wasn't sure. She kept her hand between Ren's shoulder blades, rubbing in circles until Ren rolled onto her back. Eyes half-shut, her breathing still labored, Ren squinted at her sister.

"What happened?" Akeylah asked, voice low and urgent, even though she could already guess. She knew it the moment she saw Ren limp on the ground. Seas, even sooner—she'd felt the fear in her bones, the desperate need to find her sisters, some instinct spurring her to search for them right away, despite her own hallucination in the library.

Ren coughed again. Took a moment before she drew enough breath to reply. When she did, her answer made little sense. "The true heir" were the only words Akeylah could hear.

Akeylah looked up to find Audrina bending down next to her. "The menders are on their way," the girl murmured.

Sarella stood a little off to the side, staring down at the scene, her mouth a moue of disgust.

Ren groaned, and all their eyes fixed on her once more. Suddenly, with an apparent surge of energy, Ren grasped the collar of Akeylah's gown and dragged her down, close. "The true heir is coming." With that, Ren fainted.

Akeylah and Audrina stared at each other, their faces mirror images of confusion, just as the hall outside exploded with the shouts of the menders.

❋ 2 ❋

Florencia

Ren's eyelids fluttered. In her head, all she could see, hear, smell was Burnt Bay. She saw the ships aflame. Heard the screams of the sailors as they drowned. Tasted saltwater and gunpowder on her tongue. And above it all, she listened to the blackmailer's laughter, sharp and hollow.

It's time for me to take your place.

It's time for the true heir to rise.

The true heir. She thrashed, surged upright with a gasp...and found herself staring at a roomful of people.

She grabbed the covers of the bed in which she lay and tugged them over her chest, instinctive, as she surveyed the room. Akeylah. Zofi. Audrina. Mama at her side, in a chair pulled up close to the bed.

And on her other side, a woman she didn't recognize, dressed in mender's robes.

"Hi," Ren told her audience after a pause.

"How are you feeling?" Mama caught one of her hands, pressed it between her own slim fingers.

"What happened?" Ren's voice came out like a croak. She touched her throat, belatedly registering the pain. It felt like she'd swallowed fire.

"The important thing is that you're awake," the mender interrupted, all business. She took Ren's arm roughly, turned it over to feel her pulse. "Do you know your name? The day?"

"Ren. Uh, Florencia." She glanced around the room. "And it's still Syxmonth. Countess Yasmin's funeral was two days ago."

A murmur of *Sun accept her soul* passed through the crowded room. As it did, Ren realized what this meant.

The vision. The true heir.

Yasmin wasn't their enemy. She was just another victim.

The mender flashed a mirror before Ren's eyes, tearing her back to the present. Ren flinched at the overbright reflection shining into her pupils. "Any pain?" the mender prompted.

Ren's hand drifted back to her throat.

"That's to be expected." She glanced past Ren to address her mother. "I see no residual signs of mental distress, but if her breathing slows, or if she grows confused about her whereabouts, ring the bell immediately. For the time being, what she needs is rest. She can try to eat in a couple of hours, something easy on the throat. Soup, perhaps."

With that, the mender stepped outside. Ren's mother threw the rest of the group a pointed look. "You heard her. Ren needs to rest."

"In a moment, Mama," Ren replied. Behind her mother's

back, Akeylah waved to catch her attention and widened her eyes with significance. "First, I need to speak with my sisters."

"What you need is some sleep," Mama began, but Ren slid her hand from her mother's.

"Alone, please." Ren stared at her mother until, with an exasperated sigh, Mama turned to leave. Audrina trailed after, though not before she offered Ren a quick, reassuring smile.

Her sisters waited until the door latched. Then Akeylah and Zofi hurried over, one on each side of the bed.

"What did you see?" Akeylah whispered. "Was it another vision?"

Ren closed her eyes. Behind her eyelids, the terrible hallucination awaited. Ships aflame, bodies broken across the waves of the bay. "I couldn't move," Ren said, avoiding the question. She couldn't talk about it all. About what she did. About the terrible secret she carried like a tumor inside. Burnt Bay, a rebel attack in which thousands of Kolonyan soldiers died . . . It was her fault. "My limbs, my whole body, got so heavy I sank to the bottom of the baths. Even once I realized what was happening, I couldn't move. The force was so real, *so strong*. . . ."

"It's escalating," Zofi said, fists balled. "First letters, then hallucinations, now this. What next? Will this blackmailer curse us, plant poison in our veins? Or just push us off a tower like Yasmin."

"You said something to me," Akeylah murmured. "After the baths, before you lost consciousness again. You said, 'The true heir is coming.'"

A chill trickled down Ren's spine. She felt hairs rise along her arms, at the nape of her neck. "That's what they called themself. As I was drowning, the blackmailer spoke in my mind. 'It's time for the true heir to rise.'"

"What does that mean?" Zofi interrupted.

Ren looked from her to Akeylah. "What we already guessed. Whoever's doing this to us, they want the throne. They believe it belongs to them, and they'll do whatever it takes to get us out of the way. Even kill us."

"We need to protect ourselves." Zofi's fingertips danced around the knife she wore at her waist.

"We'll likely have a couple of days." Akeylah tugged on one of her thin Eastern-style plaits. "The heir must be spent after using the Vulgar Arts twice in a row."

"Twice?" Ren's tone sharpened.

Akeylah hesitated. Cleared her throat. "I had a vision, too. Not long before yours, Ren."

Ren sat forward, then winced at a pinch in her rib cage. She sank back against the pillows. "What did *you* see?"

Her sister paused again. Ren could sympathize. She didn't exactly want to share the details of her own experience either. "A figure from my past," Akeylah finally said. Then, to Ren's surprise, she added, "My stepfather. He...he's not a nice person. To put it mildly." From the way her normally calm sister wound a plait tighter and tighter around one fingertip, Ren guessed that was a vast understatement. "The heir used him to threaten me. They said, 'Understand what I do to my enemies. You're one of them now.'" Akeylah swallowed audibly. "And then..." She straightened, seemed to recall something. "They showed me a book."

She explained how during her vision, Rozalind watched her thrash and knock a book off the shelf. Inside it, Akeylah had found a note written by the acolyte who helped Yasmin work the

Vulgar Arts. Acolyte Casca, who later met a grisly end—murder via a poisoned bloodletter.

"The note explained what Yasmin did. It wasn't a curse against a relative. And she didn't work it alone either." Akeylah drew a deep breath. "Yasmin and Andros worked the Vulgar Arts together. This curse—or tithe, whatever you want to call it—it bound their minds. Permanently."

Ren blinked in surprise. *A permanent bond?*

"What, like...mind reading?" Zofi's eyebrows rose. From her expression, Ren guessed even her best-traveled sister hadn't heard of this before.

"I didn't know that was possible," Ren said. And even if it were, why would the heir show them this book? Unless they wanted to taunt the girls. Prove just how wrong they'd been about their aunt...

"Neither did the acolyte, from the tone of this note," Akeylah replied. "He called this tithe as much a curse as a blessing, since it can't be undone. You work it, you're stuck splitting your mind with someone else forever."

"Every single thought?" Zofi frowned. "Then when we confronted Yasmin about blackmailing us..."

"Andros would've heard, too," Ren finished.

Akeylah released the plait she'd curled around her finger. "Maybe. I don't know how it works precisely, whether you choose what thoughts to share, but..."

"Either way, whether our father knows we're hiding secrets or not, this heir person could reveal them at any moment. Or worse, attack one of us again." Zofi straightened to attention, almost like a Talon. "We can't be alone, especially not somewhere vulnerable like the baths. We need trusted people with us at all times."

"So basically just each other," Ren drawled.

"Or your mother," Akeylah pointed out. "Rozalind, Danton perhaps." She ignored Ren's grimace. "Your friend Audrina, she called the menders for you. Seas, even Sarella helped."

"*Sarella?*" Ren's jaw dropped.

"She's the one who found you." Akeylah half smiled, though she also rolled her eyes. "She spent half the time I was rescuscitating you complaining about her private baths, but she did single-handedly drag you from the water before Audrina and I arrived. If not for her, I shudder to think..."

Ren did, too. She grimaced and studied her hands. She didn't know how to feel about bitter-spirited Lady Sarella suddenly acting generous, but she'd dwell on that later. "We can't tell anyone else what's going on," Ren said. "It's bad enough the heir knows our secrets. Plus, helping us may put our friends in danger. Look what happened to Yasmin."

"We can't do this alone," Akeylah protested.

To Ren's surprise, Zofi nodded. "Ren, your mother already knows something's wrong. So does your friend Audrina. And Rozalind. Sands, probably even Vidal. We don't need to tell any-one *why* we need help. But we can ask them to watch our backs. Besides, nonrelatives are good. They're immune to the heir's curses. Well, assuming the heir doesn't come from your mother's side, Ren," she added with an attempt at a smile.

Ren managed a weak one in return. "Let's hope I'm not their relative twice over." Then she groaned and sank back into her cushions.

"We'll let you get some rest," Akeylah said, intuitive as always.

"In the meantime, Akeylah and I will research the curses the heir has used. See if there's a way to defend ourselves." Zofi reached over to squeeze her shoulder. "We'll figure this out."

Ren bobbed her head. Smiled weakly as the girls left the room. A moment later, her mother returned, her face the very picture of disapproval.

"Mama..."

"I won't keep you up," Mama said. "You need sleep. I just wanted to tell you I'm here if you need me." She set a full tumbler of water on the bedside table. "Your friend Audrina had to work, but she asked me to let you know she'll visit soon."

Ren nodded, eyelids already fluttering shut. "Thanks," she managed.

Mama tucked the covers under her chin. The last thing Ren heard before she drifted off was her mother murmuring, "You're safe now."

Even half-asleep, she knew it for a lie.

❧ 3 ❧

Zofi

"Did you know Lord Rueno is our cousin from two different lines?" Akeylah asked from across the table where they sat, deep in the bowels of the library, alone save for the muttering librarian at the distant front desk. "That makes Lexana our third cousin, but twice over."

"I still doubt she's a close enough relative to work curses as strong as the heir's," Zofi replied with a distracted frown at her own book. "Keep looking into it, though."

"What have you found? Anything?" Akeylah nodded toward the textbook.

"I've been reviewing shield tithes."

Akeylah tilted her head. "Never heard of them."

"My mother taught me when I was little, but I'd forgotten.... Travelers don't find much use for defensive tithes."

"Because you prefer offense?" Akeylah guessed.

"Because we don't keep angry blood relatives around to curse us in the first place." Zofi laid the book flat. On the page was a hyperrealistic drawing of a man spread-eagled with a grayish outline overlaying his skin. "It's kind of like the impervious tithe—you know, the one that turns your skin silver, makes blades glance off you like they're hitting stone."

Akeylah squinted at the drawing. "I remember it."

"A shield tithe works like that, except it guards you against curses instead of blades. And it lasts far longer than the impervious tithe—or any tithe. It lasts a whole day, one sun cycle."

Akeylah whistled softly. "Why wouldn't people use it all the time, if it's so effective?"

Zofi traced the outline of the drawing. "Because it closes you off. Nobody can curse you, but you can't tithe either, for as long as the shield lasts. You can't heal yourself from a knife wound; you can't tithe for speed or strength, nothing."

Even boosts wouldn't work. Mother had taken great care to warn Zofi about how dangerous it would be to try, back when Zofi was little. "Boosting with a shield tithe is like lighting a fire under your own feet," she'd said. The tithe would have nowhere to go but into your veins.

"Doesn't sound so bad to me," Akeylah was saying. "Being shielded would be like being Genalese."

Zofi scrunched her forehead. "Maybe. But like Genalese soldiers facing our Talons, it would leave you defenseless against any other kind of attack, by sword or cannon or—"

"You said it lasts an entire day?" Akeylah interrupted, clearly not wanting to dwell on the morbid possibilities.

Zofi nodded. "If you perform a shield tithe at sunup, it lasts until the following dawn. It's nicknamed Father Sun's Favorite."

Akeylah met her gaze. "Do you think we should start using it?"

It would leave them vulnerable to normal attacks. But normal attacks weren't their concern just now. All she could think about was what would've happened if Sarella hadn't stumbled across Ren in the baths yesterday, or if Akeylah hadn't known what to do with a drowning victim.

"I think so," Zofi finally answered. Better to shield than die like Ren nearly did.

"Can you show me how?" Akeylah offered up her own bloodletter. "We can teach Ren when we visit her this afternoon."

Zofi talked Akeylah through it first. Then she shielded herself. One shallow, paper-thin cut and the tithe flooded her veins. She saw her body in her mind's eye, bright with the Arts. She caught all that brilliant potential and spread it out like a blanket. Wrapped it around her body as if to ward off a chill on a cold night. The moment it engulfed her, she lost the ability to feel the Arts.

It was like stuffing her fingers in her ears or pinching her nose. The world took on a duller shine, with a sense of something important missing. But that was reassuring. If she couldn't sense the Arts, the heir couldn't reach her either.

Not today, anyway.

✳

That evening, Zofi skipped dinner and started walking back to her chambers early. A day of reading had left her eyelids drooping and her head afloat.

Aside from the shield tithe, she'd found nothing else useful. Akeylah had started a list of second and third cousins, with Lexana's name at the top, but no one else stood out.

Zofi wondered whether she ought to stoop to the heir's level. "The Vulgar Arts are not to be taken lightly," Zofi's mother used to say, "but they're like any other weapon. There can be a time and a place where they're proper." Zofi had never worked the Vulgar Arts, but she'd been to the sorts of festivals where curseworkers plied their wares.

Was it possible to curse someone she didn't know? More than that, *could* she?

It didn't matter. Zofi didn't have time to ride around looking for a curseworker. And even if she found one, the thought of doing that, of tithing into someone else's bloodstream, leaving a permanent scar on her own body, made Zofi's skin crawl.

She didn't have the stomach to curse someone. Even her worst enemy.

Deep in thought, she barely noticed the footsteps behind her in the hall. Didn't register the sound of leather on leather, instead of the usual swish of satin the nobility preferred. That should have been her first clue.

Instead, assuming the footfall belonged to a passing servant, Zofi kept walking, eyes fixed on her chambers ahead. Right up until a firm hand clamped around her biceps. Even then, she didn't put up her defenses. She whirled to find Vidal at her side and smiled, on instinct.

Until she registered the dread in his eyes. *I'm sorry*, he mouthed.

The rest of the hallway swam into focus. A full contingent of Talons surrounded her. Eight, armed to the teeth. Their swords remained sheathed, at least, though their fingers lingered on the hilts.

"What's happened?" Zofi straightened, her posture mimicking theirs. "Is everyone all right?" Her thoughts raced to Ren, Akeylah, her father.

"I'm going to have to ask you to come with us, Lady Zofi," said the lead Talon, a captain Zofi recognized from the practice fields.

She frowned. "Why?"

"King's orders, my lady." His expression was stoic. "I don't know anything more."

Zofi didn't like his tone. Or the words *king's orders*. If Father wanted a simple visit with his daughter, he wouldn't send eight armed men to fetch her. Zofi glanced over her shoulder. Her chamber door was only a few paces away. Should she run? From her chambers, she could jump over the balcony, climb to the ground floor.... "Can I have a minute to dress for the king?"

"Certainly, my lady." The Talon raised a fist. Three other Talons—all women—stepped forward. "My compatriots will accompany you while you prepare."

Zofi's chest tightened. Vidal avoided her eye.

If the Talons refused to let her dress without guards, that could only mean one of two things. Either they'd been ordered to follow Zofi and her sisters, like after Yasmin's death, when the king feared for his family's safety, or...She swallowed hard.

Or these guards had been sent to arrest her.

"On second thought, this outfit is the nicest thing I own, anyway." Zofi pivoted in a way that kept the lump of her longknife hidden beneath her shirt, and took the lead, striding toward the cherry tower and the king's residence.

The Talons fell into step around her. More than once, she stole glances at Vidal's miserable, regret-filled expression.

A memory flashed through her mind. The sky gardens on the night of Yasmin's murder. Dancing with Vidal. Slipping away with him under the veil trees. His face tilting toward hers, their lips a mere breath apart when Yasmin screamed.

Zofi hadn't seen him since. But despite the weeklong absence, her pulse sped up at the sight of him. She brushed his arm as they walked, deliberate.

Vidal stiffened. After a moment's pause, he grazed a finger along the back of her hand in response.

She forced a small, sharp smile. *I'll be fine.* She didn't know if she was trying to convince him or herself.

The Keep looked eerie in the triple moonlight, which zig-zagged through the windows, casting patchwork shadows. The corridors stood empty, the only sound the march of their boots. One small Traveler girl flanked by eight soldiers dressed for battle.

It might seem like overkill, but only to someone who hadn't seen Zofi drill in a melee against these Talons. At least whatever Father thought of Zofi, he did not underestimate her.

Finally, they reached the king's suites. The captain knocked.

"Send her in," came her father's voice.

Zofi obeyed. Father looked worse than the last time she'd seen him, sunken against his bedding.

"Leave us," the king told the captain.

The Talon hesitated. "Your Majesty, we have been tasked with ensuring your safety—"

"I need to speak with my daughter," Andros snapped. "Alone."

23

"At least one soldier, Your Majesty. Please." Before the captain had finished speaking, Vidal stepped forward, silently volunteering.

Andros sighed, then nodded. The other Talons filed out, shutting the heavy stonewood doors, and Vidal fell into guard stance at Zofi's back. Zofi approached her father's bedside.

He didn't look very kingly at the moment. He hadn't left this bed without others' help since Yasmin's funeral. Tonight, he'd propped himself against the headboard, five pillows barely holding him upright, his forehead slick with sweat. The illness had eaten away at his once proud features. His cheeks were sunken, his eyelids drooping.

Zofi watched him carefully. "Father."

"Save it." His voice was a broken, crackling thing. Normally he spoke with steel underneath. Now, he sounded like an old man. "Is it true you killed my son?"

Her heart skidded in her chest. Behind her, she could sense Vidal tensing, too.

Memories flashed through her skull, rapid-fire. Blood on her hands. Puddled around her. The Silver Prince, D'Andros Nicolen, faceup and empty-eyed at her feet.

Her half brother, she now knew. With her knife in his heart.

She swallowed, throat suddenly dry as the desert. For months now, she'd dreaded this moment. Andros learning what really happened to his son. Who was responsible.

She did what she had to do; she killed Nicolen to save Elex, her best friend. But still . . .

"I don't know what you mean, Father," Zofi finally replied. Her voice came out like his. Soft. Hollow.

"I cannot put it more plainly, daughter. Did you have a hand in my only son—my *heir's*—death?"

She flinched. *The true heir.* The hairs on the back of her neck tickled. Could Nicolen be responsible for all this somehow? Back from the grave to avenge his own death?

Don't get superstitious. She dug her nails into her palms and willed her face into a worried frown. "You arrested the man responsible for Prince Nicolen's death just a couple of weeks ago, Father." She thought about Elex. The unfair, rigged trial he would have faced. The noose he'd have worn for her. She'd broken him out of the dungeons, but he still had to live on the run. "You seemed so certain that boy did it, Father. You even ordered his execution." She couldn't hide the tinge of anger in her voice, at that word.

"But it was my own child I should have looked to instead," Andros responded. Unshed tears shone at the corners of his eyes. "My sister spoke the truth. She came to me tonight, a visitation from the Blessed Sunlands. She told me of the poison in our blood. I did not want to believe it, but the look on your face tells me everything I need to know, daughter."

Zofi froze. A *vision?* "Yasmin is dead, Father," she said slowly.

"Yes. You killed her, too," he spat, anger rising. He struggled to sit forward. "She told me everything. All the sins you've committed. The shame you've brought upon this family."

"Your Majesty." Vidal stepped forward.

"Vidal, be quiet," Zofi muttered. She would not let anyone else shoulder her crimes. Not again.

He ignored her. "I was with Lady Zofi at the Sun's Ascendance, when Countess Yasmin..." He bowed his head. "When the countess passed, Sun accept her soul. Lady Zofi and I were dancing. Zofi could not have been involved."

"I did not ask your opinion," the king bellowed. "Hold your tongue, soldier, or leave."

Vidal's mouth snapped shut.

Meanwhile, Zofi's mind raced. She remembered the hallucination the blackmailer sent her. A vision of Nicolen back from the dead, taunting her. Just like Akeylah's stepfather appeared to her. The blackmailer told Zofi if she didn't leave Kolonya City, they'd reveal her secrets. Clearly this was how they'd chosen to do it—by using Yasmin's ghost as a weapon.

But Andros didn't know about the blackmail. He had no idea if his vision was real, or what caused it. "You're sick, Father. You're imagining things. Let me send for the menders."

"I am sick! Poisoned by the gods for filling this world with murderers."

"Father, please listen, you've got this all wrong—"

"Captain!" he shouted. The doors swung inward, nearly bowling Vidal over. Her gaze darted from the king to his balcony window. If she ran, would she make it?

Then what? Scale down the Keep before a Talon could fire a phantasm dart into her neck? She'd never make it down the tower, let alone through the entire city. Last time, even with Elex at her side, she'd needed Vidal's help. And she couldn't even tithe, because she'd shielded herself for the day.

Running suggests guilt. Vidal had told her that once. Back when she'd only just arrived in Kolonya. Back when running would have been so much simpler. When she thought the only thing she had to fear were secrets.

She looked away from the window. She wouldn't run. It was her word against a ghost's.

"Take Lady Zofi to the dungeons," Andros ordered. If this surprised the captain, he didn't let it show. A few Talons even smirked when he clamped irons on her wrists.

Zofi could guess what they were thinking. *Finally, we can get rid of this drifter once and for all.* Only Vidal looked sick with worry.

"Send for the menders," Zofi begged the captain. "My father needs treatment."

"If I'm ill, it's only at the sight of you, daughter." But Andros said this without venom. "How could you have betrayed me like this?" His voice broke.

"You're making a mistake, Father." Zofi started toward him. "There's more at work here than you know; enemies who want to tear our family apart—"

"I'll hear no more excuses. Lock her in the dungeons until I decide what to do with her." Only Zofi seemed to notice the quiver in the king's voice. He lowered his gaze, as though he couldn't bear to watch the Talons march her from the room.

Father's torn expression stuck with her as the captain hauled her away.

Zofi had done a lot of things others might consider unsavory. Breaking a wanted criminal from the dungeons. Killing a prince who threatened her friend. But she'd never regretted it. She did what she needed to protect her people. Now...

The Talons half dragged, half shoved her into the corridor. She stumbled, caught herself.

She used to hate the king for raising a son like Nicolen. For allowing his Talons to run roughshod over the Reaches, abusing their power. She still disagreed with many of his decrees. Yet, in the last few weeks, she'd seen another side to him. The father who wanted to teach his daughters. A king who listened to the suggestions she made.

She still didn't regret ridding the world of a violent man like Prince Nicolen. But thinking about the pain it caused Andros opened a strange new crack in her rib cage.

So this is what guilt feels like, she thought as the captain shoved her down the dungeon steps. And another thought, hard on its heels. One that let her stand straight again, even after they slammed the cell door shut.

The heir did this. One way or another, I'll make them pay.

❖ 4 ❖

Florencia

Y ou look almost as bad as I feel," Ren told Audrina with a grin, which quickly devolved into a grimace as she readjusted against her pillows.

Akeylah had stopped by last night to help her perform the shield tithe Zofi discovered. It worked but left Ren more drained than ever. The moment Akeylah departed her chambers, she'd fallen straight to sleep, only roused this morning by Audrina's knocking.

On the far side of the bed, Aud's face was drawn with concern. "Very funny. How are you feeling, honestly?"

"Lucky." Ren's smile clouded. "Thank the Sun for you and Akeylah. Otherwise..." She shuddered. She couldn't stop thinking about the water filling her lungs, drowning out the world.

"Don't thank the Sun. It's the moons who favor girls like us." Audrina winked.

It was a saying she and Ren had invented when they were young and less than faithful to Madam Oruna's rules. According to Kolonyan lore, Syx, Nox, and Essex were the lights of lovers, spies, and thieves, respectively. The moons had a reputation for disobedience, much like Ren and Aud when they'd sneak out at night to gallivant around the Keep, nicking strongwine from the cellars or midnight snacks from the kitchens.

Ren tried for a smile at their old joke, but failed.

Audrina sighed. "Besides, if you thank anybody, it should be Sarella, believe it or not."

"I should write to her. Express my gratitude." Strange as it felt to thank Sarella for anything, Ren did owe the woman her life.

"I wouldn't bother." Audrina rolled her eyes. "I tried already. Her response was, and I quote, 'I'm not some kind of monster. Just because Florencia's horrible doesn't mean she should die.' Then she stormed off."

Ren's lips twitched with amusement. "That does sound more like her."

"Speaking of unpleasant people..." Audrina hesitated. Looked away before she spoke. "Danton's been asking after you."

Ren sighed. "I know. He stopped by last night." Before Akeylah had come to visit, Ren had feigned sleep and listened to her mother and Danton's whispered conversation. He'd sounded truly concerned, voice hoarse with worry. And yet.

Danton was still engaged to marry Lexana. Something he didn't tell Ren about when, just a couple of days before announcing the betrothal, Danton spent the night in *Ren's* chambers.

She'd finally decided to trust him again. Finally opened her heart once more. And this was how he repaid her. Sun above, had he already been promised to Lexana the night they...?

"Are you thinking of seeing him again?" Audrina studied Ren from the corner of an eye.

"Of course not." Ren groaned. "You were right to warn me off him, Aud."

"Someday you'll learn I'm always right." Audrina smirked. Then her smile fell. "I am sorry, though. I know how you felt about him."

"How are you doing?" Ren asked, suddenly conscious that she hadn't the faintest clue what was happening in her best friend's life of late.

"Oh, you know. The usual. Catering to impossibly pampered ladies' every whim."

Ren grimaced in sympathy. "Who have you been assigned to?"

"Lexana," Audrina replied with a groan, surprising Ren.

"I always thought Lexana was one of the good ones. Taste in fiancés aside." In fact, she pitied Lexana. For the rest of her life, she'd be yoked to Danton, a man without honor or care for others.

But Aud scowled. "Sun above, no. Or if she used to be decent, time in the Keep has spoiled her. She has me up at odd hours escorting her through the servants' corridors, dropping concealed letters into the mail trays. Even asked me to string up privacy curtains in some unused bedchamber. Sun only knows what she gets up to in there—she had me awake all night changing the locks on it two days ago. Before...well, ah."

Before I almost died.

Ren recalled Audrina's wan face that morning, before the

attack. Aud had asked to take a nap in her bed, and Ren couldn't say no. So she went to the public baths to give her friend some privacy and much-needed rest.

"I had no idea Lexana would prove such a handful, Aud. Can I do anything to help?" Even as she spoke, her mind raced. *Sending hidden letters, building a secret hideout?*

Aud flashed a grateful look. "Would you mind asking Madam Oruna for a transfer?"

Belatedly, Ren remembered the list Akeylah had pulled together, way back before they settled on Yasmin as the likely perpetrator. Her sister had made a list of every noble descended from the outer Reaches' former royal lineages—people who'd stand to inherit if Andros died without a viable heir. *Lady D'Rueno Lexana* had been on that list.

Not only that, but Lexana was a cousin.

It wasn't much to go on, but now Lexana's behavior sounded out of character. Ren knew her as a soft-spoken girl, polite at parties, nice to her servers. Maybe that was just a front, disguising the power-hungry blackmailer inside.

Don't jump to conclusions. Still, evidence pointed to her hiding *something.*

Across the bed, Audrina groaned. "You have your plotting face on, Ren."

"I'm just thinking Lexana's behavior is off. Would you mind terribly staying in her service a bit longer? Just to learn what she's been up to."

Audrina peered at her, suspicious. "Why?"

Ren's mind raced. She needed an excuse. One besides *I think she could be involved in a blackmail plot against me.* "Well, if she is sneaking around on Danton..."

"You want to break them up? I thought you just said you were finished with him."

Ren affected a sigh. "Can't a girl want a little revenge?"

Audrina snorted. "Far be it from me, your loyal spy, to question my mistress's motives."

She said it like a joke, yet Ren still flinched, stung. "No, Aud, I didn't mean...I'm sorry. You're right, I've asked too much of you already. I'll talk to Oruna—"

"Don't." Audrina pressed her lips together, clearly still annoyed. "You want to know what Lexana's up to, so I'll find out what she's up to."

"I don't want it badly enough to keep you in a miserable situation, Aud. Your friendship means the world to me."

"In that case, what kind of a friend would I be if I left you hanging now?" Audrina's tone brightened, though it sounded forced. She rose and reached for the door. "I need to get back to work. I'll report back soon, I promise."

Ren sank back into her cushions, exhaustion and guilt warring in her chest. *I'll make it up to her somehow.* Though she knew, deep down, she'd made that empty promise before.

❋

Footsteps creaked on the far side of the room. Ren sighed and rolled over. Bright noonday sun painted the curtains. She must have fallen back to sleep after Audrina left.

Mama had returned from her morning errands. "Try and drink

a little more water." Her mother nodded toward the tumbler at her side without quite meeting Ren's gaze.

"I've had enough water." Ren searched her mother's face. Mama crossed to the window, hands wrung in a worried gesture Ren recognized. "What's wrong?"

"You'll have all the time in the world for news later. For now, you must recuperate."

She sat upright. "Why? Is the news so distressing it will send me into a fit to hear it?"

Mama dropped into a chair. "You first, Ren. Tell me about your accident."

"I told you already—"

"You did not slip and hit your head on the marble, Ren. You have no bruising anywhere, no sore spots." Ren should have known Mama's head rub last night—"to help you sleep"— was a trick. "So either you fell asleep and *nearly drowned* through sheer ignorance, or there's more to this story than you're telling me."

Sometimes Ren wished her mother wasn't so perceptive.

She couldn't tell her everything. Not about the Eastern rebels or the fact that she smuggled them information that led to Burnt Bay. The less Mama knew, the safer she was.

But she knew her mother wouldn't let up without some kind of explanation. And much as Ren hated to frighten Mama, she couldn't carry this burden alone anymore. Not all of it.

Zofi's advice echoed in her mind. *We don't need to tell anyone why we need help, but we can ask them to watch our backs.*

"I'm being threatened," Ren murmured.

"By whom?" Mama surged from her chair. "Have you spoken

34

to your father? You should have an extra guard—were you *attacked* in those baths?"

"It's . . . complicated."

Mama froze. "Have you told your father?" she repeated, slower now.

"I just said it's complicated, Mama—"

"Florencia." *Uh-oh.* Her full name never preceded anything good. "You are the daughter of a king. Your life is no longer yours entirely. You have a duty to protect yourself."

"I'm using a shield tithe, Mama. Zofi taught us—"

"One tithe performed by a foreign girl we barely know is supposed to reassure me?"

"Don't talk about her like that," Ren snapped. "She's my sister. So is Akeylah—I'd be dead right now if not for her. You need to stop talking about them like their only defining characteristics are their origins. They're just like you and me, Mama. They're family."

"*We* are family, Ren." Mama reached for her hand, but Ren drew back. Hurt flashed across her mother's face. "You've only known these girls for less than a month. You don't know their backgrounds or how they were raised. Those things are important. That's what makes a person who they are. So if you're being threatened, *attacked*, you need to rely on the family you know. The family you've had since the day you were born."

Family. She recalled Danton's warning about that. *Family either strengthens or kills you*, he used to quote at her. *Nothing in between.*

Danton might be the most poisonous viper Ren had ever encountered, but he wasn't wrong. This true heir was a blood relative. Someone with connections, spies—someone well-placed enough to not only have learned about Ren's treason, but also whatever crimes her sisters had committed far away from Kolonya City. The heir must have eyes and ears everywhere.

Ren knew her mother would never betray her, but could Mama be used as a pawn? Played by someone she trusted in turn?

"I can't tell you what's going on, Mama." Ren refused to drag her mother into this mess. It was bad enough that she, Zofi, and Akeylah were caught up in it. "Just trust me when I say I'm handling it. As you say, I'm the daughter of a king now. I must learn to face my problems without putting those I care for in danger."

She thought of Yasmin's broken body, splayed across the cobblestones below the Keep. Ren had been so sure the countess was guilty. Her death had only proven it in Ren's mind. A suicide driven by shame.

Now she realized Yasmin's death signaled something more sinister. For whatever reason—perhaps because the girls had ignored the heir's deadline and refused to leave Kolonya City by the Sun's Ascendance—the heir had escalated from covert threats to outright murder. First Yasmin. Then the attempt on Ren's life.

"Don't be silly, Ren." Mama caressed the back of her hand with a thumb. "I carried you in my womb. For nine whole months, we were the same person, you and I."

"So you always remind me, Mama."

"It's a unique bond, Ren. You'll understand one day, if you decide to have a child. The feeling of that new life within you... And Sun above, tithing when pregnant was a high like none other. The strength of two willpowers in one body..." Mama's gaze drifted.

"So I've heard. It's why Queen Suisa insisted on leading her own troops in the Fourth Genalese War, despite being seven months pregnant with the future King Floren." Because the queen, like all pregnant women, had been able to tithe with her blood as well as the blood of her unborn son. Twice the strength. Twice the abilities.

"Your namesake, I might add." Mama's eyes sparkled with humor, only for a moment. "What I'm saying is, your burdens are mine, Ren."

"I'll explain everything," Ren said. "After you tell me this news you're so worried about. What's going on out there?"

After a moment's hesitation, Mama took a deep breath. "Ren, my warning about trusting your sisters wasn't just idle speculation. At least, one sister in particular..."

Sun above. Ren's stomach plummeted. "What are you talking about?"

"It's not public knowledge yet. I heard it from an old friend, captain of the internal guard. I ran into him in town; he frequents the same abraca seller I do—"

"*Mama.*"

Her mother relented. "Zofi was arrested last night."

"*What?*" Ren flung back her covers. Leaped to her feet. "Why?" Was this the heir's doing? When drowning Ren didn't work, when the girls all began to shield themselves from curses, had the heir turned to another method of destruction?

"Lie down," Mama barked. "This is why I didn't want to tell you. You're in no condition to go running around the Keep."

Ren caught the bedpost. For an instant, spots danced at the edges of her vision. She blinked once, twice, and her sight cleared enough for her to grab her dressing robe. Normally she'd never be seen in public like this—hair sticking up in every direction, the black-and-silver robe contrasting horribly with her pale pink sleeping gown.

But news of her sister's arrest drove all other concerns from her mind.

"I need to see Akeylah." Akeylah would know what had happened. Together, they would find a way to save Zofi. Fight back, if this arrest was indeed the heir's doing.

Mama caught her wrist. "Ren, you mustn't get mixed up in this. Rumors are already circulating—they say Zofi may have had something to do with the Eastern rebellion, or possibly even Prince Nicolen's death."

One of those, Ren thought. *The other was all me.*

Technically, she didn't *know* that Zofi killed the Silver Prince. But it didn't take a genius to piece it together. Not after Zofi begged Ren to free her friend, who'd been accused of Nicolen's murder, from the dungeons. Zofi swore her friend was innocent. How could she have been so certain, unless she knew who the real killer was?

They all had secrets.

"I'm already mixed up in it, Mama. As you just reminded me, family bonds are irreversible. Zofi is my sister, like it or not." Ren tore her arm free and grabbed the doorknob.

"Florencia," Mama said in an entirely different voice. "Stop." Startled, Ren glanced over her shoulder. Her mother's expression had gone cold and hard. It was a look Ren had seen before, though never directed at her. The mask Mama put on when she was spoiling for a fight.

"You said if I told you the news, you would explain what happened in the baths. Before you scurry off to the sister you suddenly love so dearly, you owe me this much."

Ren searched her mother's face. Waited for some crack, a hint of sympathy. She found no quarter. So Ren lifted her chin, and gave none in return. "You will have your explanation once I am satisfied it is safe to give it to you. It's for your own good." Her mother stormed forward, but Ren slammed the door on her outraged shout, and hurried toward the mahogany tower.

·◦≺ 5 ≻◦·

Akeylah

Akeylah had just reached the Great Hall for the midday meal when Rozalind intercepted her. The queen's fingertips came to rest on her forearm, electric as ever. Akeylah's blood sizzled, but the excitement took a nervous bent when she glimpsed Rozalind's furrowed brow. "I need you to come to the king's chambers," Rozalind murmured. *"Now."*

"Is everything all right?" Akeylah searched the queen's gaze, startled. "Is Father...?"

"I'll explain everything there." Rozalind pressed her hand once, hard. "Bring Florencia, too, if you can find her." With that, Rozalind vanished into the swirl of nobility.

Dread pooled in Akeylah's stomach. Why Ren and not Zofi? Was Father worsening?

Akeylah hadn't gotten a chance to speak to Rozalind in private since the heir attacked her in the library. Since she'd raced off to find Ren half-drowned in the baths.

Yesterday, between visiting Ren and researching relatives, she'd been too busy. This morning, Akeylah had tried to find Rozalind, but the queen had been absent from breakfast. When Akeylah stopped by the king and queen's chambers, Talons had barred her path, sent her away.

She thought about the curse eating its way through her father's veins, and her stomach roiled. *Is he all right?*

Akeylah hurried toward the cherry tower. She'd only reached the base of the steps when she ran headlong into a tall, slim figure. It took her a few blinks to recognize her sister. She'd never seen Ren like this—hair a mess, clothes in disarray.

"Akeylah." Ren grabbed her shoulders to steady herself. "I was just looking for you."

"Same." Akeylah shrugged her sister's hands from her shoulders and tugged her into motion instead. "Rozalind needs us in Father's chambers. It seemed urgent."

"I can guess why." In a low, furious voice, Ren relayed everything she knew. Father had Zofi arrested late last night. The Talons had been ordered to keep it quiet, but this was the Keep. Word got around sooner than later.

"That must be why his chambers have been shut all day," Akeylah said. "I tried to visit, but the Talons wouldn't even let me near the doors."

"We're his daughters." Ren's mouth formed a grim line. "Just like the one he imprisoned last night."

"You don't think they suspect us, too?" Akeylah's hand drifted toward the scar on her thigh. The telltale glowing blue mark left

41

by the Vulgar Arts curse she worked against her father, albeit by accident. If the king ever accused Akeylah, he wouldn't even need to put her on trial. Proof of her guilt shone right on her leg.

"I doubt it." Ren sounded so sure that Akeylah darted a curious glance her way.

"Do you know what Zofi did? Or what Father believes she did, anyway?"

"I think so," Ren replied. "But it's not my secret to share."

Akeylah hesitated. She hated to pry, but she wanted to know how bad this was. "Is it enough to justify Father throwing her into the dungeons?"

"It's...I've done worse. I don't judge Zofi. But I understand why Father arrested her."

Akeylah cursed under her breath. In the back of her mind, she heard the heir's words. *Understand what I do to my enemies.* She was beginning to.

"We didn't leave when the heir demanded," Ren continued. "This is exactly what they said they'd do—reveal our secrets to Father."

"We don't know they're behind this. Though, it does sound like them...." Akeylah frowned as they reached the king's suites. The immense cherry stonewood doors of His Majesty's chambers were flanked by Talons, though this time the guards waved them onward.

Akeylah's mind leaped to a happier memory. The last time she entered these chambers, she'd been at Rozalind's side. *Of all the places in the Keep to be overheard, here is the least likely,* Rozalind had whispered as she drew Akeylah across the threshold.

Why is that? Akeylah had asked.

Because my husband doesn't plant spies in his own bedroom.

For an instant, all she could think about was that moment, when Rozalind's lips collided with hers. She shook her head, jarred herself back to the present.

"Lady Akeylah and Lady Florencia, Your Majesty," a Talon announced.

A thick curtain had been drawn around Andros's four-poster bed. More drapes swathed the windows, and the lanterns burned low, candles guttering in their frames.

Rozalind appeared like a spectre in the gloom. "Close the door."

Akeylah and Ren stepped inside, and the guards barred the latch behind them.

Only then did Rozalind rush forward, catching Akeylah in an embrace so tight it knocked the wind from her lungs. "Akeylah. Florencia," she added over Akeylah's shoulder with a tight smile.

"How is he?" Akeylah murmured into the queen's hair. Her normally pristine bronze curls were a tangled mess.

"Not good." Rozalind drew away, too soon, and Akeylah's arms felt empty from the lack of her.

"Can we see him?" Ren asked.

Akeylah's pulse doubled as Rozalind drew the curtain. Andros lay on the sheets, eyes open, mouth slack. Completely immobile. *No. No, no, no . . .*

But then a slow, shuddering inhale sounded, and she watched his chest rise. It fell again a moment later, his breath fluttering the sheet tucked under his chin.

Her shoulders slumped in relief. He wasn't dead. Not yet. "How long has he been like this?"

Rozalind perched on the foot of the bed. "Ever since he spoke to Zofi last night."

"You mean ever since he had her arrested." Ren took up a spot at her father's right hand.

Akeylah crossed the room more slowly. Father's dark, rich complexion had gone chalky, the color of rotten wood. His eyes stared at something beyond this world, as though he already had one foot halfway into the next.

I did this to you. Her hands shook. *This is my fault.*

"He says he had a vision," Rozalind said.

Akeylah and Ren exchanged worried glances. They both knew all too well how dangerous visions could be.

"Yasmin appeared in a dream. Supposedly, she told him Zofi murdered his son."

Prince Nicolen. Akeylah startled. Ren, on the other hand, didn't react. From that, Akeylah guessed this must be Zofi's secret. A secret she'd shared with Ren but not Akeylah.

Not that I've shared my own secret with anyone. Akeylah had no room to talk. Yet the idea of her sisters sharing confidences without her bothered her more than she cared to admit.

Rozalind spoke on, oblivious. "After Andros ordered her arrest, he fell into a fit—screaming, shouting...I called a mender. She stayed all night. Around dawn, he lost consciousness. The mender thinks the stress of his daughter's betrayal, well..." Rozalind shook her head, voice tight with sorrow. "She says it's unlikely he'll wake again. Ever."

Akeylah stepped closer, tears stinging the backs of her eyes. *Poor Father.*

Zofi's secret may have broken his heart, but it was Akeylah's fault he'd fallen ill in the first place. She reduced him to this empty shell.

"How long?" she heard Ren ask softly. "Before he..."

Akeylah closed her eyes.

"His mind is most likely already gone," Rozalind whispered. "As for the body, he's still swallowing water, and even some mouthfuls of porridge. He may yet live another week. The mender gives him a fortnight at most."

A *week or two at most.* Then Akeylah would become a murderer.

"Are you sure?" Her voice snagged in her throat. "You're sure he isn't still... in there?"

"I don't know." Rozalind wiped her eyes with the back of one hand. "I hope not. Can you imagine if he is? Lying there listening, unable to tell anyone he's here..."

A tear escaped, snaked down Akeylah's cheek.

Rozalind stood. "I should go. Give you both some time with him."

"We'd appreciate that," Ren began, but Akeylah spoke over her.

"Stay. Please." Akeylah reached for Rozalind's hand. Curled her fingers through the queen's. Then she reached down to take Andros's limp hand in her other.

Her father's fingers felt cool, rough at the tips. Calluses. She wouldn't have expected a king to have hands like that. But then, he'd never been one to sit back and lead passively. She remembered the stories of his youth. Andros leading the charge against Genal in the Sixth War.

Across the broad mattress, Ren stood stock-still, like a person frozen in time. She gazed at their father, face full of pain and regret.

Akeylah knew exactly how she felt.

"I thought we'd have more time," Ren whispered. "Now it's a week or two, and none of it with him able to offer guidance, to tell us who he wants to succeed him, or anything. . . ."

"Who knows about this?" Akeylah glanced over her shoulder at the door, thinking about the Talons on the other side.

"So far?" Rozalind cleared her throat. "The mender. You two. That's all."

"You haven't told the regional council or any of the nobles yet?" Ren spoke up.

Rozalind bowed her head. "I thought it prudent to keep this quiet for now. If you think it best to reveal the extent of his illness to court, that is your prerogative. You two are his heirs."

"You're his wife," Akeylah reminded her, though the words sounded hollow with their fingers entwined. "Maybe we can keep it quiet for now. Just until we're certain of his fate."

"I just wish he'd left some sign." Ren grimaced. "Some indication of what he wants us to do. There are no Kolonyan legal provisions for a situation like this, with multiple potential heirs. If he passes now . . . it'll be chaos."

"Then we must pray the mender finds some cure, by Father Sun's will," Rozalind whispered.

But the mender did not know what Akeylah did. The true cause of this illness. The curse Akeylah had planted in his veins. If she could find a counter to it, cure him within the next week . . . *Perhaps he still stands a chance.*

A fortnight at most, the mender said. It sounded so short, and yet, she'd only been in the Keep a little longer than that. Three weeks now, or was it four? How much had changed in her life, in that short span?

How much could she change things again?

"The menders say we have two weeks. That's two weeks left to fix this." Akeylah flashed her sister a look. "You're right. The succession isn't clear. And given present circumstances..." *Given the true heir haunting them.* "It will cause chaos once the court learns how bad he is. If we keep the extent of his illness quiet for now, it buys us time to prepare." *And time to find the heir, to stop them before they steal the crown.*

"Not a bad idea," Ren said.

"It gives us time to secure Zofi's release, as well. A dream told Father she was guilty?" Akeylah raised her eyebrows. "That's not enough proof to justify holding her."

Rozalind tensed, though when she spoke, her tone was gentle. "I know you care for your sister. But have you considered the possibility your father is right? Arresting her was his final wish. Do you want to undo it so casually?"

Yes. Guilty or not, Zofi had done no worse than Akeylah herself. "Do you think my father is right to imprison his own daughter based on a hallucination?"

Rozalind glanced down at the king. "I don't know. But I've spent nearly two years at Andros's side." Akeylah resisted the urge to flinch. She hated the reminder of who Rozalind was, her place in the kingdom. "Your father would never imprison anyone, let alone his child, without due cause."

"He's ill," Ren said. "He wasn't in his right mind."

"You didn't see him last night." Rozalind's jaw hardened. "I've never seen him so heartbroken, so torn about something, not even after—" She stopped herself short. Swallowed whatever her next words had been. "I'm just saying, don't be so quick to jump to conclusions." When she looked to Akeylah again, her eyes shone. "Someone has been threatening you."

Akeylah's pulse jumped. "How do you—"

"I'm not an idiot, Akeylah. You asked me to dig up a body so you could confront Yasmin about her past. Then there was the fit you suffered in the library, which didn't seem to surprise or faze you for long. Not to mention the way you found poor Florencia in the baths." She gestured at Ren, who winced. "It's clear to me that you're in danger. Both of you. How do you know it wasn't from Zofi?"

For a split second, Akeylah thought about it. Really thought. Zofi was the one who broke into Yasmin's chambers and brought back a note confessing to the murder of Acolyte Casca. A note that led them in the completely wrong direction.

Then there was the night in the sky gardens, when Yasmin fell. Akeylah had been dancing with Rozalind, and Ren had been with their father. But where did Zofi go? Akeylah didn't remember seeing her again, not until Yasmin had already fallen.

And of course, only Ren and Akeylah had suffered the heir's latest hallucinations—a vision that nearly drowned Ren, and another that turned Akeylah to a cowering mess.

But then, why would Zofi reveal her own secret? Why get herself arrested? It made no sense.

"We just know," Ren spoke into the silence Akeylah left, her voice hard. "And we don't have to explain ourselves to you."

Rozalind bristled. "I'm not asking for an explanation. I'm

asking you both to be careful. News of Zofi's arrest has already spread. If she *has* committed this crime, and you release her, you could be accused alongside her. Whereas now, no one can reach her in the dungeons, nor can she reach anyone else. If she is the threat, no more harm will befall you while she's trapped there. If she isn't, once proof of her innocence has come to light, you can free her at a later date. No harm done."

"Except to her reputation." Ren crossed her arms. "You of all people should understand how important appearances are here in Kolonya."

"What's that supposed to mean?" Rozalind scowled.

"Stop it," Akeylah tried to say. But her voice stuck behind a lump in her throat.

Luckily, a deafening knock interrupted. Akeylah left the two glaring daggers at each other and crossed the chambers to peer outside.

"My lady." A Talon in full uniform, leadership medals glinting on his chest, bowed. "I have come to receive my orders from His Majesty."

"I'm afraid my father is indisposed at the moment." Akeylah wedged her foot behind the door, so it would only open a crack. "I will inform him that you visited."

The Talon frowned. "His Majesty and I have an appointment. He'll be expecting me."

"Something has come up." Just a few weeks, and the Keep had made her a practiced liar.

The man's eyes narrowed. "This is urgent. We need to know how to proceed regarding Lady Zofi. Your father told us he would decide by morning whether to hold a full trial or pass sentence in private. It is now early afternoon, well past his deadline. We require an answer."

Behind her, Akeylah heard footsteps. Felt the familiar cool graze of Rozalind's fingertips at the small of her back. "Thank you so much for coming." Rozalind smiled. Akeylah eased the door open a little wider, both of their bodies blocking the Talon's view. Behind her, she heard the swish of Ren drawing the bed curtains.

"As Lady Akeylah told you," Rozalind continued, "my husband is currently occupied. But he has asked us to act as his go-betweens."

"My father sees this as a family matter," Ren said, joining them. "Not a spectacle for public consumption. He has decided against a trial."

"I see." The Talon hesitated. He clearly wanted to hear this from the king directly. But even a high-placed commander couldn't question the authority of the king's daughters—let alone two of them, plus his wife. "In that case, what are we to do with the prisoner, my ladies?"

"Release her," Akeylah replied at once. Below the hems of their dresses, she felt Rozalind step on her heel. On the other side, Ren dug an elbow into her rib cage.

The Talon's jaw dropped. "Release her? My lady, this is a dangerous prisoner, one your father instructed me to arrest with extra guards. I cannot believe his mind so utterly changed—"

"He doesn't mean to release her into the Keep," Akeylah amended quickly. The Talon wouldn't believe her if she asked him to liberate Zofi completely. But maybe she could find another way around this. A way to give Zofi her freedom without arousing suspicion.

A decision that would satisfy the heir, too. The blackmailer ordered the girls to leave Kolonya. If Zofi left now, no longer a contender for the throne, would the heir allow her to live?

Zofi, forgive me. Akeylah hated to decide her sister's fate for her. Yet she had no choice. "The king would like Lady Zofi returned to her band of Travelers."

The Talon's furious scowl relaxed, just a little, around the edges. "Banishment?"

She swallowed hard. "Yes. But we will not call it that publicly. Not until my father feels ready to confront this issue."

"But what of the girl's crimes? She is a danger to the royal family, he said so himself."

"Which..." Akeylah's mind raced. Again, she felt Ren's elbow. "Is why he would like her removed from the city, sent to a safe distance at which she can do no harm to us." Akeylah straightened her shoulders and raised her chin, a posture she'd seen Ren make when her sister wanted her way. "Lady Zofi made mistakes, but she is still a part of this family. A family that has suffered enough losses. My brother was murdered. Then my aunt. As you know, my father has been sick with grief." The Talon's face softened in sympathy. "If Father does not wish to parade my sister's crimes before the world, we must respect his decision."

Please believe me. Please.

The Talon's frown melted entirely. "I understand, my lady. But this is all highly unusual." He looked to the queen. "The courtiers will question this. My own men, too."

Rozalind huffed. "Your men will question the authority of the king and his heirs?"

The Talon's eyes went wide. "Of course not, Your Majesty."

51

"I should hope not." Rozalind's tone went icy cold. "You have your orders, soldier. Now see to it they are carried out." With that, the Talon bowed, and Akeylah slammed the door. All three of them sank against it.

"Banishment?" Ren hissed.

"I hope you know what you're doing," Rozalind murmured.

Akeylah shut her eyes. *So do I.*

✶ 6 ✶

Zofi

All night, Zofi stared at the bars of her cell, lost in thought. She curled on her side, knees up to her chest, hugging them for warmth. Yet even as she shivered, she barely registered the cold.

Play their game, Mother had told her. Zofi had tried. She tried to play the king's daughter, the promising heir, the loyal sister. She played the game, and she lost.

It was the heir's game now.

She tightened her arms around her knees. Squeezed so tight it hurt. She imagined what awaited her in the morning. Trial, certainly. Before the regional council, or perhaps in front of the whole court.

Or maybe Andros would keep things quiet. Maybe he'd confront her himself. Would he demand a blood oath? Could she lie her way out of this one?

She was sick of lying. Sick of the games.

She wished she could see her sisters one last time. She'd ask them to get a message to her mother. *I'm sorry I failed you.* Then she'd ask Ren and Akeylah for one final favor.

Beat the heir. Win the throne. Stop this monster from claiming it.

Because that's what the heir was—a monster. Andros called Zofi the poison in his blood, and that may be true. She was no innocent. But the heir was something far more deadly. The heir reminded her of Nicolen. Ruthless, willing to stop at nothing to gain power.

Zofi had seen enough corrupt Talons and townie guards to know what sort of people craved leadership for power's sake.

She'd arrived in Kolonya despising this city, this court, and Andros above all. But over the past few weeks, Zofi had come to understand the king. She may not agree with all—or even most—of his policies, yet she had seen him take advice from Akeylah on the Eastern Reach; watched him meet one-on-one with his subjects and hear their concerns; even spoken to him about military strategy herself. He'd listened. Andros was flawed, yes, but not above changing. He truly cared about his people. She could see that in him.

Not to mention, he'd given his daughters a chance. A Traveler, an Easterner, and a former lady's maid. He taught them, trained them, waited to see who proved the best fit for leadership based on merit, not their background or status.

Zofi may not always *like* her father, but she respected him.

The heir would be completely different. If she thought Kolonya was bad now, she could only imagine the depths to which it would sink under a terror like that.

Locks clanked in the distance. Zofi sat up, still shivering. They'd taken her boots when they searched her for weaponry, and her bare feet froze against the dirt floor.

Four Talons marched up to the bars. She stood.

"Turn around," one said, voice hard.

With a scowl, she obeyed. She had no weapons, and no boosts either. The shield tithe she performed last night in the library—a lifetime ago, it seemed—would wear off in a few hours, yet even so, she didn't stand a chance against this many guards. Not unarmed.

"Hands behind your back." The Talon bound tight rope around her wrists, and a moment later, another shoved a burlap hood over her face.

Her stomach clenched. Perhaps Andros had decided to forgo a trial altogether. Maybe he'd decided to march her straight to the executioner's block instead.

She struggled to keep her back straight, head high, as the Talons marched her from the cell. At some point, they crammed her into a wagon. She held her breath. Waited for the sounds of the screaming mob to greet her. Yet all she felt was warm sun on her skin, and a muggy afternoon breeze.

The wagon rattled through the city in silence, save for the occasional distant cry of a merchant or clatter of passing hooves. Nobody shouted or taunted. Nobody remarked on the bound and hooded prisoner.

Maybe Andros wanted to do this privately. That would be more

like him. Execute her with just a few witnesses. Something digni-
fied, if you could call death that. It felt like the best option to hope
for just then. Yet it didn't calm the angry churn in her gut.

I don't want to die.

When the Talons finally yanked the sack from her head, she
blinked in confusion, eyes taking a moment to adjust to the bright
sunlight.

She stood outside the city, past the portcullis. She looked from
Talon to Talon, peering beneath their lowered helms. Her heart
sank. No sign of Vidal's familiar square jawline. Another goodbye
she'd never get to make. It stung more than it should.

But not as much as the thought of her mother, her band, Elex...
all out there somewhere, oblivious to her arrest. How long would it
take before they learned of her execution? Weeks, months?

Would they mourn her, or would Elex blame her for dying,
when she'd promised to win the throne instead? She didn't even
know what Andros would do with her body. She doubted he'd
entomb his son's murderer in the Necropolis. Especially not if he
believed she killed Yasmin, too. But would he think to send her
home to Mother?

Maybe he'd simply dump her body in the River Leath, which
glittered beside her now. A traitor's death.

"Zofi."

She turned, startled at the sound of Akeylah's voice. Her sister hurried across the bridge from the city, Ren at her side. An
instant later, Akeylah's arms were around her. One of the Talons
cut Zofi's bonds, and she raised her arms to hug Akeylah back,
frowning in confusion.

"Give us a moment," Ren told the Talons. All four bowed and

crossed back over the river to the far side of the bridge. Though Zofi noticed the leader continued to watch warily.

She drew back from Akeylah's embrace. "What's going on?"

So Akeylah explained. About their father, his prognosis. A *week or two to live, at most*. And about Akeylah's quick thinking, convincing the Talons to release Zofi to her band.

"I'm sorry," Akeylah finished with a pained expression. "I couldn't think of another way to free you. At least, not an explanation the Talons would believe...."

"They aren't suspicious?" Zofi glanced at Ren.

"Not yet. Rozalind is, ah, fairly convincing at relaying 'the king's demands.'" Ren smiled faintly.

"I didn't mean to have you banished." Akeylah wrung her hands. "But I thought if you went to trial, they might, well...I mean, given the crime..." She flashed an apologetic look.

Zofi forced a carefree grin, even though she felt anything but. "Hey, better banished than imprisoned or executed, right?" She looked from Akeylah to Ren. "I'm guessing you told her?" Zofi asked the latter.

"Rozalind told us what the king accused you of doing," Ren replied. Always a diplomat.

"It's okay." Zofi waved a hand. "At this rate I'm surprised the whole kingdom doesn't know already."

"They won't if we can help it." Akeylah squared her shoulders. "We're going to manage this, Zofi. Your crime, Father's illness. We can conceal it all."

"And deal with the heir, too?" Zofi arched a brow. "Though, if you could pardon Elex, the boy from my band who took the fall for me..."

Ren nodded. "We'll clear his name."

"Thank you." She smiled and hoped it looked reassuring. "Don't spend too much energy worrying about me. I'm going home. Back where I belong." It was what she'd wanted when she first came to the Keep. The chance to go back to her band, her family. Leave all this behind.

So why did part of her feel hollow, now she'd finally been given the chance?

Because part of her family was here now.

"We brought this." Ren held out Zofi's rucksack. "I added some dried fruit, cured meat, and water. A few coins, your boots. And we talked that knife you're always waving around back from the dungeon guards."

"Thank you." Zofi accepted it with a faint grin.

"Least we could do." Ren spread her hands, apologetic.

"You two need to be careful." Zofi lowered her voice. "Make sure you both shield every day, and don't be alone anywhere you're vulnerable to an ambush." She knew she should be relieved. *I'm not about to die.* Instead, she felt a new fear, bone-deep. *I'm abandoning my sisters—my whole kingdom—in the hands of the enemy.* "With Father gone, you're all that stands between the heir and the throne."

"He's not gone yet." Akeylah's yellow-green eyes hardened. For a split second, she reminded Zofi of Yasmin. "Zofi, while you're away...I was hoping you might be able to do me a favor. It's a long shot, but I'm desperate."

"Anything, if it's in my power." Zofi frowned, and caught Ren doing the same. Clearly whatever was on Akeylah's mind, she hadn't shared with Ren either.

58

"I'm looking for a Traveler woman. A curseworker."

Zofi thought about the festivals she'd been to, the bejeweled women her mother had pointed out from time to time. *Curseworkers*, if you asked in the right way, at the right time. "One in particular?"

"Yes." Akeylah surveyed her sisters. Drew a deep breath. "The one who helped me curse our father."

Zofi's jaw went slack.

"*What?*" Ren sputtered.

"It was an accident." Akeylah tugged on one of her dark red plaits. "A horrible accident. I was trying to curse my stepfather— the man I thought was my father, Jahen, an abusive piece of..." She clamped her mouth shut. And her eyes. "It doesn't matter. What matters is I worked the Vulgar Arts against Andros instead, and I've been trying to right that wrong ever since."

Vulgar Arts? Zofi had wondered what dark secrets her sister was hiding, but even she could never have guessed *this*. "Is that what you're always researching in the library?" she finally asked.

Akeylah nodded. "So far I've found nothing. I thought the curseworker who taught me in the first place might know a way to reverse it."

"There are thirteen bands. Hundreds of Travelers spread out across the Reaches." Zofi grimaced. "I can ask around, but the chances of locating her are slim, I'm just warning you."

"Like I said, it's a long shot." Akeylah's brows contracted. "But the mender says Father will only live another week or two. A slim chance is better than none."

"Hurry it up, ladies," the lead Talon shouted from back across

59

the bridge. "That one needs to leave the city outskirts before nightfall." He sneered at Zofi.

In the distance, the sun hovered at the horizon. At the back of her mind, Zofi felt a faint tingle; the Arts flooding back into her senses as the shield tithe lost its grip. At least she wouldn't need to keep shielding herself anymore, now that she was about to ride out of the heir's crosshairs for good. "What's the woman's name?" Zofi asked.

"She never gave it," Akeylah murmured. "But I can describe her. Short, with bushy black curls like yours and a thin face, black eyes."

"You're describing nearly every Traveler in the Reaches." Zofi rolled her eyes.

"She had a scar on her face."

Zofi froze. Did she mean . . . ? *Surely not.*

"Ladies." The Talons marched closer.

"One more moment." Ren backed away to head them off.

But Zofi had eyes only for Akeylah. Her sister lifted a hand to her cheek. Traced a finger from her eyebrow to her jawline in a half-moon. "It ran along her cheek like this. It stood out, even though it was thin, because it looked silver against her skin."

A chill crept down Zofi's spine. *Impossible.*

But there was only one Traveler who matched that description. A woman who had earned her scars—quite literally—decades ago, fighting as a mercenary in the Sixth War.

Zofi's mind raced, connecting the dots. *She never lets anyone see her without a shirt on. Says the scars from the war are too disfiguring.* But what if they weren't from the war? What if the real reason she never let anybody see them was because some of those scars shone blue?

"Right, time's up." The Talons had made it past Ren, who shrugged helplessly behind them. "King's orders. You're to leave the city limits by nightfall."

She went to those fairs. She always knew who to ask for and when and where. She was probably the most connected person in the Reaches. The one people turned to for illegal things, hidden things, things no law-abiding citizen ought to know.

But then, when had their band ever respected Kolonya's unfair laws?

Akeylah watched her intently. "Do you know her?"

"I'll say." Zofi tugged her sister into another tight embrace. Whispered against her ear, where the Talons couldn't see. "That's my mother."

* 7 *

Florencia

Ren and Akeylah spent most of the night after Zofi's departure in the library, continuing the lineage research Zofi and Akeylah had begun. Every so often, Ren stole glances at her sister.

Akeylah cursed our father.

She'd always known there was more to her sister than Akeylah's quiet demeanor suggested. Ren had studied Akeylah long enough to know her sister had a well-practiced hunting face; the sort of mask one would need if, say, they'd grown up in an abusive household.

But this... This was more than Ren had expected from Akeylah. Darker.

If Akeylah had been willing to curse their father, would she stoop to cursing anyone else? Maybe the heir had been lurking right beneath Ren's nose all along....

Akeylah said she'd suffered another vision from the heir, just before Ren's. But Akeylah didn't nearly die. In fact, the heir gave Akeylah *more* information. Handed her the key to Andros and Yasmin's mental bond. It almost seemed like the heir might be helping Akeylah.

Or Akeylah herself is the heir...

Ren shook herself. She'd spent too much time with her mother lately. The heir wasn't aiding Akeylah; they were gloating. Proving to the girls that they were wrong, that Yasmin had died for nothing.

Akeylah was her sister. Ren trusted her.

She needed to. Otherwise, she'd be in this alone. *That* Ren truly couldn't face.

The morning after their late library night, Akeylah and Ren divvied up Father's schedule. They left Rozalind to babysit the comatose king while Ren met with disgruntled minor nobles and Akeylah addressed the field hands about the crop blight. With a pang, Ren thought how proud Father would be to watch them handle these appointments, so similar to the training tasks he'd given them a few weeks ago. Before everything changed.

She hoped her actions now, in some small way, would begin to make up for her sins. For Burnt Bay, for her mistaken suspicion of Yasmin, for Father's illness itself. All of it. She might not be able to heal Father, or bring Yasmin or those soldiers back, but she could keep the kingdom running in Father's stead. Support the people who remained.

Including the best friend she'd been either using as a spy or neglecting recently.

Later in the day, after her meetings, Ren invited Audrina to lunch in a private dining room. She ordered Aud's favorite fish and the nettle tea her friend loved. But when Audrina arrived, her friend barely glanced at the food. She perched on the edge of her chair, hands toying with her sleeves, one eye on the door.

"That's a lovely dress." Ren gestured at the deep blue gown with long, tight sleeves. All the rage, both in color and style. Normally Audrina wasn't one to chase trends. "Is it new?"

"Hmm?" Audrina looked down. "Oh, this." She shrugged. "One of the maids planned to throw it away. It was my size, so."

An awkward silence fell. Ren cleared her throat. "How have you been?"

"Busy working for Lexana." Aud shifted in her seat. "Busy enough I can't afford to stay long. Ren, it was nice of you to invite me, but have you forgotten what it's like below-stairs? Any moment I take to myself I have to make up fourfold later."

Suddenly Ren understood her friend's reticence. She smiled, hoping to reassure her. "Of course I remember, Aud. Don't worry. I cleared your schedule with Madam Oruna. She promised to have another girl cover your duties."

"Ren, I know you feel guilty about all the favors you've asked. But this isn't what I wanted either." She waved a hand at the food cooling on the table. "I don't want special treatment, any more than I want to be your personal spy. I just want things to go back to the way they were. Back when we were friends. Equals."

"So do I." Ren reached for her friend's hand. Aud shifted it out of reach. "Audrina, you are still my friend."

"But no longer your equal." Bitterness seeped into her friend's tone.

"That's not what I meant—"

"How can a princess be friends with a maid?" Aud's voice rose. "You're in line to become the next Queen of Kolonya, and I'm a nobody."

"Not to me," Ren replied sharply.

Audrina laughed. "No, I'm just your favorite tool." Her friend finally met her gaze. "Go on, Ren. Ask me what I learned about Lexana. I know you're dying to."

"That's not why I invited you here."

"But you do want to know."

Ren winced. "After this, I'm done with favors. We'll be back to normal, I promise."

Across the table, Audrina sat in stony silence. Finally, after a long pause, she sighed. "You were right. Lexana's having an affair."

Ren's eyebrows rose. "With who?"

"I don't know yet. But that room she asked me to curtain off? She had me escort her there one afternoon. I left the curtain ajar and saw a man enter. The room was dim; I couldn't see his face. But I certainly noticed the way he kissed her. Among other things."

Ren pursed her mouth. "When was this?"

"Two days ago."

The same night her father arrested Zofi. The night the heir

cursed him with a vision of Yasmin. If Lexana was with someone else, she couldn't have been the one sending visions to Andros. "How long did they stay in that room?"

"All bloody evening. She made me stay outside and wait for them to finish. Another sleepless night for me, just so she can have her Eastern fiancé and sample the local globe fruit, too..."

Ren groaned. "Thank you for the mental image."

"Better that than the actual image, trust me." Aud smirked. Then flashed Ren a curious glance. "What's the matter? Isn't this what you'd hoped for? It'll ruin Danton's engagement."

Ren ran a hand through her hair.

Audrina continued to study her. "Unless that's not what you were looking for after all." When Ren didn't respond, Audrina leaned forward. "You can tell me. Like you said, Ren, we're friends. If we're going back to the way things were, that means trusting each other."

This time, when Ren reached for Audrina's hand, her friend didn't pull away. "You don't know how much that means to me." Especially now, when Ren could trust so few people.

She still couldn't drag Aud into this. Not fully. But she could give her friend enough information to placate her without putting her in harm's way. "I'm being threatened."

Audrina's eyes shot wide. "By who?"

"I don't know. They call themselves the true heir—"

"What, like a secret identity?"

Ren shook her head. "Your guess is as good as mine. All I know is they want me gone from Kolonya, or worse."

Audrina's jaw dropped. "The baths..."

Ren nodded. "They..." She swallowed hard. "They used a

curse against me. To make my limbs stop working. I sank under, nearly drowned. . . ."

"A curse?" Audrina frowned, clearly thinking hard. "But only—"

"Only relatives can curse you, I know." Ren rubbed her temple with a forefinger. "That's all I know about the heir. It's someone related to me."

"Well, did this *heir* tell you what they want so badly? What in Sun's name is worth trying to drown your own relative?"

"They want the throne. Which means they need to get rid of me and my sisters first."

Audrina inhaled sharply. "What are you going to do?"

"For now? Avoid taking solo baths," she joked weakly. "Beyond that, I don't know. Keep looking for the heir. Track suspects."

"You suspected Lexana," Audrina supplied, catching on. "She's related to you?"

Ren bobbed her head. "A cousin, on my father's side. But if she was with a lover all night, two days ago, then it can't be her."

"They've threatened you again? Since the baths?" Audrina leaned forward. "Ren, who else knows about this? Your father, or someone who might be able to help you?"

She shook her head. "I can't tell anyone, Aud."

"Why?"

"Because." The truth itched to spill out. But she drew the line at admitting how terrible a person she was to the only friend she had left. "I'm sorry. I can't tell you any more."

After a moment, Audrina nodded. "Okay. I understand." Her friend gripped her fingers so hard they ached. "But if things get any worse, Ren, I hope you remember who you can trust."

Ren entered the Great Hall for dinner at Akeylah's side. At the head of the room, the king's and queen's seats stood empty. As they'd agreed after much debate, Akeylah and Ren ascended the dais to sit side by side in those chairs. Two sisters in place of a king.

Just this simple gesture caused murmurs to spread through the hall.

Ren didn't like to dwell on the chaos that would erupt if Andros died without an officially sanctioned heir. She didn't know what would happen, whether the regional council or the council of lords would force a tribunal. And what would the heir do if they saw the throne wide open for the taking?

"How did your afternoon appointments go?" Ren asked Akeylah to distract herself.

"Lord D'Quinn Cass wants the newest ship in our fleet named after him." Akeylah rolled her eyes ever so slightly.

Ren stifled a laugh. "What ego." But she faltered when she spotted a familiar face across the Great Hall. Sarella. Walking straight toward the dais, her gaze fixed on Ren's.

Next to her, Akeylah spoke on. "It's strange, isn't it, how easily these day-to-day queries can distract you. When I first came to the Keep, I judged the nobles for focusing only on their petty complaints. But now that I'm listening to them, it's just as hard for me to remember what's important. How do we keep our heads above water when everyone's desperate to drag us into the muck?"

"Like this, I suppose." Ren watched Sarella approach. "We

keep each other in check. Every day, we remind each other what matters." She straightened as Sarella reached them.

"My lady?" Sarella sank into a curtsy. "I wonder if I might have a word."

"Lady Sarella." Ren smiled. "I've been hoping for the chance to thank you. Without your aid in the baths, I fear I wouldn't be here today."

Sarella's narrowed eyes flicked to Ren. "I wasn't speaking to you. Though I do worry that my instinctive and magnanimous decision to aid you was misguided."

Ren cast her sister a wary frown. *What now?*

Sarella turned toward Akeylah. "May I speak with you alone, Lady Akeylah? I do not feel comfortable speaking about this matter in front of *her*."

Ren glanced around the room again. Was everyone staring at both of them? Or just at Ren...? "Whatever you have to say, you can tell us both, Sarella," Ren said.

Then, in the distance, motion caught Ren's eye. Audrina, dressed like a serving girl instead of in her maid's uniform. She carried a water pitcher in one hand and waved her other wildly to catch Ren's eye. Aud mouthed something Ren couldn't quite decipher.

"Lady Sarella, my sister and I were just about to begin our meal." Akeylah smiled. Ren hoped Sarella didn't notice the strain around the edges. "Might we discuss your concerns after?"

"It is urgent, my lady, and regards your sister's character. I assure you, once you hear this tale, you won't want to break bread with such a woman."

Ren finally realized what Audrina was mouthing. *Get out.*

"Lady Florencia is my sister." Akeylah's voice went cold. "I assure *you*, it takes more than mere court gossip to turn me against family."

In the distance, the main doors swung open. Audrina stopped waving and turned to stare in horror. Ren's heart beat faster as the Southern and Western ambassadors marched into the Great Hall, flanked by Lord D'Vangeline Rueno, his daughter Lexana, and the Talon captain.

Ren rose. So did Akeylah.

Rueno strode straight toward their table. Behind him jogged Lexana, eyes wide as saucers. A moment later, Danton hurried into view. He, too, mouthed something.

I'm sorry.

Dread pooled in Ren's stomach.

"Where is the king?" Lord Rueno demanded without preamble.

Ren cleared her throat. "Our father is indisposed. How can we assist you in his stead?"

"*You* cannot assist with anything," Rueno spat in her direction. "Lexana, come here." Lexana obeyed, though she kept her face turned to the floor, mouth a thin, trembling line. "Tell Lady Akeylah what you told us."

"Father, please—"

"*Now*, Lexana. This is a matter of state security."

For a heartbeat, Lexana met Ren's eye, expression unreadable. Was that fear, or something darker Ren saw written across her features? Then Lexana bowed her head once more, meek and obedient. "I found some letters. Hidden in an old, unused suite."

An unused suite you were sneaking off to have an affair in, Ren thought.

Rueno produced a stack of paper as thick as Ren's forearm. She only caught a glimpse of the first page, but she recognized the curling, perfect script even from a distance. *The heir.*

"The letters are from a known rebel sympathizer in the Eastern Reach, addressed to Florencia," Rueno said. "They contain proof that Florencia sent information to the rebellion. Including the battle plans the rebels used against us in Burnt Bay."

If a lady dropped a hatpin right now, Ren felt certain she would hear it strike the floor.

Ren glanced at Danton. The letters might be faked by the heir, but the information they contained? All too true. Danton shook his head just once, barely noticeable. *Don't say anything.*

Panic clawed at her throat. Everything she'd worked for. The reputation she'd carved for herself. Her new position in the Keep. It would all come crashing down now.

Lexana picked up the thread. "Josen, the king's personal valet, is responsible for cleaning the study where the king kept his plans. He told me Lady Florencia returned his study keys one evening, a few months before Burnt Bay. Lady Florencia claimed she found Josen's keys in the chambers of the lady she served at the time."

"That would be me," Sarella piped up from somewhere on the edge of the crowd. "There were no keys in my chambers that evening. I believe Florencia stole them herself."

You were so blind drunk that night you couldn't remember your own name. Ren clenched her jaw to swallow the retort. It wouldn't help.

71

The Talon captain spoke up. "Until recently, we could not fathom how the Eastern rebels knew our ships were coming, or when to fight back. But with assistance from within the Keep..."

"With all due respect, Captain, I heard nothing about this from my Eastern contacts," Danton interrupted.

"And just how effective have *your* contacts proven at garnering us intelligence, Ambassador?" Ambassador Ghoush raised a brow.

Ren sat forward. If she didn't speak up now, Danton would hang himself, too. She may hate him for his betrayal, but she couldn't let him die. "My lords," she started, but froze.

Under the table, Akeylah's foot dug into hers. *Wait.* Ren stuttered to a halt.

Akeylah glanced Ren's way. Could she see the guilt written on Ren's face? Did her sister know this was true?

If so, then Akeylah had become a very adept liar over the past few weeks.

Akeylah turned back to the crowd with a bewildered expression. "Lady Florencia was born here. She grew up serving you all. She is the daughter of your king. What motivation could she possibly have to smuggle information to rebels in a Reach she's never even visited?"

"Well..." Lord Rueno narrowed his eyes. "I—"

"How could an honest man like Lord Rueno fathom the twisted mind of a girl like her?" Sarella scowled. "Florencia served as my personal maid for years, where she proved entitled and greedy. Perhaps the Easterners paid her for this information."

"The key word there, my lady, is *perhaps.*" Akeylah kept her tone gentle. "None of us know what happened. We will wait upon my father's judgment before we take action."

Shouts rose at the back of the hall. Somewhere, a man cried, "Arrest her."

"She killed my son," a woman yelled.

Rueno cleared his throat. "My lady, if we could see His Majesty at once—"

"Given the nature of this accusation and my father's delicate condition, I believe it best if I speak to him personally," Akeylah replied, with only the briefest stutter. Under the table, Ren pressed her knee against Akeylah's for support.

"Of course, my lady." Rueno and the captain exchanged glances. "But please inform him we are eager to hear his decision as soon as possible. From him, naturally."

"Naturally." Akeylah offered a polite smile. "I'm sure his summons will reach you soon. Captain?" Akeylah turned to the Talon. "Would you please escort us to the king's chambers?"

Only once they began to move through the crowd did Ren understand Akeylah's request. Her sister wanted the captain to prevent any furious Kolonyans from attacking the traitor behind Burnt Bay. Muttered curses followed them across the Great Hall.

Hatred I deserve.

Outside the Great Hall, Ren pretended to trip. Akeylah knelt to offer her a hand. "I'm as good as dead," Ren hissed. "Distance yourself from me. Protect the throne."

Akeylah glanced over her shoulder at the captain. "I have a plan." Then Akeylah raised her voice. "Please help my sister. She's twisted her ankle."

The captain grabbed her arm and yanked Ren upright. "Get up, traitor."

Akeylah cleared her throat. "Innocent until proven guilty,

Captain. Escort Lady Florencia to her chambers and place a guard on her door—for her safety as much as ours. I will send word when Father is ready to see her."

As she strode away from her sister, Ren felt the heir's chains close around her, as tangible as physical shackles. *Two sisters down. Only one to go.*

·∘8∘·

Akeylah

"I need your help doing something irresponsible," Akeylah greeted Rozalind the second the queen's chamber doors shut behind her. In her arms, she carried a pile of clothing she'd just pilfered from her father's suite.

"My favorite." Rozalind smiled, but it faded at Akeylah's serious look. "What is it?"

Akeylah tossed the clothing on the bed and launched into the story. Lexana's accusations, the chants to arrest Ren. The evidence, such as it was, of Ren's crime. Rozalind listened in silence, although her eyebrows rose higher with every new detail.

Akeylah understood. *Burnt Bay.* She knew Ren's crime must have been serious, but...

Still. Akeylah had seen the papers Rueno held. She'd recognized the handwriting. How much of what Rueno said was true, and how much had been fabricated by the heir?

"Now Rueno is demanding to hear Ren's sentence from Father himself." Akeylah held up a narrow waistcoat and matching silk trousers. "Do you think this would fit me?"

Rozalind dropped onto the bed. "Well. People had to discover your father's condition eventually. I know you'd hoped for more time to prepare, but—what are you doing?"

Akeylah had stepped into the silk trousers and begun to tug them up under her skirt. "If Rueno has his way, he'll get the court to sentence Ren to death. She doesn't stand a chance. Not for a crime like this." Akeylah secured the trousers and peeked to check the scar on her thigh. *Good.* The glow didn't show through the dark silk.

"Burnt Bay was a horrible atrocity, Akeylah. Aiding rebels in committing it...You said Florencia asked you to distance yourself from her. Perhaps you should listen." Rozalind's voice faltered as Akeylah pulled her shift dress over her head.

Only then did Akeylah realize, face flushing, that she wore no slip beneath. She turned around to fasten her father's waistcoat. It was too big in the shoulders and pinched tight at the waist. Still, it fit well enough to pass a distant inspection.

"None of this explains why you're dressing in Andros's clothes," Rozalind pointed out.

"Just a test run. This is where the irresponsible part comes in." Akeylah took a deep breath and met Rozalind's gaze in the mirror. "I'm going to use a camouflage tithe."

Rozalind's eyes shot wide. "Akeylah, no."

"It'll only last a couple of minutes, so I need you to act as go-between. We'll arrange it for tomorrow morning, first thing." By then, her daily shield tithe would have worn off. It would be a risk—she'd be open to the heir's attacks until she was able to shield herself again. But saving Ren was worth it.

"You can meet Rueno and the Talon captain in the sitting room," Akeylah said to Rozalind. "Tell them I—I mean, the king—has a terrible flu. Then you escort them in, and I'll whisper my instructions. We can say I lost my voice, too, because if they hear me speak they'll figure me out in a second," she muttered, more to herself than to Rozalind.

"This is madness."

"It's our only option." Akeylah strode toward the queen.

Rozalind rose to meet her. "You're putting yourself in danger for a wanted criminal, Akeylah. What if the tithe wears off too soon? If you're caught doing this..."

Akeylah captured Rozalind's hands. Held them to her chest. "If I don't try, how can I live with myself?" She held the queen's gaze. "She's my sister, Roz."

"Your sisters are proving bigger liabilities by the day. What if Ren is guilty, just like Zofi may be? Think about all the soldiers who died in Burnt Bay. And think about Kolonya—without Zofi or Florencia as options, you're the only heir. The only leader left. You can't make yourself into a criminal just like your siblings."

I already am. Akeylah bit back the retort. She understood where Rozalind was coming from. First Zofi was accused of murder, now this?

Growing up on the shore, Akeylah had seen ships sink. She could imagine what Burnt Bay must have looked like after that attack. If Ren really did supply the rebellion with battle plans, then her sister had blood on her hands. A lot of it. But Akeylah understood how that felt. No executioner's noose could strangle you tighter than guilt.

No hangman could bring those soldiers back from their graves either.

"We've all done things we regret," Akeylah whispered. "Me more than anyone."

"I cannot believe that." Rozalind dropped Akeylah's hands to cross her arms instead.

Akeylah hesitated. Studied the queen's expression. She might lose Rozalind once and for all if she told her this. Rozalind may hate her, may never look at her the same way again. But Rozalind believed Akeylah was innocent. That wasn't true.

Akeylah couldn't let her sisters take this fall. If Ren went down for her crimes, Akeylah would be next.

"I'm the reason my father is dying, Rozalind." She said it louder than she meant—too loud. She checked over her shoulder, but the doors were still shut, no sounds of life beyond.

The queen shook her head. "You mustn't blame yourself, Akeylah. Your father is ill—"

"No, he isn't. He's cursed. *I cursed him.*" It was easier to say this time. Ever since telling her sisters the truth. "Look." She yanked on the trousers she'd donned. Drew them down far enough to reveal the bright, damning blue scar on her thigh.

The reason she'd never gone further than kisses with Rozalind. The reason she'd hidden from the maids ever since she arrived in the Keep. The reason she couldn't let Ren swing for her crime. Not when Akeylah had done something just as terrible, perhaps more so.

The queen's lips parted. She stared at the scar. Took a step backward.

Akeylah's heart wrenched. *Now I lose her, too.*

"Why?" Rozalind finally managed, the word barely a breath.

"I didn't know who I was." Akeylah retied the trousers around her waist. "My stepfather beat me, almost killed me more than once. I thought it was him I was cursing."

For a moment, Rozalind shut her eyes and inhaled sharply. When she opened them again, her expression seemed carefully controlled, almost blank. "So it was...an accident."

"A terrible one." Akeylah's hands shook. She curled them around her father's shirtsleeves. "One I've tried to set right. I've looked everywhere for some way to reverse it—"

Understanding bloomed across Rozalind's face. "Your time in the library. The healing tithes you're always researching." The queen swore under her breath. "All this time I thought you were looking for a cure the menders missed."

"I didn't know where else to turn." Akeylah dared a step forward. "Rozalind, please believe me, I never meant for any of this to happen."

Rozalind spun away. Stared at the narrow passage that connected her rooms to Andros's. "Is this what you're being threatened over?"

Akeylah shut her eyes. "Someone else knows my secret, as well as what my sisters are hiding. We thought it was Yasmin. That's why we asked for your help with that acolyte's body...."

"Gods, Akeylah."

"I understand if you hate me now," Akeylah murmured. "I would. If it were my husband." Her voice barely cracked on the word. She was getting better at saying it.

When she opened her eyes again, pain twisted across Rozalind's face. But she moved closer again. Approached until she stood just inches from Akeylah. Close enough that Akeylah caught her familiar, ocean-sweet scent. The queen's breath grazed her lips.

She didn't say anything. Only searched Akeylah's eyes.

Rozalind must despise her now. Rozalind, the dutiful queen, the obedient daughter who sailed across the sea and wed a stranger to forge peace. She might sneak around with Akeylah, but only because her husband had given his blessing to extramarital affairs.

What did Rozalind know of secrets? Of the crushing weight of guilt Akeylah carried?

Yet. "I could never hate you," Rozalind said in a voice like the ghost of a whisper. She reached up, agonizingly slow, and caught one of Akeylah's plaits. Brushed it off Akeylah's shoulder, her fingertips grazing Akeylah's collarbone. "No matter what you've done, Akeylah, *I know you*. You're a good person."

"How can you say that? After what I just told you . . ."

"You told me it was an accident." Rozalind traced up Akeylah's neck. Cupped her cheek. "You told me you've been trying to fix it. What is there to hate in that?"

"I *cursed* someone, Rozalind, my own father—" But she broke off. Because Rozalind leaned in and kissed her.

The protests melted away. Akeylah caught Rozalind's cheeks,

drew her closer, and Rozalind's hands went to Akeylah's waist to untie the trousers once more. They puddled at Akeylah's feet, and she stepped forward, into Rozalind's arms.

She had nothing to hide anymore.

They'd have to prepare soon. Go into Andros's chambers and move the king somewhere safe, set up a reception area, practice what Akeylah needed to tell Rueno. But they had all night for that. So when Rozalind wrapped her arms around Akeylah's waist and walked her backward, toward the bed, Akeylah moved with her.

Right now, Rozalind was all she could see.

※

Thank the seas for Rozalind's ability to tithe. Akeylah doubted they could have managed the next morning if Rozalind hadn't been able to lift Andros all by herself and carry him into the adjoining rooms. As her tithe faded, Rozalind tucked the king into her bed, while Akeylah rearranged the king's reception wing.

They were interrupted briefly when Zofi's Talon friend Vidal stopped by. He begged permission to ride after Zofi, to escort her safely to her band. Akeylah granted it gladly, though she did so with the door half-shut, praying Vidal didn't notice anything amiss inside.

Now, tucked into her father's bed, wearing his clothing, with a bloodletter hidden underneath the sheets, Akeylah wondered if this truly was the right course of action. Rozalind had ordered the king's mender not to speak about Andros's illness until the royal family announced it. But Akeylah knew from experience how long secrets lasted in this Keep—less time than it took milk to turn. What if the mender had told someone about the king's condition already? Or what if said mender heard about the king holding an audience with Rueno and the captain, and asked how they'd received orders from a comatose man?

On top of all those worries, not to mention the fear of what would happen if the tithe faded too soon, Akeylah felt all too aware of her vulnerability. She'd foregone the shield tithe today. It left her senses brighter, sharper...but uneasy, too. Like stepping outside on a rainy morning back east—the fresh air was nice, yet a chill accompanied it.

In the adjoining sitting room, she heard Rozalind's voice. "Lord Rueno, Captain, thank you for coming so quickly."

Too late to change my mind.

Akeylah turned the bloodletter so the point jutted into the crook of her elbow. Rozalind spoke in a low, urgent tone, relaying what Akeylah had asked—*the king is not well, he's lost his voice, this conversation must be brief.*

She drowned out the queen's voice. Focused on her father instead. His facial features, the silver of his hair, the thickness of his neck.

She could only approximate him—camouflage tithes couldn't disguise your height or body build. But the bedding piled around her would help. She just needed to perfect his face.

The doorknob rattled. Rozalind. *Here goes nothing.*

Akeylah dragged the blade across her skin. The tithe swept over her. The Arts sang in her veins, neon-bright with promise. They felt stronger after several days of shielding, almost overwhelming. She harnessed all the potential and channeled it into a mental image of Father.

Father, lying in this very bed. Father, breathing weak and labored, skin wrinkled with age. The same man she'd spent the morning gazing at, willing back to some semblance of life.

In the end, the tithe was easier than she'd anticipated. Father already occupied so much of her imagination, it took little effort to shape her facial features into his.

When she opened her eyes, Rueno and the Talon captain regarded her seriously. Behind them, luckily out of their line of sight, Rozalind had frozen in shock. Akeylah hoped that was because she'd done too good a job with this camouflage and not the other way around.

She began to cough, hard. With one hand, she reached limply for Rozalind, who recalled herself and darted across the chamber to catch it.

"Yes, my love, I'm here." Rozalind bent close enough for Akeylah's—or, rather, the king's—lips to graze her ear.

Akeylah kept her voice low, half-growl, half-whisper. "Tell them...I have decided what to do about Florencia."

Rozalind relayed her words, then turned back to Akeylah.

"Your Majesty, we are deeply sorry for all your woes of late." Lord Rueno bowed. "I'm grateful you take this matter as seriously as we do. The court is anxious to see justice served."

"As am I," said Akeylah-via-Rozalind. "But exactly that. *Justice.*" She laid on that word hard enough to justify another series of coughs. "Not the judgment of an angry mob."

Lord Rueno and the captain exchanged glances when Rozalind repeated those words.

"Captain, you are to confine Lady Florencia to her chambers. Post double guards on every entrance, the servants' passages included." Akeylah knew they had to at least make it *look* like they were trying. "As for the evidence against her, Lord Rueno, you will give me these letters and any other evidence you have collected."

"Of course." Rueno bowed. "But, Your Majesty, the serving boy—"

"Once I have familiarized myself with the letters and their contents, I will hear Josen's testimony," Akeylah continued. Then, on an impulse, she bluffed, "I will also hear from other witnesses who may wish to speak to me in private." That should buy them a little more time. "Only once I have heard from every voice in this case will I pass my judgment."

"Your Majesty, if I may…" Rueno stepped forward. "I understand your desire to hear all the facts. But this was a very serious breach, if the allegations prove true. Do you think confinement to her chambers will really be sufficient to secure such a traitor?"

"You tell me, Captain." Akeylah's voice dripped with sarcasm, through Rozalind, as she looked at the Talon. "Are our Talons trained enough to secure a single young woman?"

The captain's mouth twitched at the corners. "I believe we can handle it, Your Majesty."

Rueno ducked his head. He may be stubborn, but he knew when to hold his tongue, too.

"Now, you have heard my decision." Akeylah glanced at Rozalind. She didn't have much time left. The tithe ached. Made her want to crawl out of her skin. "Captain, see it done."

Then she sank into her loudest coughing fit yet. Underneath

the thick blankets, her fingertips tingled. She clenched her teeth as the tingle became an itch became a burn.

"I'm afraid I need to ask you two to leave now." Rozalind placed a firm hand on both men's shoulders. "If you see the mender on your way out, send her in, please."

"Roz...alind," Akeylah growled. *Get them out of here*, she thought, desperate.

At a glance in her direction, Rozalind reached for the curtains around the bed and casually flicked them shut, far enough to obscure Akeylah from view.

Everything burned. Almost as bad as a Vulgar Arts curse. She could feel her face start to split, like a sunburn peeling open, as it began to change back. She flung a hand across it and moaned in agony. She wished she had as much practice at tithing as Zofi. Her sister would likely be able to hold this tithe longer than she was managing.

"Is he quite all right?" Lord Rueno hesitated on the threshold.

"He will be," Rozalind promised. "You have your orders, gentlemen. Thank you for coming by." With that, she slammed the bedroom door and collapsed against it.

With a final burst of itching, followed by a sensation like plunging her entire body into a cool bath, Akeylah's face returned to its normal shape. She levered herself up on one elbow to peer around the curtain. Rozalind held her ear to the keyhole.

Only once the sounds on the far side faded did the queen let out a sigh of relief. "That was too close." She glared at Akeylah.

"I know." Akeylah flung back the covers and surged to her feet. "But it worked."

"You need to be more careful." Rozalind stepped toward her, expression serious. "You take all these risks to protect others. What about protecting yourself?"

"I protect myself." Even as she said it, she recognized the irony of the statement. In posing as Andros, she'd left herself vulnerable to the heir. From the depleted scratch in her veins, it'd be a few hours yet until she'd have the strength to shield herself again.

Rozalind reached her side. Akeylah's skin burned with the memory of the queen's fingertips. All the places they'd explored last night. "Not when it counts," Rozalind whispered.

Akeylah lifted a hand to cup the back of the queen's neck. Their foreheads touched, and she lost herself in the queen's sea-deep gaze. "I'm more worried about you," Akeylah murmured. "You're a foreign queen, daughter of the country we've been at war with for centuries. Have you thought about what will happen if Father dies?"

"Of course I have. I've thought about that possibility every single day since I arrived in the Reaches. Why do you think I'm so worried about you?" Rozalind grazed her thumb along Akeylah's jawline. "You're almost as foreign as I am here, Akeylah. You may be half-Kolonyan, but that's not the half people will see if they learn what you've done. You need to be smarter. Take care of yourself above all others, even your family."

Akeylah closed her eyes. Savored the queen's touch, her scent. "I can't do that. I have to take care of the people I love, too, or I'd never forgive myself."

"People you love." Rozalind's whisper set her veins alight. "Where am I on that scale?"

The corners of Akeylah's lips curved upward. "Somewhere near the top," she admitted in a barely there breath.

"Let's make a deal, then, love." Rozalind tilted her head. Akeylah mirrored her until their lips were a hair apart, so close she felt the warmth radiating from the queen's skin. "I protect you, first and foremost." Rozalind's mouth brushed Akeylah's as she spoke. "And you protect me. That way we'll both be safe."

Akeylah smiled, wider now. "Deal."

❊ 9 ❊

Zofi

Two days. Two days, and still Zofi had yet to find anyone on this gods-forsaken road willing to sell a horse to a Traveler.

Despite her trustworthy boots, which her sisters had thankfully squirreled away in the supply bag they'd brought her, her feet throbbed. She'd made as much progress as possible—walked over a dozen leagues per day. By the end of the first day, she'd left behind the busy merchant stalls, which only stretched about forty miles north of Kolonya City. By the end of the second, she found herself passing dozens of small roads, footpaths to the outer settlements dotting Kolonya proper. Each one nestled into village-sized clearings in the Ageless Jungle.

Late on the second evening, a thunderstorm struck, and she gave up trying to sleep in the muddy patches under the trees. Instead, she dug into the supply of coins her sisters had added to the rucksack. It was enough to pay for room and board in the next village she found.

The town, Vinesland, had been named for the houses woven into the tree canopy with vines, the floors and walls and roofs all stitched together like a giant bark-and-leaf quilt. Her room was a five-by-five-by-five-foot square, which she climbed into via a rope ladder as high in the trees as Ilian Keep towered above Kolonya City. For once, as she stretched along the floor, she was grateful for her short stature. Ren would have to bend near in half to fit in this bed.

The proprietor of the inn swung past—literally, as the paths among these treetop homes were just hanging vines. He left a bucket of fresh water, another bucket of hearty stew, and a curt note. *Please leave by first light*, it read in clumsy block letters. *Don't want other lodgers to see you. Sure you understand.*

Sands forbid any respectable lodgers see a Traveler sleeping in the same establishment. That would be bad for business.

Zofi tore up the note. It left a bad taste in her mouth, even though the stew was delicious, heavily spiced with an extra portion of meat. That was all money could buy you. Food, a roof over your head, fresh water.

Not respect. Not equal treatment.

She'd left her chance at winning that behind in Kolonya. And unless Zofi found her mother in time, unless Mother knew a cure for the curse she'd helped Akeylah work, Father would die. His blood would be on Akeylah's hands, a secret the heir wouldn't hesitate to use against her Eastern sister.

How long before they all fell? Before Akeylah and Ren were banished, too. Or worse, if the heir had their way. Zofi could only imagine what sort of a twisted tyrant this "true heir" would make.

Then again, from the outside, people might say the same about her. Or Akeylah. Zofi had murdered her own brother—never mind that he'd been a terrible person. Akeylah had cursed her father—never mind that she didn't know who she was or that she'd been desperately trying to escape abuse.

If Andros had been honest with his children from the start, if Zofi had known Nicolen was her brother, if Akeylah knew her true parentage . . . none of them would be in this situation.

Then again, Zofi might never have grown up the way she did. She may never have known the freedom of a Traveler band, might not understand the world the way she did now, from the bottom-side up.

Much as she hated the straits they were in, Zofi couldn't bring herself to wish things any different. She loved her mother, her people, the life she'd had.

The only thing she regretted was letting the heir threaten it all.

The next morning, Zofi followed the proprietor's request. She departed well before dawn, her waterskin freshly filled and her belly full of cold leftover stew. On her way back to the merchant's road, however, Zofi flashed her curse finger at Vinesland in general.

She had to stay focused. Find her mother, learn what in sands' name kind of curse she'd taught Akeylah. Send Akeylah the cure as fast as possible. Only then did they stand a chance. With Andros healthy and restored to himself, her sisters might be able to buy more time. Fend off the heir.

If they couldn't win the throne themselves, then at least they might be able to stop it from falling into the worst possible hands.

Back on the merchant's road, for the first time in weeks, Zofi prayed. She prayed to the sands to keep her sisters strong. She prayed her own journey would grow easier soon. She'd already been on the road three days. Without a horse, she'd need a miracle to reach Mother's camp before Andros's time ran out.

Sands guide me to my mother swiftly. Let me find Father a cure.

And let Mother explain why she never told me she was a bloody curseworker.

Zofi always knew her mother had secrets. It was a game they played, when she was little. "How many secrets are you keeping?" Zofi would always ask.

And Mother would smile, her silver scar flashing under the moons. "As many as there are grains of sand in the desert."

After learning she was the daughter of a king, Zofi supposed she shouldn't put anything past her mother. But his status aside, hiding a father was not unusual. Unless a baby was fathered by another Traveler in the same band, the usual custom was to conceal his identity.

But selling cursework at underground festivals to strangers... How did Mother get into the Vulgar Arts in the first place? Who taught it to her, and why?

Perhaps Mother had been like Akeylah. Desperate, in need of a way to strike back at a relative who abused their bond. How much did Zofi really know about Mother's past?

Her past, come to think of it. Anyone Mother might have learned to curse would be a relative of Zofi's, too.

Her head throbbed. Too many possibilities. She couldn't contemplate them all.

Hooves thundered on the road behind her. Zofi stood to the side, half-concealed in the underbrush, until a pair of merchants rode past, trailing a rattling wagon. She waited until they faded from sight ahead before she began to walk again.

A Traveler walking alone could never be too careful.

Morning songbirds began to whistle. Monkeys chattered in the branches. Every now and then, one would swing into her view upside-down and peer at her while she walked, checking whether she had any food to steal. Zofi waved her empty hands, and the monkeys bared their teeth in disappointment, swung back into the trees.

My mother is a curseworker.

Mother, who spent hours telling stories around the communal fires at night—sweeping sagas about the First Six or Traveler Queen Claera, or even personal tales of towns where she'd negotiated her way out of tight corners. Duels she'd won and damsels she'd rescued.

The same mother who let Zofi sleep in her tent for weeks after the Silver Prince's death.

Zofi shouldn't be surprised. If anyone in the Reaches would have forbidden knowledge about the Vulgar Arts, *of course* it would be Deena. But why had Mother offered that knowledge to an outsider? She taught Akeylah how to work a Vulgar Arts curse strong enough to fell a king, but she never shared the knowledge with her own band.

That went against every bone in Zofi's body. Your band was your family—they shared everything. Food, money, weapons, any advantage they managed to grasp in a world set against them. Yet Mother hid this enormous capability.

Hooves sounded again, louder. This time, Zofi didn't bother to move off the road. Dawn had already lit the sky, and there were gaggles of other passersby here and there. She felt safe enough not to hide in the bushes.

The hoofbeats slowed.

Zofi's shoulders tensed. Had she made a mistake? Her hand drifted to her longknife. She glanced back, expecting trouble, and froze.

"Zofi?"

Behind her stood an enormous stallion. Eighteen hands high, his pelt bright silver, he snorted in greeting. Next to him paced a familiar chestnut mare, a grinning boy in a Talon's leather vest on her back.

Despite herself, an answering smile split Zofi's cheeks. "What in sands' name are you doing out here?"

"Looking for you." Vidal dismounted in a cloud of dust. "I can't believe you walked this far already. I doubled back twice, thinking I must have ridden past you."

She shot her eyes skyward. "Have you no faith?"

Then his arms were around her, and Zofi sank into them, more grateful than she cared to admit for the familiar embrace. "My mistake," he murmured into the nest her hair had become after three days' hard journey without a scarf to tie it back. "Next time I'll take into account the fact that you walk as fast as a horse yourself."

She snorted, the sound muffled by his leather tunic. "Not nearly." Then she tilted her chin back to assess him. Aside from a faint sheen of sweat on his brow, he looked good.

Better than good. He looked as handsome as he had the night of the Sun's Ascendance when, dressed in full uniform, he'd swept her across the sky gardens in a flawless dance. She hadn't been this close to him since. Hadn't been able to wrap her arms around his waist or feel his chest rise and fall against hers. Or to watch his lips part, trace the edges of them and wonder how they would feel pressed to hers, the way they'd almost done that night...

"Did the king send you?" she asked, tearing herself from his arms. The last thing she needed was to get distracted—or dragged back into the king's dungeons. Not now, when she was so close to home. *Back where I belong*, she reminded herself. *Back with my band.*

"Nobody sent me," Vidal replied, too quick. The tension in his tone made her suspicious.

"You're a Talon. You have to follow orders."

"I...requested new orders."

She frowned. "And your leader allowed that?"

He bowed his head. "Our leader is dead."

Of course. Yasmin had led the Talons. With her dead and Andros incapacitated... "But your other commanders. Your captain, or whoever is in charge now..."

"I went over his head. Appealed to the source of power, so to speak."

Her eyebrows rose. Last her sisters told her, that source lay comatose in bed. "My father?" she ventured, careful. She wasn't sure whether word of his condition had spread throughout the Keep yet.

The corners of Vidal's lips quirked. "Not quite. But Queen

94

Rozalind and your sister Akeylah were happy to grant me leave to accompany you. They both agreed our army won't miss one Talon for a few days."

Zofi reached up to touch the silver sand-stepper's nose, and he huffed out an excited breath, then stamped his hooves.

Vidal, for his part, watched with concern. "Your sister was worried about you. A Traveler alone on Kolonyan roads…"

"I can take care of myself," Zofi replied. "I've spent my entire life on the roads, I might add, and my entire life being a Traveler, too." She thought angrily about the innkeeper who asked her to leave. The traders she'd attempted to barter with, who had refused to sell her even a wizened old nag of a pony. That last thought, at least, softened her. "I'm grateful for the horse." Zofi reached up to pat his flanks. "But you can't come with me, Vidal. I'm not riding into my band's camp with a Talon in tow."

"At least let me escort you to the camp itself. If I can't come in with you, then I'll return to Kolonya City alone afterward."

"I'll stand out like a stubbed thumb with you riding next to me."

"I can take off the uniform." Without another word, he tugged on his vest stays. It fell open, and she had to tear her gaze away from his bare chest. "I have another shirt in my saddlebag," he added, and she could've sworn she heard a smirk in that tone.

It made her want to kick him. "I don't need an escort." She set her jaw, stubborn. When she finally turned to look at him again, he'd thrown on a simple cotton shirt. But she could still see the sharp outline of his muscles beneath it, and try though she might, she couldn't make herself dislike the view.

"Then I won't serve as your escort." He smiled, too damned winning for his own good. "I'll simply join you as a friend."

She didn't deign to answer that. Without another word, she swung up into the stallion's saddle. Then she wrapped her hands in his mane, leaned down along his neck, and kicked him into motion. Wind whipping through her hair, Zofi smiled—her first real smile in what felt like a lifetime.

And sure enough, when she stole a glance over her shoulder, there was Vidal riding hard after her, a matching grin painted across his face.

Right then and there, she made a silent decision. *If he can keep up, I'll let him stay.*

❈ 10 ❈

Florencia

Five days since the mender told them Father had a fortnight to live. Two since she'd been confined to her chambers, pending Andros's judgment about her actions.

About the treason I committed.

Last night, unable to sleep, Ren had curled up on the floor beside the thin wooden servants' door and listened to the guards posted outside her chamber gossip while they played crowns, an old dice game.

"Confinement. That's all for now."

"Why such a light sentence? If she really did it..."

"We don't *know* that," the first Talon, a woman, scolded. "Stop believing every whisper you hear passing through the halls."

Ren couldn't help it. A faint smile touched her mouth.

But then the woman continued speaking. "First His Majesty's health, now this."

"That's not a rumor—everyone knows he's been bedridden since the countess's funeral," the male Talon retorted.

"With grief. Not some deadly virus. Or, what did Niven claim it was? *Poison?*" Even through the closed door, Ren could practically hear the woman roll her eyes.

"I never said I believed Niven. But you have to admit, it's strange. He arrests one daughter, banishes her without even publicly stating her crime. Now another is accused of treason. And not a peep from our king?"

"Our king has better things to do than reassure a grunt like you." The woman laughed under her breath. "Besides, Captain Lindle received the order to confine the girl from Andros himself. The king was well enough for that."

Ren frowned. That couldn't be right. They must be confused. Unless her father's health had improved. Could Zofi have found a cure for the curse already?

Ren squinted at the flicker of the torchlight under the door as the Talons shifted topics. For a while, they talked about girls, then complained about their commanding officer. Finally, Ren levered herself up off the floor and retreated to bed, where she stared at her canopy instead.

At some point, she must have drifted off, because she awoke to a series of knocks.

"My lady, a visitor," called the Talon outside the main entrance.

"One moment," she cried, and did her best to put on a presentable outfit. She might be a prisoner in her own bedroom, but that didn't mean she needed to look the part.

Finally, when she was satisfied with the girl in the mirror, chin-length hair hot-combed into obedience and a few daubs of paint to cover the worst of her sleepless night's damage, she threw on an ornate robe and sat at her writing desk to give the illusion of productivity.

"Send them in." She expected her sister, or perhaps Rozalind, come to relay news of Andros. Maybe even Andros himself, if the Talons' whispers were to be believed.

But when the doors opened, she slumped in her chair. "Oh, it's you."

Danton pushed back his hood and shut the door before he responded. "You always know how to make a man feel special, Florencia."

"I do when he is." She leaned her chair back onto two legs and studied the ambassador. The morning sun painted deep hollows under his cheeks, and in profile, his nose looked sharper, fiercer. "You shouldn't be here. Haven't you heard what I've been accused of doing? Aiding rebels within the Reach you represent."

"All the more reason for me to meet with you and glean any information I can about said rebel correspondents. At least, that's the reason I've given the council." His face clouded. "Florencia, seeing you locked in here, hearing the rumors...I'm afraid for you. If this goes to trial...." His voice cracked. "I can't lose you."

He meant it. She knew him that well. Recognized the pain and fear in his expression.

But it didn't change what he'd done. She still remembered how it felt at the Sun's Ascendance when Lexana slipped her arm through his and called him her fiancé. Just two days after Danton had lain in Ren's bed all night, his lips tracing a familiar path across her body.

"I'm sure your fiancée would soothe away your pain," she replied, unable to keep the bitterness from her tone.

Danton moved closer. "Florencia, I've been trying to catch you alone since the Sun's Ascendance, to tell you the truth. Lexana and I, it's a sham."

She had to laugh. "Why, because she's cheating on you, or because you never cared for her in the first place? The latter I could've guessed. You've never truly cared for anyone but yourself, Danton."

He flinched. Ran a hand through his dark auburn hair. "Lexana needed a cover story. She's in love with a commoner, a servant boy her father would never approve of. She asked me to pretend to marry her, in exchange for her father's dowry. It would've been more than enough money to supply Tarik with food, medicine, everything we needed to survive this year."

Tarik. Always Tarik. "Enough to help your rebels build better weaponry, too?" Ren asked, tone scathing.

"Absolutely not." His hand dropped back to his side, clenched. "I'm never helping them again—not after...."

Not after the reason I'm locked up in here, she thought angrily. Not after the rebels took the plans Danton and Ren stole for them, and used those plans to kill thousands of Kolonyans.

"Every last coin was going to go toward rebuilding our country. It would've created an alliance between the Northern Reach and Tarik, given Tarik a fresh start."

"Would have. Past tense? What disturbed your plans?" She crossed her arms.

"Me." He locked eyes with her. "I'm going to confess."

It took a moment for her to understand. When she did, she scrambled to her feet. "Danton, no."

"It's the only way, Florencia. They'll kill you for this. You know as well as I do that correspondence is fake. But Lexana showed me the letters. They're damned convincing; whoever forged them used a real rebel seal, code words only the rebellion uses. The only way to prove you're innocent is to show the council the real letters. The ones addressed to me."

"You'd be executed in a heartbeat. I'm still Andros's daughter; they'll hesitate before hanging me. But you, you're an Easterner, no noble ties . . . You can't." She didn't remember moving toward him, reaching out. But suddenly she was clutching his hands to her chest, their faces inches apart.

Danton searched her gaze. "I thought you hated me."

"That doesn't mean I want you to *die*."

"I've brought you nothing but misery. You, the person I love most in the world." He said it so easily she forgot how long it had been since she last heard him say *I love you*. It seemed like yesterday. It always did when they stood like this, so close she felt his breath on her cheeks, almost tasted his lips on hers. She still craved him, even when she hated herself for it.

Nobody kissed her like Danton.

"Let me do this for you," Danton whispered. "Let me shoulder this one burden for you when I've failed to carry so many others."

Only now, standing this close, did Ren notice the unkempt bedraggle of his hair, the uncharacteristic stubble along his jawline. He looked like he hadn't slept in days.

"Danton." Her voice cracked. "I don't want you to die for me.

All I want is for you to trust me. To be honest with me. Like with your engagement—you could have told me about it, rather than letting Lexana blindside me with the news."

"I wanted to, but Rueno demanded we keep it confidential until the contract was finalized, and I didn't realize Lexana would..." He shut his mouth. "You're right, I should have told you. But it doesn't matter now. What matters is that I do the right thing. Clear your name."

She shook her head. "Even if I let you, it wouldn't make a difference. The person who forged those letters? It's me they want to destroy. They'll take you down, too, if you get in their way, but your death would solve nothing. They'll still come for me. And without you, I'd just have one less ally, one less person I trust to lean on." Her voice softened.

He raised a hand, tentative. His thumb grazed her cheekbone, a touch light as air, yet it reverberated through her entire body. "Who's doing this to you, Florencia?" His brow furrowed, came to rest against her forehead. "When I found that boy outside your chambers, the one with the phial of blood...Do you think the same person sent him as forged the letters?"

"I believe so." Ren gritted her teeth. She'd almost forgotten about that boy. Just one more mystery in a stack growing far too tall for comfort. What else was the heir capable of?

"They can't have *that* much influence. Not unless they're royalty." He smiled faintly, but sobered when she didn't join in.

"It's someone related to me. That's all I know." She backed away from Danton, all too aware that if she kept touching him, she'd do something stupid. "Well. That and they want the throne. They'll stop at nothing to remove my sisters and me from their path."

Understanding dawned on his face. "Zofi."

"They went for her first. Now it's my turn."

He frowned and watched her pace across the room. "But nothing has happened to Akeylah?"

"Not yet."

Danton looked pensive. "So it's a relative of yours in line for the throne. . . ."

"It's not Akeylah." Her sister had helped her research Yasmin. *Who turned out to be innocent.* She'd rescued Ren from the baths. *Or did she just know when to arrive because she'd cursed Ren in the first place?* "She's being threatened, too. It just hasn't been made public yet."

"I see." Danton arched a brow. "And you've seen these threats yourself."

Rozalind had seen Akeylah have a fit in the library. And Ren had seen one of Akeylah's blackmail letters, back when Ren and Zofi first confronted Akeylah about being their enemy. But what did that prove? Akeylah could have faked a fit for Rozalind, could have penned the letter she showed Ren and Zofi herself.

"I trust Akeylah," she heard herself say. But she couldn't help thinking of Akeylah's secret. The curse she worked against Andros. She said it was an accident, but that accident brought the sisters here, to Kolonya. If Andros hadn't fallen ill, he would never have summoned his illegitimate daughters, never have offered them a chance at the throne. . .

Plus, the curse meant Akeylah knew how to use the Vulgar Arts. If she'd been willing to curse her own father, what would stop her from cursing a sister or two?

Danton was nodding. "Of course. But just to be on the safe

side, why don't I ask around about her? The forger had seals from the rebels, knew code words they use. Perhaps Akeylah has met some of my contacts before." When Ren still hesitated, Danton pressed a hand to his chest. "Please, Florencia. If you won't let me trade my life for yours, at least let me do this."

"You know I still hate you, right?" But she said it with a smile.

He grinned. "I can live with that." He turned to go, then hesitated on the threshold. "Hatred is not the opposite of love, Florencia. To hate a person, you must still care about them."

"You said it, not me." But in spite of everything, her smile lingered long after he'd gone.

·≈[11]≈·

Akeylah

The first day of Ren's confinement to her chambers, Akeylah woke up and shielded herself immediately. Only after the half-smothering, half-calming sensation stripped away her connection to the Arts did she agree to meet the council of lords.

The council was a gathering of the highest-ranking nobility from Kolonya and beyond. Lord Rueno was an absolute boor the entire time. He complained of her father's absence at every turn, questioned every word she said. Akeylah was forced to remind him, rather more sharply than she liked, just how much her family had been through in recent weeks.

After the meeting, lord after lady crowded her schedule all evening, until Akeylah could hardly squeeze in a moment to slip to the powder room, let alone breathe.

The second day, she woke, shielded herself again, and spent the morning hearing complaints about property tax laws, land feuds, all the endless petty wars nobles waged against one another.

All the while, Ren's words echoed in the back of her mind. *Every day, we remind each another what matters.*

She wished she could slip away and visit her sister. But every time she tried, another urgent request arose.

In lieu of visiting, at the end of each of her endless meetings, Akeylah eased into the topic of her sister. By the time she was through with her appointments, she had talked at least a few nobles into a fury over "Lady Florencia's undeserved public slandering."

"After all," Akeylah found herself repeating, over and over, "we haven't even begun a proper trial, yet she's already being condemned. Is this any way to treat a king's daughter?"

By the second evening, the muttering in the Great Hall started to shift. Now, Akeylah overheard people who variously supported or pitied her.

"I hear Eastern rebels forced Lexana to make it all up," one minor noblewoman said.

"Well, *I* heard that Traveler girl cursed her from afar. Lady Florencia had no idea what she was doing when she sold us out, poor dear."

At that, Akeylah bristled, but when she turned to search out the gossip, she couldn't tell who among the sea of faces at her table had spoken.

She didn't know what to do. She couldn't buy one sister's

innocence at the price of the other's. But she could not afford to correct every rumormonger in the Keep either.

The one good thing about her breakneck schedule was it left her no time for worrying.

The third morning, instead of burying herself in the library to hunt for countercurses the way she'd planned, Akeylah went back to the royal chambers. She had the regional council meeting later that afternoon, but for now, she needed a respite. Between Father's illness, Ren's confinement, and the political machinations... It was too much. She needed to feel alive again.

She needed Rozalind.

Outside Father's chambers, a Talon stopped her. "Delivery came for your father while you were at breakfast, my lady," he said as he handed her a box swathed in black velvet. "We checked the contents, to be safe. Just a wooden doll and a letter."

"I'll take it to him, thank you." She reached out to accept the package.

Only once he'd laid it in her arms did the Talon add, "It's from your stepfather, I believe, my lady. Jahen dam-Senzin. That was your old surname, no?"

Her blood went cold.

Would Jahen send her father a package? He hadn't shown his face in court since the day she arrived, and thank Mother Ocean for that. What could he possibly have to say to the king?

"Did you read the letter?" she asked. She couldn't imagine what it would be about. Unless... She thought about the forged letters the heir created for Ren. The last vision the heir cursed Akeylah with—her stepfather towering over her, fists balled.

Unless this package isn't from Jahen dam-Senzin at all.

The Talon, meanwhile, seemed affronted. "Of course not, my lady. We don't read His Majesty's private correspondence."

"Of course not." She forced a smile. "Thank you."

The Talon opened the door for her, and Akeylah caught her breath until she spotted the curtain drawn around the bed, hiding Father from view.

"Akeylah?" Rozalind's voice drifted from behind said curtain.

"I'll be right there," Akeylah called as she beelined for the bathing chamber attached to the king's bedroom. Inside, she dropped to her knees, the package cradled in both arms, and peeled back the lid.

Her breath caught.

A *wooden doll*, the Talon had called it. But it was more than that.

From its dark red plaits to its painted-glass eyes, even to the style of gown it wore, a loose chiffon dress Akeylah could've sworn must be cut from the same fabric as the outfit she wore to the Sun's Ascendance . . . In every detail, the doll was an exact miniature of Akeylah.

Except for two differences. The golden crown on its head, a replica of her father's. And the puppet strings attached to the doll's arms, legs, and head.

A thought struck her. She raised the doll's skirts. Sure enough, on its thigh, the doll had a bright blue line inked onto its wooden leg. A Vulgar Arts "scar" of its own.

Her heart raced as she laid the doll carefully back into its nest. Beside it sat a letter. She recognized the handwriting at once. *His*

Majesty D'Daryn Andros. She unfolded the letter with trembling fingers.

Dearest Akeylah,

I expect you've intercepted this letter. Naughty girl. It was addressed to your father. But then, you clearly don't mind impersonating him, do you?

Her heart thudded.

I'm sure you're wondering why I've spared you so far. Don't worry. I haven't forgotten you. One might even say you're my favorite.

But alas, little puppet, being the favorite comes with certain responsibilities. When I tell you to do something, you obey. Listen, and I'll protect you. Refuse, and, well...you've seen what I do to those who are not in my favor.

Your first task is to put the traitor behind Burnt Bay on trial, immediately.

Oh, and shield yourself all you like, puppet. But ignore me, and I'll make those you love suffer in your stead.

They'd signed the letter *The True Heir to Kolonya and the Outer Reaches.* A chill settled over Akeylah's skin. Sank into her veins.

"Akeylah?" Rozalind knocked on the door. "Is everything all right?"

"Is the mender still here?" Akeylah barely managed to keep her voice from trembling.

"She just left. Do you need me to call her back?"

Akeylah unbolted the latch. Yanked the door open. Rozalind took one glance at Akeylah's stricken expression and caught the letter before Akeylah could protest. Skimmed it. Then Rozalind's arms were around her, and thank Mother Ocean for that, because Akeylah didn't know if she could stand on her own. She buried her face in the queen's shoulder, shaking.

"We'll figure this out," Rozalind whispered against her temple.

"How? They want me to put my sister on trial. If she's convicted, treason is punishable by death."

"*If* she's convicted," Rozalind replied. "There's no way to know how a trial would go until we hold one."

Akeylah jerked from her grasp, stung.

"What's the matter?" Rozalind's brow creased.

"You agree with this monster?" She snatched the letter back, shook it at Rozalind. "You think I should do it. Arrest her, make a spectacle of her."

"It's Kolonyan law, Akeylah. If she's innocent, a trial will prove it."

"And if she's not?" Akeylah's throat tightened with grief.

"Then the tribunal will deliver an appropriate punishment to fit her crime. Akeylah, I'm sorry, I know you care about your sister, but she made her choices. At the end of the day, Florencia has no one to blame except herself. If she's guilty," Rozalind added quickly.

Akeylah stared at her in stunned disbelief. "You're just like all the other nobles. In your mind you've already condemned her."

"I never said that. But you must distance yourself from her, Akeylah. Sympathy toward a suffering sister is one thing—we can explain it as familial pity, once you're crowned—"

"Once I'm *what*?" Her eyebrows shot skyward.

"Collusion, however, is another thing," Rozalind spoke over

her. "We cannot seem too close to Florencia, or people will question your authority. 'First one heir spies for Eastern rebels, now an Easterner sits on our throne.' 'Can we really trust anyone who isn't Kolonyan?' You can't afford those kinds of questions so early in your reign."

Akeylah stormed across the room. "Crowned. Reign. You seem to think this a foregone conclusion, Rozalind. But there's still this blackmailer to contend with, even if my sisters are denounced. And have you given up on your husband already?"

"*Already?*" Rozalind flung her arms up. "The mender told us he'd live a week, two at most. That was six days ago."

"Zofi's looking for a cure—"

"A cure you've been seeking for over a month now, with no progress. When will you learn that you need to plan more than one step ahead in this game?"

Akeylah folded her arms. "My father's life, my sisters' reputations, those are games?"

"To someone in this Keep, they are. I've been here for a year and a half, Akeylah. You think the past, what, *month* since you arrived has been difficult? This court changes you in ways you haven't even begun to comprehend. You learn how to hit first in order to survive. You can't..." She pressed a hand to her stomach. Shut her eyes, as though in pain.

Akeylah started toward her, but Rozalind flinched away. "Roz..."

"Don't. I'm trying to keep my promise to you, Akeylah." When Rozalind met her gaze once more, she looked hard. Furious. "I'm trying to protect you. But I can't save you from yourself." With that, Rozalind swept out of the room.

Akeylah stared, long after the door slammed. She should go after her. Chase her down, make her talk.

Instead, all she could think about was the first argument she'd had with Rozalind. Back when Zofi had been accused, and Rozalind encouraged Akeylah not to release or pardon her. Now she was doing the same to Ren, and talking as though Akeylah were already queen.

Akeylah didn't want this. She didn't want a throne, a crown. She just wanted the people she loved safe, once and for all.

✳

The doorknob to the solarium turned. The gems set in the knob reflected the sunlight overhead, sent a flurry of bright snowflakes dancing across the map of the Reaches on the central table.

Akeylah stared at those white sunspots and willed this meeting to go quickly.

"My lady." Ambassador Perry of the Southern Reach greeted her.

"Ambassador Perry." She smiled in welcome.

Ambassadors Ghoush, Danton, and Kiril filed in behind him. "Is His Majesty still indisposed?" asked Ambassador Ghoush, the pucker-mouthed woman who represented the Northern Reach, the moment she entered.

"I'm afraid he is not yet feeling well enough to leave his chambers. But he sent me in his stead." She gestured to a scribe in the corner, furiously copying notes. "I will bring him a transcript of everything we discuss, along with any urgent queries that need to be resolved."

She only hoped she wouldn't need to impersonate him again anytime soon.

"For a week now, we've been hearing these excuses." Ambassador Kiril of the Western Reach scowled. "I have never known Andros to suffer this much from a mere cold or flu."

"We have our best mender attending him, Ambassador," Akeylah replied.

"Not that we don't appreciate your being here, Lady Akeylah." Lord Perry inclined his head in her direction. "But we hope your father recovers soon. We need him more than ever."

Akeylah folded her hands on the table. "We had best get started, then. The first item on the agenda is the crop shortage—"

"If you'll forgive my impertinence, Lady Akeylah," Kiril butted in. "Before we move on to the set agenda, I had hoped to discuss the matter of your sister Lady Florencia."

"What about her?" Akeylah set her teeth on edge behind her careful smile.

Ambassador Ghoush laughed. When Akeylah didn't join, she sobered. "Well, I think I speak for all of us when I say that four days' time seems more than sufficient for a cursory review of the evidence. Is there enough to imprison the girl or not? My people are in an uproar."

"Mine as well." Ambassador Perry grimaced. "Some have gone so far as to call for her head, even in spite of her noble birth. Ambassador Danton, I'm sure you understand, given the Eastern Reach suffered grievous losses in Burnt Bay, too."

"It's funny," Danton replied, without his usual swagger. "More Easterners died in Burnt Bay than any other Reach, and yet, I don't hear these barbaric cries for execution from my people." His voice went sharp.

"Well." Akeylah leaned forward in her seat, eager to avoid an all-out fight. "I'm sure we can all appreciate the high emotions involved. Many people lost loved ones on those ships."

Danton narrowed his eyes. "So you agree with those baying for your sister's blood."

She flinched. Danton had always been the one ambassador she counted on for support. His relationship with Ren, fraught though it may be at times, usually made him agreeable to the sisters' suggestions. "Of course not, Ambassador. I'm merely suggesting we all feel strongly about the situation. We must take care so that our emotions don't lead us to false conclusions."

"So your father doesn't plan to put Florencia on trial." Ghoush's mouth thinned.

Akeylah swallowed hard. *Here it was.* She should agree to a trial. It's what the heir demanded. Seas knew the heir could ruin her as easily as they had her sisters. By this time tomorrow, it could be Akeylah's head these ambassadors were demanding. Or worse.

Ignore me, and I'll make those you love suffer in your stead.

She thought about her father. About Ren, or even Zofi. Would Zofi still think to shield herself, out on the road? And there was Rozalind, of course. At least the queen shared no bloodline with the heir, couldn't be cursed. But there were other ways to make people suffer. . . .

But giving in to the heir's demand meant sacrificing Ren, and for what? The brief illusion of safety. After she subjected Ren to a trial, there would be another demand, and another, until the heir took the throne at last.

Could Akeylah really be so easily controlled? *Was* she a puppet after all?

"We don't believe there is sufficient evidence to justify a trial,"

114

Akeylah said. "Yet," she added, when it looked like Ghoush was about to protest again.

Danton, who'd relaxed at her first statement, tensed at the final word.

She avoided his eye and cleared her throat. "Now, if we can return to the agenda. The crop blight is our first item of business."

Ambassador Ghoush folded her hands on the tabletop. "As I understand it, the agricultural guild has produced a cure that worked on the farms surrounding Kolonya City."

Akeylah nodded. "But we'll need to distribute it to the outer Reaches as soon as possible if we want to avoid mass famine. Especially the Reaches with short crop-growing seasons..." The meeting droned on.

More than once, she caught Danton studying her, gaze narrowed.

She didn't like keeping Ren locked up any more than he did. But while she couldn't release her sister, she wouldn't force her into a worse position either. She would not cave to the heir's demands.

Akeylah didn't know why the heir singled out Ren and Zofi for punishment. Or why they'd decided to manipulate Akeylah instead. But she'd spent too much of her life being beaten. Too much time on the floor, cowering. No more.

If the heir wanted a sister they could easily control, they picked the wrong one.

❋ 12 ❋

Zofi

Falling back into the Traveler stride was easy. A relief, almost. She'd been able to make only minor headway on foot, but on horseback, they rode all day and well into the night.

The next morning, Zofi roused Vidal before the sun so they could ride throughout the early morning. At midday they broke to nap in the heat, then started again in the afternoon.

Vidal proved much better at maintaining this grueling pace than she'd expected. Maybe there was something to be said for the Talons' training after all. By nightfall, she expected him to quit. Instead, he rode without protest until a rare desert thunderstorm gathered on the horizon, obscuring the moons. Only then did Zofi decided to camp, to avoid the worst of the damp.

They removed the horses' tacks and pitched the double tent Vidal had brought.

"Impressive." She inspected the tent. "Is this why you signed up to become a Talon? All the fancy equipment that comes with the job?"

He laughed. "Hardly. I signed up because ever since I was a little boy, for as long as I could remember, I wanted to serve Kolonya. All the Reaches," he quickly amended. "The same way my father served, and his mother before him."

"What's so appealing about a life of servitude?" She scrunched her forehead.

But Vidal's face lit up. "It's not servitude. It's protecting people. Helping people. I surrender some personal freedom, but I gain so much more from becoming a piece of something greater than myself. Together, we Talons keep the Reaches safe."

She worked on the campfire in silence, digesting. She could understand sacrificing a little bit of yourself to build something bigger. Wasn't that what her band did, after all? They stuck together through thick and thin, not because they had to, but because they chose to. Together, they were stronger. Together, they were *more* than they could ever be apart.

Now, tent raised and a merry campfire blazing in anticipation of the rain that would soon try its best to douse the flames, Zofi huddled next to the Talon she was starting to understand. Their thighs touched as they squeezed onto a makeshift bench built from rolled-up rucksacks.

She wondered what a passerby would say if they chanced upon the two. A Traveler and a Kolonyan riding through the desert together. A strange pairing, most would think.

Zofi longed for a world where that wouldn't be strange. Where

Travelers could ride with anyone they liked, aspire to any position they wished.

She could've started that. Been a Traveler queen like Claera, helped her people.

"Are you all right?" Vidal leaned across to thrust a spit of meat—a hare Zofi had shot earlier in the day—into the coals. "You're uncharacteristically quiet."

"I'm hungry, that's all." She lifted her hands to the fire. The warmth tickled her palms, yet did little to quell her surge of regret.

I failed my band. She would not be queen. She'd been forced out of Kolonya, sent home with her tail between her legs, and a Talon in tow, no less.

"Are you worried we won't catch up to your band in time?" Vidal's brows furrowed. "You said they'd be out west this time of year. We're almost to the swamplands—"

"We should reach them by tomorrow morning." Tomorrow, which would mark a week since her departure. If she'd had a horse all along, she could have made it to her band in two days, three at most. But since she'd had to walk for so long at the start . . .

She prayed she wasn't too late.

"Then what's bothering you?"

She hated how, in just the few short weeks they'd known each other, Vidal had learned to read her so well. "Just . . ." She gestured vaguely at their camp. Overhead, the rain clouds thundered. "This. My banishment. I'm on my way home to announce my failure."

"What do you mean?" Vidal turned the hare over.

"My mother wanted me to play the Keep's games. Elex wanted me to win the throne. Instead I got myself thrown out in disgrace."

"Surely your band knew what you were up against."

"That's just it." Her fists balled. She thought about all the judgment, all the prejudices and hatred she'd faced, simply for who she was. "I was supposed to—I *wanted* to change all that. I wanted to sit on the throne, not for me, but for them. I thought if I was crowned, maybe people would stop treating Travelers like we're less than human."

Vidal refilled her cup from their waterskin. Then he contemplated his own mug for a long moment. "I don't know if that alone would have done much. People have their prejudices. It will take a long time to change those, whether or not you're queen."

She rolled her eyes and drained her mug. "Somehow that doesn't lift my spirits."

"*But.*" He nudged her with an elbow. "Queen or not, you can still work toward that. You don't need a throne to change people's minds."

She looked at him. Found herself distracted all over again by those dark hazel eyes of his. They flashed with the lightning overhead.

"You didn't need a throne to change my mind, after all," he murmured.

"You're different."

He laughed, soft and breathy. "I'm nobody. Just an anonymous minion, remember?"

Oh, she remembered. *Anonymous minion.* That was what she

had called him the first time they spoke. After she awoke in a carriage bound for Kolonya City, her whole life turned upside down by one phantasm dart. She glanced at his lips, at the ghost of a smile that danced there. Felt the corners of her own mouth lift in response. "No, you aren't."

He bent closer.

A sharp crack from the fire startled her, and she whipped around, hurriedly grabbed the poker. Rain had begun to fall around them, soft but gaining force. They wouldn't have long to finish roasting this hare. She prodded a large chunk of wood, and flames burst forth.

When she dared a peek at him again, Vidal turned the hare on its spit, carefully avoiding her gaze. "Tell me more about your band," he said after a silence that was too long, too electric.

Think about Elex, she reminded herself. Elex, who she'd see again soon. Elex, who Ren had promised to pardon.

Elex, who she'd barely thought of since the night she bid him farewell. Elex, who she cared about but who only knew the old Zofi. The Traveler she used to be. Not the hybrid she was now. Half-Traveler, half-Kolonyan.

She swallowed hard. "What do you want to know?"

"Whatever you want to share. Your history, maybe? Your legends? I only know Kolonyan ones. I'm sure you must have your own."

"Plenty." She grinned and stirred the fire again. "Who do you want to hear about? Kolonyans normally love the stories about Traveler Queen Claera, King Ilian's wife."

To her surprise, he shook his head. "I've heard those. I want the ones I wouldn't have learned growing up. Who came before Claera? What other queens were there?"

She laughed. "Queen is a misnomer, really. Claera took the title when she wed Ilian. But our bands don't recognize royalty. Each band has its own leader, though there's no election or crowning. It's just whoever volunteers to take on the burden of leadership, for as long as they care to bear it. When they've decided they're done, someone else steps up to fill their shoes."

Vidal's eyebrows rose. "Is it always so peaceful?"

"No," she admitted. "But it's usually more or less democratic."

He grinned. "What happens when it isn't?"

"Anyone in the band can challenge a leader they believe is making unfair or selfish choices."

"Challenge them how?" Vidal blinked. "Combat?"

"Such a Talon." She nudged his knee with hers. "No. To a testing."

"What's that?" Vidal propped his chin in his hand, balanced on one knee as he listened.

"Well, the Travelers started out as wisdom keepers. Back in the day when the First Six came over—you know, the first six ships that settled the Reaches?"

"I thought it was the First Five."

Zofi snorted. "They always erase us. Even in history. Watch it, by the way, that's burning." She reached over to take the hare from him. Sheepishly, he released it, and their fingertips brushed as he handed it over. She flipped the meat. "There were six ships. Five settled the Reaches that exist now. The sixth was the Traveler ship, captained by Nova. She decided that rather than settling in any one Reach, her people would move among them all. In exchange for free passage, and support from the other Reaches— resources, food, water—the Travelers brought knowledge from Reach to Reach. Those first Travelers were menders, counselors, historians, storytellers who had memorized the histories of Genal, and priests of the old religion. The one that came before the Arts."

"How do we not learn about any of this?" Vidal asked.

She shrugged a shoulder. It brushed against his. The heat from his arm sent the hairs at the back of her neck to attention. "Perhaps because your people devalue history now. Over time, our jobs changed. At first, we chronicled the new histories—the events and legends that sprang up in each Reach. We carried stories from one Reach to another, kept the Reaches united.... You might say Travelers were the bloodstream of this continent. Respected, revered even, for the knowledge we bore."

"What happened?"

"The Arts. When they first appeared, Travelers collected information about their use from all over the Reaches, the same way we catalogued all knowledge. We recorded new tithes, unique uses for the Arts, all sorts of research. When King Ilian proposed to Claera, it was because of her experience with the Arts. He wanted that knowledge for himself—though of course Claera didn't know it at the time. She trusted Ilian. Loved him." Zofi's voice hardened. "But after she was crowned and began to teach the Arts to more Kolonyans, rumors began to spread. Rumors about some of her practices being ungodly. About Travelers learning witchcraft, becoming evil curseworkers. It was because tithing was still new, of course. People always fear the new and

122

different. The Arts weren't embraced Reaches-wide yet, not the way they are today."

"But they worked the Vulgar Arts, too," Vidal said. "They knew curses. I can understand why that unsettled people."

Zofi shook her head so hard her curls bounced against her cheeks. "Back then, there was no distinction between the Vulgar and the Blood Arts. Not until nearly a century later, when acolytes of the Sun laid out the edicts to govern 'proper' tithing." Zofi made quotes with her fingers. "By then, of course, the damage had already been done." She flashed him an angry glance. "People hated us. Just for the knowledge we tried to bring them."

"If all that is true, though, without Travelers..."

"The Reaches wouldn't be the continent we know today. No." She smirked. "Ironic, isn't it?"

Vidal fell silent for so long that this time, Zofi nearly burned the hare. She removed it from the fire, propped the stick in the sand to cool. By the time it had cooled enough for her to rip off a leg and pass it to him, Vidal was gazing into the flames, lost. Zofi elbowed him.

"It's a very depressing story and all," she said, "but you do still need to eat."

He accepted the leg. Bit off a chunk and chewed. "Do you think it's needed again?" he asked once he'd swallowed.

Zofi helped herself to a leg of her own. "What do you mean?"

"That knowledge. Not about tithes—about the Reaches. Our history. Our *real* history, not just the pieces Kolonya tells us."

"I think it's always needed." She bit into the leg. A spurt of juice ran down her chin. She caught it and licked her finger. *Sands.* There was nothing quite like this. Meat fresh off the spit, with rain falling all around, and a warm, friendly body to share it with. Swapping stories over the fire as though she were already home.

Without thinking about it, she leaned closer to Vidal. She tried to tell herself it was for warmth.

She almost believed it.

"Maybe that's what you need to do now," Vidal said.

"What do you mean?" She chewed another mouthful of hare.

"You can't be queen. And that's a shame, because I think you would've made a damn fine one."

She snorted again. "Sucking up won't win you any more of this hare."

"But you can still help change people's minds. Help change the Reaches—by telling that story. That story, and any others you think the world needs to hear."

"People don't want to hear Traveler stories any more than they want to let Travelers stay in their towns and sleep in their fancy inns."

Vidal reached across her and helped himself to another haunch. She tried not to think about how his arm brushed along hers. "So make them listen. Trick them into it if you have to—hide it in plays, tell stories to the children, or write it in books."

"That all takes time and money and sponsorship from higher powers."

"You have time," he answered. "As for money and sponsorship, look, Zofi..." He touched her knee. Waited until she looked at him. "You might be in exile, but you are still the daughter of a king. Nothing can change that. And from what I've seen of your sisters, they care for you and love you still. One day, one of them will take your father's place. They may not be able to overturn his edict, or lift his ban, but they will be able to support any actions you take."

Assuming it's one of my sisters who wins this thing, and not the enemy who forced me out in the first place. She fought away the thought. "We'll see."

Vidal just grinned and reached up to tuck a stray curl behind her ear. "That doesn't sound like the Zofi I know. The Zofi I know would say 'I'll make it happen no matter what.'"

A faint smile touched her lips. "Yes, well. Maybe the Zofi you know underestimated just how much stands in her way."

His expression softened. Turned serious. "The Zofi I know could take on the whole world, if she needed to."

Their eyes locked, and her heart skipped. It took effort this time to tear her gaze away, to shift the topic to some joke about him shivering from the rain. It was picking up now, beginning to fall in sheets. They finished eating, kicked sand over the fire, and retreated into the tent.

But when they crawled inside, the steady torrential rain overhead punctuated now and again by deep rumbles of thunder, Zofi took one look at their separate sleeping cots and tugged her mat next to his. Without a word, she spread both blankets across the joined bed.

Vidal watched her for a moment. Then he reached over and tugged her to him, their bodies hot as furnaces beneath the covers. "Are you sure?" he whispered into her hair.

In response, Zofi pulled his face to hers. Their lips collided.

He tasted like smoke from the fire, like the earth after rain. He was warm and solid and real, his body taut against hers, and as her lips parted to let him in, the world shrank to just the two of them.

For the first time since she'd left Kolonya, something finally felt *right*.

❄ 13 ❄

Florencia

Four days. Four days of pacing her chambers. She counted twenty steps from the main entrance to the bathing chamber. Ten steps bed to window, ten more from bed to serving entrance.

Ren had long since memorized the voices of the various Talons outside. She'd nicknamed the ones by the serving entrance Gabby and Snarky, the former always complaining about something, the latter responding with bemused sarcasm. But even Snarky didn't defend Ren when Gabby went on a tirade about his cousin who drowned at Burnt Bay.

When she wasn't listening to Talon gossip or counting steps, Ren occupied herself as best she could. Mama visited a few times, though she usually brought more disheartening tales. Stories of nobles arguing in favor of Ren's execution. Lord Rueno was the loudest of them all.

Audrina wrote to say she'd visit when she could. Ren wrote her more than a few letters in response, though she tried to stick to mundane details. The sort of things they used to talk about, back before their friendship strained under the pressure of Ren's new position. She hoped Audrina read the letters, understood that Ren wanted things to go back to normal between them.

Not that it would much matter, she supposed, if Rueno took her head.

She wrote to Akeylah most often. She begged for news of their father, word from Zofi, updates on what was happening in the Keep. Akeylah sent back one-line answers. *No change in Father. No word from Zofi. Keep under control. More when I have time.*

None of the details Ren craved. *What's happening out there?* she wanted to scream.

The only information she'd received so far had been from Danton. He told her about all the appointments Akeylah had been taking—the council of lords, individual petitioners, even a regional council meeting yesterday. In it, Danton told her, Akeylah had spoken against putting Ren on trial. She supposed that was something. Though from his description, it would only be a matter of time. The other ambassadors pushed for more direct action. Ren knew Akeylah wouldn't be able to delay much longer.

On the morning of her fourth day locked in this bedroom, the sort of chamber she'd once coveted, but which now felt impossibly small, Mama visited again, this time carrying breakfast.

"Mama." Ren flung herself into her mother's arms before she had a chance to set down the tray. It had only been two days since Ren had seen her, but that felt like an eternity in here.

"Wait a moment, Ren, you're going to spill the sheep's milk,"

Mama scolded. Then she set down breakfast and scooped Ren into her arms. The two embraced until the Talons left.

Only then did Mama kiss her cheek and draw back to study her, gaze sharp as a stormwing's. "What have they been doing to you?"

"Nothing, Mama. I told you, I'm fine."

"These vultures have you locked up like a criminal. That's about as far from *fine* as you can get." Mama's lips twisted into a scowl. "I told you not to trust that Easterner."

"Akeylah's trying to help, Mama. Danton says she stalled the regional council from putting me on trial."

Mama scoffed. "Some help that is. You wouldn't need anybody to stall anything if that girl would just publicly denounce these ridiculous charges. I'll bet she's the one who concocted this story in the first place, to get you out of her way. You're the best-suited candidate, after all—the most natural heir."

At that, Ren turned away. She crossed to her windows. Through the panes, she could see all the way to the Living Wall. The River Leath glinted beyond its leafy canopy, a distant flash of silver wrapped like a bracelet around Kolonya City.

Spread under her feet was the city itself. The terra-cotta rooftops of the merchant's district, the brightly colored tents of the marketplaces, the white-painted brick of the scholars' quarter, the dark stone of the Necropolis. So many people. So many lives.

She wondered how many had relatives on the ships at Burnt Bay.

Only when Mama crossed the room to stand beside her did Ren speak again, in a whisper. "The charges are true, Mama."

For a moment, Mama fell silent. Her eyebrows rose, then lowered again, even deeper thunderclouds than before. "Who made you do it? Did the rebels force the plans from you?"

"Shh," she hissed, because Mama's voice had risen dangerously close to a volume the Talons might overhear. "Nobody forced me, Mama. I did it of my own volition." Well, mostly. "I didn't think anyone would get hurt. The rebels said they wanted to escape, not attack us."

Mama swore.

"I've regretted it every day since. But that won't change anything. It won't give all these people their families back." She gestured at the city. "Perhaps this is what I deserve. Perhaps I should just tell Akeylah to go ahead and call a tribunal."

"*No.*" Mama narrowed her eyes. "You're right, Ren, you cannot change the past. Which means there's no sense in you sacrificing yourself, or all your hard work—all *my* hard work, too, I might add—to get you this far. Leaders make mistakes sometimes; it comes with the territory. But letting your sister exploit you—"

"Akeylah didn't do this. Or at least, I don't think it was her." Ren had nothing left to lose now—the whole city knew her secret. She might as well unburden herself to the one person who would understand. With a heavy sigh, Ren told her everything. From the blackmailer's threats to Yasmin's death and Zofi's banishment. By the time she stopped speaking, her throat felt dry, and Mama had taken a seat right there on the windowsill.

"So when you collapsed in the baths..." Mama began.

Ren nodded. "The so-called heir cursed me."

"And when that didn't work, they spread this story." Mama pursed her mouth. "Well, whoever they are, they're smart, unfortunately. You really believe the Eastern girl is innocent?"

Ren spread her hands wide. "I've seen a blackmail note she

was sent. Whether she penned it herself or not, I can't be certain, but she told me the secret the heir is using against her. I don't know why she would admit her own crime if she's the one behind these attacks."

"To throw suspicion off, perhaps." Mama tapped her chin, lost in thought. "Unless it's someone else just as close to the throne."

Ren's brow lowered. "Who else is there?"

"Why, the current queen, of course."

Mama said it so matter-of-factly that Ren almost rolled her eyes. "Mama, I told you, this person has been using the Vulgar Arts. They're related, probably within one or two generations, to perform curses this strong."

"Exactly," Mama replied. Only when Ren's face remained blank did her mother's begin to clear in comprehension. "Oh, Ren, I'm sorry, I just assumed you would have heard from your friends in the serving quarters...."

"Heard what?" Ren crossed her arms.

"I've been visiting Madam Oruna for the past few days." Mama patted the windowsill beside her. After a moment's hesitation, Ren sat. "I thought it would be a good idea to keep an ear open for any potentially useful gossip."

I learned from the best, Ren couldn't help thinking.

"The most interesting thing I learned was what the queen's chambermaids relayed to Oruna. They say Rozalind's sheets have been spotless for the last three months."

Ren frowned. "That's hardly surprising. I doubt she and Father shared beds often, especially since he fell ill—"

"No, Ren, you mistake my meaning. *Spotless.* Even when all three moons are high."

Ren's eyes widened. "But..."

"As for Rozalind," Mama continued, "she's summoned girls in the wee hours at least three times over the past couple months. Emergency cleaning services. The queen told anyone who asked that it was a bad case of food poisoning, but she refused a mender's inspection. Then last week, Rozalind ordered a dozen new shift gowns tailor-made, with much wider waist measurements. The same day, she dismissed her personal attendants. I can guess why, if she wants to keep this quiet."

"She's pregnant?" Ren hissed. "But that makes no sense. Father would never have recognized me or my sisters if he knew he had a legitimate heir on the way."

"That's the kicker." Mama cast her a pointed look. "Andros must not know. Believe me, I spoke to him just after he summoned you. All he could talk about was how he regretted putting you in this position, how he'd hoped his young wife could have supplied a true heir."

"Maybe it's not his," Ren mused.

"Knowing how the queen's tastes run, I doubt that." Mama lifted a brow.

"Then why would she hide something that affects the whole kingdom? She could've spared Andros months of worry. He could have left my sisters and me ignorant of our heritage."

"That I don't understand," Mama admitted. "It does seem a strange decision. But you said this heir person was a relative. If Rozalind *is* carrying Andros's child, your sibling..."

Ren's stomach dropped. What did Mama always tell her? *For*

nine whole months, we were the same person, you and I. Pregnancy made women as strong as two people. It combined twice the will-power, twice the Arts ability in one body.

"But she's Genalese," Ren said. "She can't tithe."

"*She* can't. Her half-Kolonyan child can."

"Is that possible?" Ren's voice dropped to a hushed whisper. "Has anyone...I mean, when was the last time anyone from the Reaches wed someone from Genal?"

"We all descend from Genal if you look far enough back," Mama pointed out. "Check the history books from three or four hundred years ago. You'll find plenty of examples of half-Genalese children tithing the same way any native of the Reaches can."

Ren's body went cold. This changed everything.

If Rozalind was pregnant with Ren's half sibling, then for the duration of that pregnancy...Rozalind was as good as Ren's sibling, too.

For hours after her mother's departure, all Ren could do was turn that information over and over in her mind.

Rozalind is pregnant. And for some reason, she'd elected to hide it from Andros, from everybody in the Keep. Did Akeylah even know? She and the queen were...close. How much had Rozalind shared?

Why hide this?

If Rozalind had told Andros months ago, he'd never have summoned Ren, Akeylah, or Zofi. He wouldn't have needed to. He had a legitimate heir on the way.

Now...if Andros never recovered, Rozalind would find it

difficult to prove the child's parentage. The court would want to know why she'd concealed the pregnancy. Why Andros didn't acknowledge the heir himself.

Moreover, if he *did* recover, how would she explain to her husband that she'd hidden a secret this huge?

Ren's head swam.

Late in the afternoon, another knock came. This time, the Talons introduced her guest with all the formal flourishes that preceded a royal entrance.

"Akeylah." Ren rose from her writing desk on shaky legs. *Does she know?* Was her sister working with Rozalind, or was she another pawn of the queen's?

The moment she stepped inside, Akeylah swept across the room to kiss Ren's cheeks. "I'm so sorry I didn't visit sooner," she said as the Talons bowed out of the room. "I keep trying to sneak away, but my schedule is packed. Between the council meetings and the nobles demanding attention..."

Once the doors shut, Akeylah collapsed onto the bed. "Honestly, I don't know how Father does it. Ruling is exhausting."

"I wouldn't know." Ren kept her tone carefully even. "Personally, I've had all the time in the world for relaxation, caged in here."

Akeylah winced. "I apologize for that, too. It's only temporary, until we can clear your name."

"We?" Ren asked, voice sharpening as she studied her sister's expression. She didn't want to believe Akeylah knew about Rozalind, or that she'd been helping the queen all along. But Ren knew how close the two were. Despite Ren's warning to Akeylah about sneaking around with their father's wife, Danton informed her that Akeylah now spent every night in the king's and queen's conjoined suites.

Was it mere coincidence that Akeylah was the only sister whose secret wasn't exposed?

"Yes, we. You and me. We'll clear this mess up together." Confusion warred with worry on Akeylah's face. It seemed genuine, but Ren knew all too well how easily lying came to some courtiers. Maybe Akeylah's innocent shy behavior had been an act all along.

Whoever they are, they're smart, Mama had said. Akeylah was smart. Smart enough to fool everyone for this long?

"I doubt I have any say in the matter." Ren lifted her chin. "From where I'm sitting, it's you and your girlfriend holding the reins now."

"Rozalind is trying to help us," Akeylah started, but Ren spoke over her.

"Are you working with her? Is that why she's left you unscathed?"

"I don't know what you're talking about. I'm still being threatened by the heir." Akeylah lowered her voice to an angry whisper. "I just got another message yesterday morning."

"Care to share proof? Because from where I'm sitting, you look like the only one who's escaped this reckoning." Ren gestured at the barred doors on either side of her chambers. "Sun above, if I didn't know any better, I'd say you could be the heir yourself. After all, you've already used the Vulgar Arts against one family member."

Akeylah flinched as though slapped. "At least I told you about my crime, Ren. So did Zofi, for that matter. You're the one who kept yours a secret from everyone, even us."

"A secret?" She laughed. "The whole world knows what I've done by now. But yes, you've got me pegged. I'm a criminal mastermind who locked myself in my own chambers. It's all part of my evil plan to let someone else usurp the throne."

"Ren, this is what the heir wants. They want to get into our heads, make us distrust one another. We cannot fall for it."

"I'm worried you already have, Akeylah." As far as Ren could tell, Akeylah was telling the truth. But she could still be Rozalind's pawn, whether she knew it or not. "What message did the heir send you?"

Akeylah balled her fists. "They said they'll hurt people I love unless I obey their orders. Which I've already disobeyed, by the way, since they demanded I put you on trial at once."

"Thank you for that," Ren replied, serious. That seemed to mollify Akeylah somewhat. "But has it occurred to you there might be another reason the heir isn't treating you the way they treated Zofi or me?"

"Because I'm weak? Easier to manipulate?" Akeylah's mouth twisted bitterly.

"Because maybe part of her does care about you, even though she's using you for her own gain." Ren spread her hands, palms up. "Or maybe she thinks having you beside her will legitimize her claim. Once Father dies, you two can wed and she can have the baby, raise it as both of yours."

Akeylah's body went very, very still. "You're not making any sense, Ren."

Oh, Sun above. Did Akeylah truly not know? "Rozalind hasn't told you?"

"What do you have against her? She's Genalese, Ren; of all the people in the Keep, she's the only one who couldn't possibly—"

"She's pregnant, Akeylah."

In that moment, Ren knew Akeylah was on her side. The way her sister's face, her whole body, crumpled...nobody could fake that. Not even a trained actor with the best hunting face in the world.

"That's not possible." Akeylah's voice came out wooden.

"Maids notice everything," Ren said, gentler now. "Clean sheets for months, bouts of morning sickness, new, loose gowns Rozalind had tailored..."

"She would have told me."

Ren rose from the desk, crossed to sit beside Akeylah on the bed. "Akeylah, think about it. You hardly know her. I warned you about getting too close...."

Akeylah turned her face away. Swiped angrily at her eyes with the back of her hand. "Even if she is..." Akeylah couldn't say the word. "Even if she's in that condition. It still doesn't mean she's capable of all this."

"Pregnant mothers can tithe or curse with their child's blood. I don't know what happens if the mother is Genalese, but since her child is half-Kolonyan..." Ren stopped speaking when Akeylah's mouth went slack. "What is it?"

"The tithing..." Akeylah whispered. She swallowed hard. Spoke again with her eyes shut tight. "I didn't understand it. Neither did Rozalind—she told me the ability came on her suddenly, and she couldn't figure out why."

Ren swore. "You knew she could tithe? Why didn't you tell us?"

Akeylah tugged at one sleeve. Wound her fingers through the fabric. "I didn't think it relevant. She's not related to us. What did it matter?"

Ren grimaced. Stared down at her lap.

"Even Rozalind didn't know why she could suddenly tithe."

"She wouldn't," Ren said. "She wasn't raised here; she doesn't understand how the Arts work."

Her sister drew a shaky breath. "Look, even if she's pregnant." This time, her voice barely shook. "We can't be sure she's the heir."

"You're right. We need proof."

"How?" Akeylah met Ren's gaze.

"You're closer to her than anyone. And from the sound of it, you've ignored the heir's demand, so they'll be gearing up to punish you somehow, soon. If you stick to Rozalind's side, never let her out of your sight—"

"I have duties to attend to," Akeylah protested. "And I've needed Rozalind to stay and look after Father while I do."

"How long has it been, a week already?" Ren looked up, out the window. "Either Zofi will be sending the cure in the next couple of days, or..." *Or Father will be dead soon, anyway.* "Do you think you can delay your other duties that long, at least? Push back any nonvital meetings and stay with Father and Rozalind for now?"

Her sister nodded, though her mind looked far away.

Ren reached out, touched Akeylah's shoulder. "I apologize for accusing you earlier. When I suggested you were working with her. I just... I had to be sure."

"It's all right." Akeylah managed a weak smile. "I'd have done the same."

Ren didn't believe that. Akeylah was always the kind one, the softest sister. But she appreciated the lie. It made Ren feel a little less bad for distrusting one of the few allies she had left.

Ren forced a faint smile as she rose to walk her sister out. "For what it's worth, Akeylah, if you need to talk any more about this... Well." She gestured at her bedroom. "You always know where to find me."

❧ **14** ❦

Zofi

The next morning, Zofi spotted a familiar tuft of black tumbleweed curls at a farmers market in a small marsh-side town, just half a day's ride past the edge of the desert. "Norren!" She stood up in her saddle to wave. Beside her, Vidal started and reached for his sword before he realized she was grinning like an idiot.

"Zofi?" The old bear of a Traveler, almost wider than he was tall, paused in the middle of haggling over potatoes. "Am I seeing things?"

She kicked her feet from the stirrups and slid off her silver stallion.

By the time she'd dismounted, Norren had abandoned the potatoes entirely to gape at her horse instead. He knew exactly how much an alpha like this would fetch at auction. "Well, if it isn't Her Highness the princess visiting in style," he joked.

Zofi slapped his shoulder, and only then did he recall himself and pull her into a crushing hug. "Nice to see you, too. How's Rull?"

"Oh, you know, as big a pain in my rear end as that brat has ever been." He grinned. To hear him talk, you'd never guess Rull had been his exclusive partner for the past fifteen years—rarer than a double lunar eclipse by Traveler standards. "What in sands' name are *you* doing here, child?" He squinted at Vidal. "And riding with a king's Talon, no less."

"Don't worry, I won't bring him to camp," Zofi was saying while Vidal dismounted.

"How can you tell I'm a Talon?" Vidal glanced at his attire. He wore a simple cotton shirt, leather breeches, and unmarked boots. His uniform sat balled at the base of his saddlebag.

"Besides the stallion?" Norren pointed at Vidal's waist, where his horn dangled. "Only Talons carry stormwing horns."

Vidal cursed. "You told me it would pass for a drinking horn, Zofi. That nobody would notice the carvings."

Her eyes sparkled. "My bad. I should have said nobody but Norren here, who's got the best eye in the Reaches for the finer details of anything he might be able to pawn."

"Give you a hundred kolons, if you're looking to sell." Desire flashed in Norren's eyes.

Vidal swept into a bow, one hand clasped protectively around the horn. "Thank you for the offer, sir, but I'm afraid a hundred kolons wouldn't pay for half the menders' treatments I'd need if my commander found out I'd sold this."

Norren burst into laughter. "*Sir.*" He slapped Vidal's shoulder, then turned to wink at Zofi. "Don't worry about bringing the boy to camp. Not if he's *with* you."

She didn't like the way Norren's eyes sparkled when he said *with*. She narrowed hers. "I need to speak to my mother."

"Of course. But I thought you..." He shook his head. "Well, I didn't know *what* to think, truth be told. First those Talons dragged you off, then Deena told us all it was fine, they'd come to crown you a princess." He guffawed again, louder. "Can you imagine that? A princess, our Zofi." Norren mimicked an elaborate curtsy, and Zofi elbowed his side, hard.

"Don't you dare start."

But Norren maintained a steady stream of *my lady*s and assorted affected titles all the way through the marshlands. Unlike the oasis towns, which by necessity had to huddle together around their lone source of water, villages out here in the Western Reach tended to sprawl. This one consisted of at least a hundred houses on stilts, dotted throughout a swamp that stretched as far as the eye could see in every direction. Here and there, portions had been walled off to grow rice and grains, but most of it, as far as Zofi could tell, remained wild.

They walked several feet above the marshes on a wooden path that varied from ten feet at its widest down to narrow foot-wide bridges Zofi had to tiptoe over. At the first of these, she and Vidal were forced to tie their horses to a hitching post, the animals unable to cross.

"I can stay and watch them," Vidal offered.

"No need," Norren said. "Enough people have seen you

by now. Even if this area was known for thieves, which it isn't, nobody is daft enough to steal a Talon's ride."

Finally, far ahead, she spied a structure that reminded her of a tree house without the tree. A massive four-level series of wooden platforms, it stood open to the elements, save for the tents pitched around the edges. And clustered around those tents, she saw them.

Bette and her kids. Her partner Rez. Mia. Lek. Ora. Dozens of familiar faces, one after the other. More materialized as she drew closer, and shouts started up along the platform.

Finally, emerging from one of the tents on the first level, his hair cropped shorter than the last time she'd seen him, his cheeks thin from weeks on the run...

Elex.

She walked as if in a trance. It felt like drifting backward through time to an earlier version of herself, a less complicated one. To the Zofi who only knew half of her life, half of her story.

She was still aware of Norren on her right, shouting greetings. Vidal on her left, close enough that their fingers brushed with each step. She glanced over, found him staring at Elex, too. Of course. They'd met the night she sprang Elex from the dungeons. The night Vidal turned traitor to help Elex escape.

They nodded to each other, expressions solemn.

Then Elex's eyes caught hers. She still felt a skip in her heart, a warmth under her skin, yet it felt different this time. Confusing, because now, standing between him and Vidal, she could still feel Vidal's kisses on her mouth, his hands on her bare skin, *all over me...*

She didn't know how she felt. Not anymore.

"Zofi. What are you doing here?" Elex asked. "Is everything all right?"

She hauled herself onto the wooden platform beside him. "I'm fine" was all she managed to get out before Elex wrapped his arms around her, pulled her into the tight, crushing embrace she'd always loved—the kind that always used to make her feel safe, secure, *home*.

He smelled the same. Like electricity after a storm. But holding him, she didn't feel that relaxation, that release anymore. She felt taut as a bowstring.

She wriggled out of his arms. "What about you?" she said. "I would've thought you'd still be on the run."

Elex looked stung when she backed away, but only for a moment. "I don't know how you managed it, Zofi." He grinned. "But a pardon came through, clearing me of all charges. I got word of it in the town where I was camped out just a couple days ago."

She forced a smile. "The crown owed me a favor." Mostly true.

At least one good thing came of her exile. Elex was free now. But he must have read the conflict on her face, because his smile flickered. Faded.

"It was the least I could do, after everything," Zofi added.

"But if you're here, then . . ."

"It's a long story." She did need to talk to Elex, but not now. First she had work to do. "It'll be better told around a campfire with a strong beverage. Have you seen my mother?"

"Top platform." He pointed. "You'll see her tent. Watch the ladders, they're rickety."

Already a week had passed since she left Kolonya City. Father would only have a few days left. If Mother knew of a cure, Zofi had to send it immediately. After that, she'd have all the time in the world.

After that, whatever happened back in Kolonya had nothing to do with her anymore. That fact hurt more than she expected.

She glanced over her shoulder. "Vidal. My mother has something I'll need to send to the Keep as fast as possible." Her gaze drifted to the horn at his waist. "Do you think you might be able to make use of your, ah, pet?"

He followed her eye. "Is it a written message, or something larger?"

"Written."

He nodded. "Should be doable. Find me whenever you're ready."

She couldn't wait to see how *that* went over with her band. A Talon summoning a stormwing right into their camp. Still, it relaxed her somewhat. Stormwings rode the thermals, so high above the ground they usually looked like specks in a clear sky. Vidal's bird should be able to carry a message to Akeylah in no time. Assuming Mother had the answers they needed.

❄

For a moment, Zofi just stood outside her mother's tent. The tent she'd shared for weeks before her capture by the Talons. Before she'd been stolen away to a whole new life.

It looked smaller than she remembered. Dingier around the edges, like a faded painting.

When she drew back the flap, she found Mother crouched

over a mug of mint brew, a crude hand-drawn map spread before her. Zofi watched, and her eyes began to sting.

I'm back, she wanted to say. The words stuck in her throat.

Mother bent closer to the page and spoke without looking up. "Either ask me for whatever you need, or close the flap. You're letting all the vampyre flies in."

Zofi stepped forward and let the tent flap shut. Cleared her throat. But the lump only grew, until it threatened to make the sting in her eyes spill over into tears.

Finally, Mother looked up.

"Oh, sands alive. Zofi." Mother sprang to her feet, and Zofi barely had time to extend her arms before Mother pulled her into a hug so tight it was difficult to breathe.

That was fine. She didn't need air. Not right now. She buried her face in Mother's neck. Much to her embarrassment, a couple of tears escaped to wet Mother's shoulder.

"It's okay, baby." Mother kissed her cheek once. Twice. A third time. Then she pulled back just far enough to start kissing her other cheek.

Zofi squirmed out of her arms. "Mother," she groaned, even as she wiped her eyes. "I'm fine."

"What are you doing here?" Mother kicked some stray camping supplies off her sitting mat and gestured at the pillow. Zofi sank onto it, and Mother sat so close their knees knocked.

The story poured out of Zofi. The blackmail, the heir, the threats. Her banishment. "I failed," she finished in a whisper. "I couldn't play their game. Not well enough to win."

To her surprise, Mother laughed, albeit gently. "Nobody expected you to win, Zofi."

She snorted, then accepted a handkerchief to press against her nose. "Gee, thank you, Mother. That makes me feel so much better."

"What I mean is you had the deck stacked against you from the outset. You went to court, you met your father's family, played the hand life dealt you. Now...I'm just glad to have you back home."

Oh, right. Belatedly, she remembered she was mad at her mother. "Why didn't you tell me about any of this? My father, my bloodline, the throne..."

Mother sighed. "I won't insult you by saying that your father asked me not to, although he did. And I won't say it was for Traveler tradition either, because the situation was more complicated. But, Zofi, whatever I think about your father's decisions, he had a point here. If nobody knew you existed, nobody could hunt you. And people would have, believe me. Your blood alone would fetch more on the black market than our band has earned in decades."

"Again, you always know how to make me feel better," she muttered. Then she leaned forward. "Even now, Mother, you aren't telling me everything."

"If I told you every secret I have, Zofi, we'd both be sitting in this tent until we died of old age." Mother smiled, though she sobered when Zofi didn't join her.

"Why didn't you tell me you're a curseworker?"

Her mother hesitated. Only for a split second, yet it was enough. Then she laughed and raised her tea mug. "Would you like some? Fresh-picked mint, from just down the swamp."

"Mother." Though she did take the mug and drink, deeply. It

stung on the way down. Mother must have laced it with a little something extra.

"I've been a lot of things in my life, Zofi." Mother watched her closely. "Not all of which I'm proud of. But first and foremost, I'm your mother. And while I hope I'm your friend as well, being a mother—it's not like being friends with somebody. There are certain things you don't share with your children, dangerous things...."

"Spare me the lecture, Mother. It's true, isn't it?" She eyed the silver scar on her mother's face, so familiar that to Zofi it seemed a part of her skin. Like something she'd been born with. "Didn't you trust me enough to tell me?"

"Zofi, darling, of course I *trust* you. It's the rest of the world I don't. If someone learned what I am, I wanted you to have a clean conscience. They couldn't arrest you for covering up an illegal business you had no idea existed."

"So you put the whole band in danger to sell curses at black markets?"

"Some of the band know," Mother said, and if Zofi thought the betrayal hurt before, that was nothing to the sting of it now.

"Who?" She scowled.

"A few elders. Enough people to cover my tracks and get the rest of you to safety if I was ever taken. Look, it doesn't matter who knew, Zofi. It was never about that. Or about money. It's about doing what's right. Sharing knowledge, the way Travelers have always done. I help people with cursework, yes. Rarely, and only when I see true need."

"Is that why you helped Akeylah?"

Her mother frowned. "Who?"

"An Eastern girl," Zofi said. "Red hair, on the tall side, quiet... She said you helped her curse her abusive father."

Mother's frown remained. "I did help a girl who fits that description. My first commission in a long time. But anyone would've done it. You only had to take one look at her bruises to feel for her."

Zofi searched her mother's expression. "So you didn't know, then, who she really was."

"Zofi, what are you talking about? How did you come to meet this girl?"

"She's Andros's daughter," Zofi replied. "My half sister."

For a moment, Mother didn't react. Then her face crumpled, as the realization struck. "*Sands,*" she groaned under her breath. "That's why—"

"Why Father summoned us bastards, yes," Zofi interrupted. "He's dying. Akeylah was raised like me—ignorant of her background. She thought she was cursing her abuser."

Mother shut her eyes. "That poor girl. And Andros, gods, what have I done? A death like that, there's so much pain...."

Zofi sat forward. "Help me, Mother. There has to be some way to fix this. A countercurse."

"Not one you could perform," Mother said. "Because you did not work the initial curse. But Akeylah can. It takes a great deal of the Arts, and it may be too late—"

"Just write down how it's done." Zofi dug through Mother's trunk until she found writing supplies. Tossed a quill in her direction. "If there's any chance of saving him, Akeylah will take it."

Mother hesitated. Then she flashed Zofi another look, expression unreadable.

"What?" Zofi asked as she flung some paper and an inkwell her mother's way.

"I just can't believe you're home."

A strange sensation flooded her, as she watched her mother write the instructions.

Being back here didn't feel unusual. Everything remained the same—the people, this tent. Even Mother, with her countless secrets, was the same person she'd always been.

But Zofi wasn't.

And much as she wanted it to, the word *home* no longer quite described this place.

·⚜ 15 ⚜·

Akeylah

Rozalind can't be the heir. She recited the refrain over and over as she strode through the Keep, until it became a sort rhythmic prayer. *She can't.*

The Vulgar Arts left scars. Akeylah would have seen them on Rozalind's body.

But it had been dark, the night they'd finally lain together. And while she'd seen plenty of the queen, she hadn't exactly studied *every* inch. How noticeable had her own scar been that night? She didn't remember.

Other memories chased that one. Rozalind arguing to keep Zofi imprisoned. Wanting to put Ren on trial. Rozalind's reaction when Akeylah admitted she'd cursed Andros—the queen had seemed surprised, but had she been *that* shocked, given what Akeylah confessed?

She thought about the tithing. When Rozalind first showed Akeylah her ability, Akeylah thought Rozalind was sharing a huge secret with her. It made her trust Roz, drew them closer.

In reality, Rozalind had been lying all along.

She was carrying Father's child.

Akeylah's stomach churned. Surged. She clamped a hand over her mouth just in time to hold the sickness in. A passing servant shot her a look of concern, but Akeylah waved him away, soldiered on down the hall.

Rozalind had hidden her pregnancy from everyone. Even from Akeylah. *What else is she hiding?*

Akeylah thought about her most recent message. The puppet so carefully designed, in a gown just like the one Rozalind's tailor sewed for her. *Dearest Akeylah,* the heir wrote. *One might even say you're my favorite.* It sounded almost tender, compared to the other threats.

The heir promised to protect her if she played the puppet right. Was this Rozalind's idea of leniency? Maybe she liked Akeylah just enough to make her a pet. A girl to warm her bed while Rozalind ruled the Reaches.

She felt sick all over again. She had to stop, press her forehead against a window, and take several deep breaths.

By the time she made it back to the king's chambers, she had herself under control. At least, so she thought. Until Rozalind greeted her, face drawn with worry.

"The mender's here," Rozalind said the instant the doors closed. "It doesn't look good."

Are you carrying his child? Akeylah wanted to scream the question. Sob it.

Are you the one tormenting us?

She swallowed the cry. Followed Rozalind to the bedside with difficulty. "What happened?" Her voice sounded odd. Curious and detached.

"I couldn't get him to swallow any water at lunch," Rozalind said.

A week or two, the mender told them a week ago. Still no word from Zofi. No cure.

"It won't be long now, I'm afraid." The mender released Andros's wrist with a sigh. "I won't be surprised if he goes tonight. Maybe tomorrow morning or evening at the latest. Some people hang on in cases like this. But I would stay close, ladies."

"There's nothing we can do?" Akeylah's voice cracked.

"Only make him as comfortable as possible."

She closed her eyes. They'd failed. All those books she'd read, stacks upon stacks in the library. All Zofi's efforts, come to nothing.

And Akeylah had no one to blame but herself. She did this. She killed her own father.

"Call me if there are any other changes," the mender whispered, then ducked out.

Akeylah heard the rustle of Rozalind's skirts as she approached. "You should stay here today," Rozalind murmured. "If there's anything urgent, I'll handle it."

Why, so you can get some practice taking his place? His heir should be the one handling any urgent concerns. Was that what Rozalind hoped to do now?

Akeylah squeezed her eyes shut. She feared if she looked at the queen, she wouldn't be able to stop. She'd stare and stare until she couldn't hold it in anymore, until she screamed for the truth. *Tell me you're not carrying my father's child. Tell me you aren't the one cursing my sisters and me.*

"Akeylah."

"Yes?" Akeylah asked after a beat.

"What's wrong?"

"My father is dying," she replied, voice hollow. "Am I not allowed to grieve?"

"Of course you can. I'm grieving, too. I care about Andros. But...look at me, please."

Akeylah finally looked up.

Rozalind stepped closer. "Did something happen when you visited Florencia this morning? You seem...angry."

Akeylah turned her face to the wall instead. "Rozalind—"

"Talk to me." Rozalind touched her bare arm. The contact made Akeylah's skin tingle.

Her eyes burned. "There's no fixing this."

Rozalind's hand dropped away. "No. All we can do now is be here for him."

"I'm not talking about my father," Akeylah spat. The vehemence in her tone surprised even her. But she leaned into it.

Anger was easier to handle than sorrow. Than pain. Than the crushing weight of the realization that the girl she trusted, the girl she'd fallen for, the girl she'd just begun to realize she *loved*... had been lying to her all along.

She clenched her fists so hard her nails dug into her palms. "Are you pregnant, Rozalind?"

The queen's face shuttered at once, like a trader's house with boards suddenly nailed over the windows. Rozalind tore her gaze from Akeylah. Stared at Andros instead.

"Seas below." Akeylah shoved away. "So it's true. You're carrying my...*my father's child?*" Her throat tightened. Her stomach churned again, sick with grief, nauseated at the idea.

Half of her wanted Rozalind to deny it. Claim it was another affair. Something, anything.

But Roz shrank in on herself. Deflated. "It happened three months ago. Long before you came here, Akeylah, and I swear, the moment I learned I was pregnant I stopped lying with him. Gods, even before that, we barely ever..."

Akeylah sucked in a sharp breath through her teeth. "You've been hiding it from me this whole time, and that's supposed to make me feel better?"

"I've hidden it from *everybody*. Even your father didn't know. *Doesn't* know."

"Why in Mother Ocean's name not?" Akeylah flung her arms wide. "You could have saved us all of this. He need never have brought me to court, or my sisters; I'd still be at home, ignorant of my heritage—" She stopped short. *And still pinned under the thumb of an evil man who hated me.*

Rozalind shook her head, hard. "No, Akeylah, I...Andros and I got pregnant once before, a year ago. I lost the child a couple months in. He was so heartbroken, I couldn't...I couldn't bear to tell him again. Not until I was certain the baby would survive this time." She winced. "Then he fell ill, and I thought...Well, imagine the chaos if he passed away and I lost this child, too. Who would inherit? This way, I thought you three could be—"

"Your backup options?" Akeylah hissed.

"Yes," Rozalind admitted in a whisper.

Akeylah stared.

She wanted to believe it. Wanted to believe the only thing Rozalind had lied about was the baby. That was bad enough. But now... how could she trust anything the queen said?

"Was any of it true?" Akeylah's lips trembled. "Anything you ever said to me?"

Rozalind flinched as though she'd been struck. "Akeylah. Yes, everything... everything you and I have, that's true. I should have told you about all this from the start, I know, but I was afraid it would change things between us, and that's... You're the only thing in the world I'm sure about right now."

She shook her head. Took one step backward, then another. "How can I trust you? If you were willing to hide this, what else are you keeping from me?"

"Nothing, I swear—"

"Seas below. Ren was right." Her heart clenched like a fist. "I don't even know you."

Rozalind's eyes shone in the dim light. "Akeylah, please..."

She never finished the sentence. A deafening shriek interrupted, like the stormwing horns the Talons used on the practice fields, only much louder.

The outer doors burst open. Talons stormed the room. "What was that?" one barked.

Akeylah blinked in surprise. "I was about to ask you the same thing."

The shriek sounded again, closer. It almost sounded as though it were coming from...

"Stand back, my lady," one guard advised while the other crossed to the window, still hung with heavy blackout drapes, to conceal the king.

The Talon yanked back the curtain.

Outside, the largest bird Akeylah had ever seen perched on the balcony. Its razor-sharp talons curled around the stonewood railing, and it cocked its head to one side, curious. A *stormwing*. She'd never seen one this close before.

As they all stared, the bird let out another piercing shriek and extended one leg. Only then did Akeylah notice the metal tube tied above its talon.

The guard opened the window and unbound the tube, as though this were perfectly normal. "Message for you, Lady Akeylah," he said with a glance at the side.

Akeylah stepped forward to accept it. The metal felt cold as ice under her fingertips—probably from the height at which the bird flew, far above the clouds. On the outside, her name was scrawled in messy handwriting. No titles. Just *Akeylah*.

"Zofi," she breathed.

❋

Akeylah read and reread Zofi's mother's note half a dozen times. Deena said she'd need to use the same scar. Reopen it to work the curse again, but in reverse this time. Where before, she'd been planting a seed, now she needed to tear that plant out by its roots.

In theory, it should work. Just one problem—Akeylah had shielded that morning. It wouldn't wear off until dawn.

By the time Akeylah had finished committing Deena's

157

instructions to memory, it was well past sunset, but the mender had said Andros was fading fast.

Akeylah knelt at his bedside. "Hold on, Father," she whispered. "Please."

On the far side of the chambers, Rozalind sat behind the king's desk, watching. Akeylah couldn't stop thinking about Ren's warning not to let the queen out of her sight. If Rozalind was the heir, she couldn't do anything with Akeylah a few feet away. Not unless Rozalind wanted to let all her secrets slip out at once.

Still, just because she had to be in the same room didn't mean Akeylah needed to acknowledge the queen's existence.

They spent the night like that. Akeylah kneeling beside her father, counting his every breath with her own held. Rozalind perched at his desk, until exhaustion overtook her, and she laid her head down to sleep on the hard stonewood surface.

The only break Akeylah took from their standoff had been to pen a quick note to Ren, to reassure her sister they had a cure, an end goal in sight. Father only needed to hang on for a few more hours, until she could perform it.

Finally, after the longest night of her life, predawn light painted the curtains.

Akeylah crossed to the desk first. Satisfied the queen was still asleep, Akeylah tiptoed past her into the bathing chamber.

Please, Mother Ocean, let this work, she thought as she knelt on the tile floor and gripped her bloodletter in a trembling fist.

The pain was worse than she remembered. When she reopened the scar on her thigh, sparks exploded in her vision, and her breath came so sharp she thought she might faint.

She didn't.

She ignored the pain flaring at every nerve ending. Focused her mind instead, the way she'd done on the beach months ago.

It was easier this time. Easier to look past her own bloodstream, to turn with that extra sense and survey the other bodies nearby—her close relatives. Siblings and parents.

This time, she counted the bodies.

She couldn't see any features, of course. Not faces or body shapes or anything identifiable. Only people's insides. Hearts, veins, muscles, nerves. Yet she noticed, now that she knew what to look for, subtle differences.

Andros was easy to find. His veins ran black with the curse she'd planted. She could smell it on him—vomit and bedpans, nostalgia and regret.

But there were other shapes in the darkness. Other relatives.

She recognized Zofi first. Her veins ran hotter than anyone else's, the blood brighter, the pulse faster. She smelled like running on a windy beach, or diving off a cliff into the sea.

Florencia's blood ran slower, smelled of perfumed dances and sly sideways smiles.

And beside Ren, another presence. Vast and wild, dancing around the edge of her perception. This person felt harder to sense, almost... *hidden*. She couldn't see their veins or heart or pulse. The scent, however, was harder to mask. This thing smelled familiar. Like sweat and fistfights and screaming at the top of your lungs, *The world is so damned wrong.*

She tore her mind from the black hole of that presence, refocused on the task at hand. Healing Father.

Akeylah concentrated on his outline. She reached into his blackened veins, and groaned as the stench filled her nostrils, invaded her mouth. He tasted of bile, of guilt and loneliness. She wanted to puke. She wanted to lie down and die alongside him.

Last time, this part had been simple. She'd planted a seed—a tiny drop of cursed blood. Now, she had to rip up a whole root system. Tear out the venomous plant she'd grown in him.

Her forehead creased in concentration.

The curse wove through his veins. It had grown enormous, from that one drop. She reached for his body as though pushing through a membrane, until her fingertips curled around the black poison.

It was slippery, hard to grasp. She raised both hands, wound the curse's roots around her knuckles and *pulled*.

Somewhere in the distant corner of her mind still connected to reality, she heard a shout of pain from the adjacent room.

She ignored it, yanked harder. Threw all her weight into this, fists clenched so tight they shook, her whole body leaning away from her father's. She channeled all her weight and focus behind the movement.

She felt the curse begin to give. The black web creaked, and a few tendrils snapped. In those places, she glimpsed clean red bloodstream, Father's veins beginning to return to normal.

Underneath the regret-rot scent of the curse, she caught whiffs of another scent. A smell like sunrise on a craggy cliff or an over-strong abraca brew. She gritted her teeth, wrenched at that black web again. This time, she couldn't tell whether the cry of pain came from herself or her father. But she bent into it, pulled and pulled and pulled until, with a sharp cracking sensation, the curse *broke*.

Akeylah fell backward, and the world slammed into view. The

tile floor, dotted with her blood. The glow from her scar, twice as bright now, lighting the whole room.

She moaned. It *hurt*.

But Akeylah was used to pain.

She tugged her knees to her chest. Curled around her wound, and let the pain sweep her away. At some point, cool arms wrapped around her, lifted her up. It took all her remaining energy just to open one eye.

Rozalind was carrying her to bed. Then her eyelids fluttered shut, and she forgot about anything but sleep.

* 16 *

Florencia

Day five of her confinement crawled.

Over a week had passed since Zofi left, since Father fell unconscious. Last night, Akeylah sent word that she had the cure in hand. Ren prayed for good news. Sun knew they needed it.

As for Ren, she couldn't stop turning the latest discovery over in her mind. *Rozalind*. A princess of Genal and a queen of Kolonya. A queen who might be carrying Andros's only surviving legitimate child. If so, then the words *true heir* described Rozalind's unborn child better than anyone else in the Reaches.

But why hide her pregnancy from the king? That was the one piece of the puzzle Ren couldn't snap into place.

Why bring the girls to court only to drive them away again?

She was spared from chasing that question in circles late in the afternoon, when a visitor arrived with her dinner.

Ren waited until the Talons left before she embraced her friend. "How are you?"

Audrina laughed, her breath stirring Ren's already messy hair. "You're caged inside your own bedroom and you ask how *I'm* doing?" The girls broke apart, and Ren surveyed her friend while Audrina laid out the dinner tray she'd brought with her.

Aud wore another new dress, jet-black with long sleeves. Darker than Aud usually preferred, though it was still within the parameters set for maids' outfits. Nice, but not too nice.

Can't have the ladies you serve feeling inadequate.

Ren smiled when she spotted the contents of the dinner tray. Audrina had brought all of her favorites—globe fruit, Lyra the cook's specialty bread, a fluffy white variety only the nobles were allowed. Even a pot of bright-yellow Northern curry topped with hackley leaf. "Isn't this out of season?" Ren reached for a spoon to stir the hackley into the thick, creamy stew.

"Lyra owed me a favor. Anyway, you're a lady now, you can eat whatever you want."

"I'm a prisoner; I'm pretty sure I'm not allowed any such considerations. Besides, I thought we agreed not to give each other special treatment anymore." Ren raised an eyebrow.

"This doesn't count," Audrina protested. "I'm just comforting a friend in need." She peered around Ren's chambers with a groan. "Sun above, Ren. I can't believe your tormenter went so far as to invent a tale this immense. Is there no way to prove your innocence?"

Ren shut her eyes.

After a minute, Audrina let out a slow breath. "I see. The accusation is true."

Ren swallowed around a lump in her throat. "I would have told you, Aud, but I couldn't bear the thought of my only real friend left hating me."

"How could I hate you?" Audrina cocked her head. "I know you, Ren. You care about this country. If you were willing to turn against Kolonya, you must have had good reason."

Ren pursed her mouth. "Just the same tall redheaded reason I do anything foolish."

"Now, *him* I hate." Audrina crossed her arms. "Is Danton working for the rebellion? You should use that as leverage—clear your name and lock him up instead."

"I can't do that," Ren said, voice low. "Me, my father might spare. An outer Reach ambassador, they'd hang."

"Well, he should have considered that before he betrayed Kolonya. We give him a place to live in the Keep, offer him a cushy ambassadorship, and this is his thanks?"

Ren ran a hand through her hair. "He didn't know the rebellion would take things as far as they did. He just wanted to help his Reach—and so did I. The rebels are terrible, but so is what we've done to the other Reaches. Despite everything...I can't watch him die for me."

Audrina swore softly. "You still love him."

"No, I..." But the denial died on her lips. Right now, with nobody but her best friend to hear, Ren couldn't keep lying. Not even to herself.

Her shoulders sagged. Everything he'd done, every decision he made—helping the rebellion, offering to take the fall for her, Sun above, even his sham marriage to Lexana. Those were all decisions Ren would have made, too, in his shoes. If Lexana's dowry would've been large enough to support his Reach for months, how could she blame him for wanting it?

Danton was like her—once he set his heart on a goal, he'd stop at nothing to achieve it. Like when Ren swore she'd raise herself up out of the servants' chambers.

Look at me now. She'd lifted herself out of that muck, all right. Straight into a sinkhole.

"My mind and his work the same way," Ren finally answered. "I love him the way I love myself—I can't help it, in spite of all the terrible decisions I make."

Audrina sighed. "Just remember, love clouds our judgments, Ren. It lures us into forgiving sins that ought never to be pardoned." Audrina's fists tightened, and suddenly it occurred to Ren that her friend wasn't talking about Danton anymore.

"I'm doing it again," Ren said. "Only talking about myself. How are you, Aud?"

For a moment, Ren thought her friend might actually respond. Then Audrina reached for Ren's bread. "Oh, just the usual. Work, babysitting noblewomen..."

"Really?" Ren arched a brow. Audrina grimaced, and Ren took a guess. "Your parents?" They were a constant point of contention in her friend's life. They never approved of anything Aud did. Growing up, they'd always complained they shouldn't have had her, that she cost more trouble than she was worth. Even after she came to work in the Keep, they remained unimpressed—she could never work hard enough to earn their favor.

Audrina turned the bread over and over in her hands. "Things are actually better with my mother now. But my father..." She drew in a sharp breath. "I just want him to say he's proud of me, just *once*."

"Sun damn him if he can't see what a caring person you are." Ren reached for her hand. "You don't need the approval of a man like that. You've got friends who love you like family."

A ghost of a smile appeared on Audrina's face. "Thanks, Ren."

"No, thank you for putting up with me. And for giving me another chance when I was being such a self-involved jerk."

Audrina's smile widened. "I'd give you a million chances. But I'll also tell you if you're being a jerk—that's what friends are for."

Ren couldn't help but laugh. "I need that reality check these days."

"No headway, then, on figuring out who's been doing all this?" Audrina frowned.

"None. Just...well." Ren tilted her head. "Did you know Rozalind is pregnant? My mother told me rumors have been circulating through the maids."

Audrina's jaw dropped. "I didn't, no. Then again, I rarely talk to the other girls—Sun above, if she's carrying your half sibling... do you think it could be her?"

"It's possible. But I don't understand why. Apparently Andros doesn't know she's with child, but if she'd just told him, my sisters and I need never have been dragged into this."

Aud tore off a fresh piece of bread and chewed for a moment. "Well, there's the obvious explanation. She's Genalese." Audrina said it as though this explained everything. When Ren didn't respond, Audrina gestured impatiently. "She's a princess of Genal. Her child is the potential heir to the Sun Throne. That baby would be eligible for both the Kolonyan and Genalese thrones. And what does Genal want more than anything?"

"To reconquer the Reaches..." Ren said slowly.

166

"Four hundred years of wars haven't achieved that. But what if Rozalind found a way to do it without bloodshed? What if her father the king sent her here, under the guise of forming a peace treaty, with this goal in mind all along?"

"It still doesn't explain why she would let Andros publicly acknowledge us. We're the competition. Our very existence undermines her claim on the throne."

"Exactly." Audrina nodded as though Ren had just proven her point. "If she let you all stay hidden, someday you might rise up to bite her in the backside. Especially if she makes moves to do something hugely unpopular, like reinstating Genalese rule over the Reaches. Better to get you three out in the open now. Ruin your reputations, destroy you publicly, so there's nobody with even a hint at a counterclaim. Then, when she takes the throne, Kolonya is out of options. The country has no choice but to follow her into any mess she wants."

Ren let the idea digest. "Sun above. And if Father dies now, she won't even need to wait for the child to grow up. She'd become regent in the baby's stead."

Audrina lifted one shoulder, let it fall. "It's what I would do, in her shoes. The best option is to become the only option."

Ren's expression darkened. "Not if we can help it."

✢ 17 ✢

Zofi

To celebrate Zofi's return, a huge bonfire had been built in a clearing of the swampland, on high ground. Massive torches burned around the outer rim, each one laced with sweet-smelling fruit peels to keep the vampyre flies at bay. Even now, with Essexset approaching, the party was still going strong. Every Traveler in the band had come out, though a few rotated back to the campsite on watch, making sure not to leave it entirely unguarded.

Zofi's heart ached. If she seemed insecure, a little out of place and not quite home yet, nobody seemed to mind. They kept her drinking horn full and her plate overflowing, and no one asked what had happened in Kolonya. Her band knew Zofi would only talk once she felt ready.

As for her other home, well, the stormwing had flown back to Vidal at sunset, holster empty, letter delivered. Akeylah must have received the cure. She would either work it or not. Andros would recover or he wouldn't.

None of that was Zofi's concern anymore. Kolonya was another lifetime, one she needed to forget.

She'd grown up on the move, leaving town after town in the dust. Why did this feel so much more difficult?

She whirled across the dance floor, trading partners every few bars of the song that Ina and Kant fiddled. Off to the side, little Pyra had picked up her mother's flute to join in, and Zofi was startled at how good the girl had grown in just the few weeks Zofi had been away.

What else has changed?

She pushed the thought to the back of her mind and grabbed Bette's hand to swing across the muddy, trampled grass. Her breath came short, half from the dancing, half from laughter. When Bette finally swung her to a halt, she stumbled off to the side, dizzy. There, she spotted Norren's partner, Rull, teaching Vidal the jump-twist.

Or trying to.

"No, no, left foot first, watch me." Rull demonstrated again, making sure to move slow enough that Vidal could trace the individual steps.

Vidal hopped left foot first this time, but when it came to the twist, he stumbled off-balance and nearly collided with little Pyra midnote. "Sorry!" he blurted, and backed away, one hand clamped over his mouth.

In the other, he held a drinking horn. A large one.

Zofi burst out laughing. He spun to glare at her, and she pointed at his feet. "What happened to the suave dancer I met in the sky gardens, hmm?" she called.

"He drank a lot less—what did you call this again?" Vidal shook the horn. A few drops of Heine's clear moonshine splashed onto an innocent passerby. "Oh, Sun above, I apologize."

"He's never tried moonshine," Zofi explained to the woman, a local from the town where they were camped.

"Oh, I don't mind." The woman scanned him up and down, a small grin touching her lips. "I do not mind one bit." She sidled closer. "Tell me, handsome, are you spoken for?"

Now it was Zofi's turn to press a hand over her mouth, to stifle her grin.

Vidal glanced from the woman to Zofi and back again, blinking fast. "Um...I...er...Am I?" he added with a confused glance in Zofi's direction.

"You tell me," Zofi replied, eyes bright with amusement.

"I'll take that as a yes," the villager said with a quick wink at Zofi.

Zofi practically skipped to Vidal's side to pluck the drinking horn from his fingers. "Let me guess. You filled it to the brim?" She peered inside and cursed. Only a few drops remained.

"Isn't that what you do with..." Vidal hiccupped. "With cups?"

"Not these ones." Zofi laughed. "And certainly not when it's moonshine filling 'em. Come on. Let's get you tucked into bed." Zofi offered an arm.

"It tastes like paint," he complained as he looped his arm around her neck. "I much prefer strongwine."

"I'll bet." She wrapped her other arm around his waist and began the slow plod toward the campsite, about half a mile through the swamps. She hoped there weren't any particularly narrow or precarious bridges along the way or Vidal might wind up face-first in that swamp.

"Need a hand?" Rull offered, but Zofi just handed him Vidal's empty horn.

"We'll manage. You go have fun."

They made it a few yards before Vidal stopped to peer over his shoulder. The motion threw them both off-balance, and it took Zofi a minute to right them once more. "Your people are nice," Vidal said. Or slurred, rather. "I didn't...expect..."

"Didn't expect them to welcome a Talon so easily?" She smirked. "Me neither, truth be told. I guess my word carries more weight than I thought."

"Everybody loves you." His voice rose louder. "*Evvverybody.*"

"Well. They're my family. They have to," she joked. She tugged him back into motion, and together they swayed across the first wooden bridge between here and home.

"Some like you...more than family." His voice went low.

Her heart throbbed. She didn't need to ask. She knew what he meant.

She'd spent all evening dodging Elex. She hadn't felt ready to talk yet, even though she'd caught him approaching more than once. She kept pulling Bette or another Traveler out onto the dance floor instead and pretending not to notice him.

It was a conversation she didn't even understand how to begin.

"If you mean Elex..." Zofi started.

Vidal nodded so hard they nearly tripped sideways off the bridge.

"Whoa, hold it together." Zofi caught him around the waist. Swung him to a halt. They stood face-to-face—or, well, her face to his chest. He was so much taller than her. But he bent closer, and the Noxlight caught his eyes. Made that muddy hazel-brown color seem deep and dark as the marsh they stood above.

"I saw him watching you, Zofi. Every time you started to dance, or every time you were talking to somebody else. Anytime he didn't think you'd notice."

"Vidal," she whispered.

"Look, I'm not an idiot." He ran a hand across his eyes. "You've got history, that's obvious. And I know whatever happened with us . . . It was just one night with some guy you hardly know; some guy from a whole different world. But Zofi, I have to tell you."

"You're drunk, Vidal." She caught his hands. Tried to tug him toward camp. "Let's just go to bed." She didn't want to hear this. Not here, not like this.

But Vidal didn't move. Instead, he twisted his arm free of her grasp, and touched her shoulder. Waited until she lifted her gaze to his. "I want you to know it was real for me, Zofi," he said, voice soft and quiet. "*You* are real to me. Whatever happens now, whatever you choose . . . I don't regret anything."

Her breath slowed. Threatened to stop altogether when he leaned in. His mouth was so damn close she could almost taste him again, like clean hay and fresh-cut grass and winning a fight. Her eyelids fluttered. Drifted shut. She felt his eyelashes brush her cheek, his warm breath on her lips.

Someone coughed.

Vidal's hands slipped off her arms. They both turned to find Elex.

"Zofi. Vidal," Elex added, a beat too late. Like an afterthought.

Vidal took another step backward. "Zofi, I'll see you back at camp?"

"Wait," she started to say, worried about his balance on these swamp bridges. But Vidal had already retreated across the first, and his gait seemed far steadier now. The fresh air must be helping. That or the head rush of what he'd just said to her.

You are real to me.

"Sorry," Elex said. "I didn't mean to interrupt."

After a minute of silence, Zofi cleared her throat. "You didn't," she lied, unconvincingly.

"A Talon, huh?" Elex raised a single bemused eyebrow.

"He's not like most Talons," Zofi said, dodging the question. "He's really open-minded, and he's nice, and..." *And part of me is worried I might break his heart.*

"I'm not judging." Elex raised one shoulder, let it fall. "He seems...yeah. Nice."

Zofi walked to the side of the wooden bridge. This one was only a few feet wide, so she wanted to leave room for any passersby. She sat on the edge and let her feet dangle above the marsh. "Sorry for avoiding you," she said.

After a pause, Elex sat beside her. "Are you ready to tell me what happened back in Kolonya? You said you needed some drinks first; your breath smells like it might be time."

She snorted. "Maybe a few drinks past time," she admitted, though the cool night air had dimmed the spin in her head to a lower, pleasant hum.

"When I left, you were being blackmailed...." Elex watched her carefully.

"They told the king what I did. I've been banished from Kol-onya." She shut her eyes to avoid his stare. "Learning about it may very well have been my father's last act. He fell sick afterward, and as far as I know, he hasn't woken since."

"Sands, Zo."

When she opened her eyes again, the pity on his face nearly killed her. "Don't look at me like that."

"Like what?"

"I already know how terrible the situation is; I don't need you feeling sorry for me on top of it."

"That's not sorrow you're seeing, it's guilt." Elex's voice dipped so low that Zofi looked at him, startled. "It's my fault you're in this mess. If I hadn't provoked the prince that night—"

"Don't you dare." She grabbed his chin, turned his face toward hers. "Nicolen—" She cast a quick glance around, remembering too late that there were villages around here, other people dotting these marshes. But she saw nobody in hearing distance. Just a few figures silhouetted against the fire, fields away.

Still, when she spoke again, her voice was lower. "Nicolen was a horrible person. Half brother or not, I'd do what I did a million times over if it meant saving you, Elex. And it was my decision to attack him, I'll remind you. You can't shoulder responsibility for my mistakes without stealing my victories from me, too."

"But your father—"

"I got along just fine without him my entire life." She flinched, though, when she said the words. Her hardened voice lost some of its edge. "I wish I could have known him better, but I'll take what little time I got. Better that than none at all."

"And the rest of it? The throne, your sisters?"

She tried and failed to sound lighthearted. "No longer my concern. My future's here, with the band. Where I belong."

Elex softened. Took her hands and laced her fingers through his. He was warm, even in the chilly predawn air. "As nice as it is to have you back, Zo, I feel like you're not..." He hesitated.

"Not what?"

"Not *here*." He searched her gaze. "Just a couple weeks ago, I begged you to leave Kolonya, come home with me. You wouldn't even *consider* it. What changed?"

"Well, the whole being banished thing, for a start." She laughed once, bitter, and twisted her hands from his.

He laughed, too, but with disbelief. "So that's it? You're giving up, just like that. Since when do you take orders so obediently?"

She scowled. "What do you want from me, Elex? First you beg me to come back. Then I do, and you complain that I'm here."

"I want you to get what you want, Zo. I want you to win this thing. Remember? You promised me you would."

"It's over. I lost."

Elex crossed his arms over his broad chest. "Why, because they told you so?"

"What am I supposed to do, march back there and let them hang me for murder?"

"Look, if you were here of your own free will, I'd welcome you back with open arms. Sands, I'd be throwing you this party myself. But you're only here because you gave up. You let them decide your fate. And that's not you, Zo." He reached up to gently tug on a stray curl of hers, and the graze of his finger tickled her skin. "You're never going to be happy like this. You're never going to truly be home. Not until you decide to be."

She understood, then, the sorrow in his gaze. Felt it mirrored in her own. Because he was right, damn him. It's why her homecoming had felt ever so slightly off, why nothing here fit her anymore, like a shoe she'd outgrown. Because she didn't choose this path herself.

"Elex..."

"When you love someone," he said, and that word sent a rush into her veins, "you don't hold them in a fist." He held up a hand, palm open to the night sky. "You let them chase what their heart desires, because when they're happy, you will be, too."

He stood, then, and she watched him go, heart sinking with the realization.

This wasn't home anymore. And wouldn't be ever again, not unless she was the one who decided to come here. Right now, she was following someone else's command.

She needed to take back the reins of her own life.

⊲ 18 ⊳

Akeylah

This is a role reversal," a voice said, deep and sonorous, and loud enough to wake her from a fitful dream.

Akeylah's eyelids fluttered. *Father? That can't be right*, she thought as her memories flooded back. He was still bedridden, unconscious. Dying.

Yet, when she finally managed to crack her eyelids, there he sat, alive and well, in a heavily cushioned chair beside her bed. He was even smiling.

"Father." Her voice cracked. She levered herself up on an elbow, and the king's chambers swam around her. She was in his bed. The freshly opened scar on her thigh throbbed. An ache deeper than just the knife wound.

Andros held out a glass of water. "I'm the one who's supposed to be bedridden. Not my healthy young daughter." He tsked, though he nodded with approval when she took a long drink.

The water burned going down. Everything burned—her veins, her temples, even her eyeballs thudded in their sockets. Her leg worst of all. It felt on fire, alight with pain. She could almost sense the glow, brighter than ever. Had her father seen it? Did he know?

"Your illness..." She hesitated.

His smile widened. "Is gone. From what I hear, I was well beyond death's doorstep. All the way to the entrance of the Blessed Sunlands, when I was called back to this realm. A miracle, my guards are calling it." He checked over her shoulder. The room was empty. He bent closer. "My wife and the mender, on the other hand, tell me otherwise."

Her face went hot. He must have seen the scar. Realized she was the culprit. *This is it.* He was going to imprison her like Ren. Or banish her like Zofi. "Father, I am so sorry—"

He held up a hand.

Or worse. Have her executed. She would deserve it. A traitor's death. She nearly killed him, after all. Her own father.

"It took bravery to do what you did, Akeylah."

She blinked. Whatever she'd anticipated, it wasn't this. "I..."

"Rozalind told me how you researched night and day. That you refused to stop until you found a tithe to heal a relative. Healing another person's body is, technically, a use of the Vulgar Arts—the scar on your thigh should remind you of that. Father Sun sent those marks so we'd know never to tithe into another's blood. But in this case..." He flashed a quick wink. "I think we may make an exception."

Oh. She dared to breathe again.

Rozalind didn't tell him everything. He didn't know Akeylah was the reason he'd fallen ill in the first place.

"I've explained to the mender who treated you that a king enjoys certain privileges," Andros went on. "The privilege to bend the rules, at least a little, when it pertains to his own life. We're going to keep this our little secret, with the understanding you will never flout the Sun's law again." The corner of his mouth rose. "Does that sound agreeable?"

"Of course, Father." She ducked her head. Drank another gulp of water to soothe her throat.

"Good. Now, I'm afraid the scar will last a lifetime—nothing we can do about that. In the meantime, I have spoken to the dean in charge of the University. I'd like you to enroll in some basic courses. This knowledge you've stumbled across may come in handy in other situations. Sun knows we ought to review our categorization of Blood and Vulgar Arts sometime soon—I'll add it to the councils' future agendas."

Her head swam. She couldn't think about the councils, about anything except the miracle sitting beside her.

"I'm just grateful you're all right, Father." Akeylah smiled through a sudden sting at the back of her eyes. *Father.* He would fix all of this. He'd help them stop the heir. He'd calm the nobility, restore order throughout the Keep. Or, seas, throughout the whole Reaches.

Everything was going to be okay. They'd done it.

I fixed him.

"As am I, daughter." He studied her. "I dreaded the thought of dying too soon. I left so many things unfinished, but you were my greatest regret of all. Not assuring my daughter's place in the kingdom. At least I am certain about it now."

She struggled to sit upright, despite the throb in her skull. "About what, Father?"

"My rightful heir."

Her stomach flipped. *No.* "Father, about my sisters—"

"Rozalind has filled me in. Zofi obeyed your orders and departed the kingdom quietly—for that I will spare her. As for Florencia, the charges against her are too great to ignore."

"She's innocent, Father."

"Your loyalty to your family is a winning quality, Akeylah." He smiled, indulgent. "It's why I'm certain I have made the right decision. But in Florencia's case, I am afraid your loyalty is misplaced. Proofs against her continue to stack up, though of course, her guilt and subsequent sentence must be determined in a fair trial. Rozalind and I are discussing the best time and place for that."

Rozalind. Lying to the king about Akeylah's scar, and now encouraging him to name Akeylah his successor, to push forward Ren's trial. Was she doing this because she truly believed Akeylah would be the right choice? Or did she have other motives?

Being the favorite comes with certain responsibilities…

Akeylah steeled her spine. She was nobody's puppet. "It sounds as though Rozalind has done a thorough job of updating you on everything that's happened since you fell ill, Father. But did she also tell you her own good news? You may not need to name a successor after all."

Her father froze. The wrinkles on his forehead deepened as his brows climbed toward his hairline. "You mean…?"

"She's with child."

Andros leaned back in his chair. "But we've not . . . it's been . . ."

"She's several months along," Akeylah added. "She admitted she didn't tell you yet because she worried about the child's viability—"

"And I'm glad that she did not," Andros said, stunning Akeylah into silence. Now it was her turn to stare wide-eyed.

"If she'd said something sooner, I would never have gotten to know my other children." He extended a hand, and she took it, fighting a sudden lump in her throat. "I thought I was doing the right thing, all those years ago. Hiding you away from the Keep, safe in your ignorance. Now I realize what a disservice I did, to you most of all, Akeylah, but to your sisters, as well. Zofi may never have committed such an atrocity; Florencia might have learned true loyalty for her country. . . ."

Akeylah tried to imagine that. A life here with Andros. A life without Jahen's beatings. Without her siblings to follow his lead, taunting and tormenting her. She could have grown up surrounded by true family, by a kind king who, albeit flawed, at least loved her.

Who would she be in that world? She'd never know.

But she liked who she was now. Who she'd grown into, despite her hardships. "It's enough to be here now, Father," Akeylah replied. "It's enough to have this second chance."

He smiled, the stormwing's-feet at the corners of his eyes wrinkling. "I'll let you rest now, daughter. If you're well enough to be on your feet tomorrow, I think we should hold a summit in the Great Hall. Confirm your acknowledgment as my heir."

She blinked in surprise. "But Rozalind—"

"If I learned anything during my illness, Akeylah, it is never to trust in uncertainties. Rozalind and I have conceived a child together before. We lost that child. I'd much prefer a known quantity, a daughter I trust, to bear the title of heir apparent."

This was wrong. She couldn't be queen. She barely held the Keep together for one week. "Father, please, I am not the right choice for this. I'm not ready—"

"The best leaders are those who accept the crown as a burden rather than claim it as a prize. You are the best choice, Akeylah. The *only* choice." With that, he moved to stand. But halfway from his seat, he groaned and reached for a cane propped beside her bed.

"Father? Are you feeling all right?"

He waved her off. "It's nothing. My usual aches and pains." His expression went wry. "Try never to age, Akeylah; it is not a pleasant experience. But, I suppose it is better than the alternative."

He waved over his shoulder as he hobbled out.

Akeylah laid back on the cushions and stared up at the ceiling of her father's bedroom, wondering how in the world she could accept the title of Andros's heir, when a single week of acting on his behalf had nearly destroyed her.

Akeylah slept straight through the afternoon and into the next day. When she woke, she found a rack of gowns she didn't recognize, newly made and all in her size. Alongside the gowns were instructions from her father to come to the Great Hall as soon as she was ready.

Akeylah didn't think she'd ever be ready.

Underneath Father's message, she found a trio of letters from Ren. No wonder—Ren must be desperate for news. A pang of guilt struck. But Akeylah had been too exhausted to even consider writing until now. Even just skimming the first note, which begged Akeylah to send word about Father, made her head throb and the writing swim across the page.

Akeylah set the letters aside and forced herself out of bed.

The countercurse had taken a toll. She walked with a limp, favoring the leg she hadn't abused. Her body felt stiff, run dry.

She wasn't shielded, she realized, belated. Yet the mere thought of lifting a bloodletter made her nauseated. To judge by the dullness in her senses, she doubted she could have managed a tithe, anyway. She had no reserves left; she'd spent everything on Father.

It was worth it. Her heart swelled at the memory of his voice, his smile. Him telling her he was grateful for the chance to know her.

Even the prospect of becoming his official heir scared her less now that Father was back. She'd never experienced this—having a parent to lean on, a role model. She had so many questions to ask him. Now they'd finally have time.

She scribbled two quick, jubilant notes. One to Ren and one to Zofi, the same contents in each. *It worked. Father is well again, stronger than ever. I am working to convince him of your innocence.* To judge by his conversation about wishing he'd spent more time with his daughters, Akeylah felt certain she could talk him into pardoning both Zofi and Ren, given time.

She sent Ren's letter with a serving boy, and Zofi's with a girl who promised to run it up to the aerie. Then she dressed in the least ostentatious of the new gowns, a dark emerald dress with half sleeves that set off her auburn hair to perfection.

If this proved to be her first act as the heir apparent, she wanted to strike the right note. Elegant but not over-the-top.

A pair of Talons waited outside Father's chambers, and Akeylah wondered briefly whether Father was maintaining the heightened security because of his condition or because he didn't trust Florencia, even with her locked in her chambers. The guards marched her all the way to the vast double doors of the Great Hall. There they bowed and took up positions outside, while Akeylah continued in.

It was early, so she didn't see any other nobles here yet. Just servants laying out place settings and arranging fruit baskets.

She didn't see her father either. But the dais at the head of the room was set for three people, she noticed. That used to be Andros, Rozalind, and Yasmin.

Now she'd take her aunt's place.

A couple servers drifted close enough for Akeylah to overhear their conversation. "I guess even kings and queens have marital spats," one man murmured.

"How long you wager before the Genalese madwoman starts throwing plates?" the other snickered.

Somewhere in the distance came a crashing sound, and both men cackled. Akeylah didn't hear anything else they said, because she was already hurrying toward the sound, her nerves jangling.

Something was wrong.

Even kings and queens have marital spats. Where was Rozalind? Akeylah had promised Ren she wouldn't let the queen out of her sight. Then she went and left Roz to her own devices for two whole days.

She reached the back of the hall, which had fallen silent. She froze, trying to figure out which of three passages to take. Then a faint sob sounded from the rightmost corridor, and Akeylah raced that way, heart rabbiting in her chest.

The short corridor led to an anteroom off the Great Hall. To judge by the cloaks and scepters that lined the wall, it was a dressing room of sorts, for royals to prepare before events.

Another sob drew her gaze past the fur cloaks and dress crowns to the far side of the room. The world slowed. Her heartbeat pounded in her ears, deafening.

Andros lay on the ground, mouth open in a silent scream. Black spiderwebs wove under his skin, raised the veins on his arms, crept up his neck. A curse, it had to be, though it looked faster and far more painful than the one Akeylah had used.

And there, beside him, skirts hiked up around her waist, a bloodletter clenched in her fist, slick and red ...

"Rozalind." Akeylah forced the word out through frozen lips.

Everything inside her shut down.

The queen turned as if in slow motion. The blade dropped from her fingertips, clattered across the stonewood floor. Cherry stonewood, not so very different in color to the blood staining it now.

On Rozalind's thigh pulsed a vibrant blue scar, just like Akeylah's.

"Akeylah." Rozalind's voice cracked. Broke. "It's not what it looks like..."

"What have you done?" Akeylah whispered. Then Father moaned aloud, and she forced herself to move. "Help!" she shouted. The word echoed through the open door, into the corridors. She dropped to her knees beside her father and pulled his head onto her lap.

Andros stared up at her with horrible, empty eyes. He groaned again, a sound like worlds crashing, kingdoms burning. The blackness reached his chin, unfurled across his face.

Akeylah grabbed her own bloodletter and dragged it across her forearm, but she felt nothing. No taste of possibility, no tingle of the Arts. The countercurse had run her dry.

"Someone help!" she screamed again, and finally, *finally*, she heard running footsteps. "Father, please hold on," she begged.

He turned toward the sound of her voice. Suddenly, with a surge of energy, Andros grabbed her wrist. His grip was crushing, powerful. For a brief instant, his vision seemed to clear. "Akeylah..."

"Save your strength, Father," she whispered.

But he dragged her down until her ear was beside his mouth. "Don't...let her...use you."

"Who, Father?" She turned to look at him. That's when she saw it. The moment the light faded from his eyes.

His hand slipped from her arm, and his head dropped backward. She held a palm above his parted lips. No breath warmed her fingers.

Boots crashed into the room. "It's the king," someone shouted. "Call the menders!"

Somewhere, bells clattered. But it was too late. She already knew it, even as someone dragged her away from him, and brown menders' robes swirled into view.

Only then did she think to look. The rest of the world flooded in, a dream she'd almost forgotten. She spun, searched every corner.

Rozalind was nowhere to be seen.

❊ 19 ❊

Florencia

The bells alerted her first.

They started to toll before the first star appeared in the sky. Hundreds of bells, all across the city, some large and booming, others high-pitched and too bright-sounding for the occasion. This kind of clamor could only signify one thing.

The death of a king.

Ren launched from her window and snatched up Akeylah's letter. Reread it, as though her sister's words could reverse whatever had just gone wrong. *Father is well again.*

So why this death knell?

What went wrong? Ren wondered. *The heir.* Rozalind.

Nausea rocked through her. Even though she knew this might happen, even with a week to brace for it, Ren hadn't really let

188

herself believe they'd lose Father. Not so soon, not without any instructions on how to carry on in his stead. They needed more time.

It isn't fair. Akeylah reversed the curse. He was improving. Akeylah even hinted he might forgive Ren one day, or at least hear her side of the story. Ren had felt hopeful today, for the first time since being locked in here.

Now it all came crashing down.

Ren crossed to the doors and pounded on them. "Guards! What's going on out there?" she demanded when the Talons didn't respond.

"Keep's on lockdown," came a muffled reply. "Remain where you are."

As if that was any great change. "Why are they tolling the bells? Is it my father?"

"We know as much as you do, my lady." The guard's tone thickened with annoyance.

"Well, send a messenger to find out," Ren snapped. Stony silence was her only answer.

Frustrated, she stormed back to the window. Pressed her face to the glass, and peered at the neighboring towers. Specifically the cherry one. She watched shadowed figures move across it, backlit by the windows on the few corridors that faced outward.

Above the tower hung Nox, full and bright, its yellow light usually her favorite of all the moons. Tonight, it seemed sickly. Reminded her of a dying man's yellowed eyes.

She didn't notice when the first tears fell. Only when one dripped onto the window and streaked down the glass.

Father.

He'd died thinking—no, *knowing* Ren was a traitor. She'd betrayed him, betrayed Kolonya. She had planned to make up for it one day. To work hard, pay for her sins in sweat. She'd dreamed of forging a better Kolonya, a fairer one for all its people.

Now look at her. Trapped in this tower. Barred from any chance of reconciliation with her father, hated by the people whose approval she'd longed for.

So what are you going to do about it? asked a little voice in the back of her mind. *Stay here and meekly await your trial? Subject yourself to the heir's whims?*

If she was already as good as dead, no harm in risking her life now.

Ren shoved away from the window and crossed her chambers again. She knocked harder this time.

"What?" shouted the same Talon.

"Is my father dead?" Ren asked the impassive stonewood door. She let him hear the pain in her voice. "I deserve to know that much."

She heard a heavy sigh. Finally, the locks turned, and a brown-eyed, broad-nosed Kolonyan face appeared in the crack. "You're right. I'm sorry for your loss, my lady."

She shut her eyes. Her lungs ached, as though the breath had been sucked from them. "Did he . . ." She licked her lips, suddenly dry. "Was it peaceful, at least?"

"I don't know, my lady." She looked up and found him staring at her in concern. "The Keep has been placed into lockdown. That's a procedure we only use in cases . . . Well. Cases like Countess Yasmin's, Sun accept her soul."

Cases of murder. So the heir got to him after all.

"I see," she managed to reply. Her throat, her chest, everything felt tight. Dizzy.

And yet, her earlier resolve crystallized. *I can't stay here. I can't just wait and see who the heir murders or imprisons next.*

"I'm not feeling well." She pressed a hand to her forehead. "Can...you send..." She didn't finish the sentence, but fell into a swoon. She made sure to sell it, flinging her arms wide when she hit the stonewood.

The Talon cursed, and shoved inside, calling for a mender. All the while, Ren's mind raced. *What would Zofi do?*

First, she'd have armed herself before fainting. But Ren didn't keep weapons in her chambers, and besides, the Talons had confiscated anything sharp, even her bloodletter. She'd been shielding herself with a pen every morning, the sharpest implement she could find.

A female Talon knelt in front of her face. "My lady?"

Ren fluttered her eyelids. "Mama," she moaned. Then she pretended to faint again. It took effort not to smile at the Talons' renewed cursing.

"What do we do?" the front-door guard asked. "Orders are to keep the nobles in their rooms, at least until the queen is found."

The queen?

"She's a sick girl," the woman replied. "She just lost her father. She wants her mother. What harm can there be in that?"

A pause. Finally, the front-door guard sighed. "Fine, fetch her mother."

"Ren." Mama knelt beside the bed the Talons had lifted her into. "Can you hear me?"

She felt her mother touch her forehead with the back of a hand, but she waited until the other voices—the Talons and a mender who'd pronounced her unharmed but for shock—faded. The moment the lock jangled, Ren's eyes flew open.

Mama startled. "Honey, are you—"

"I'm fine," she whispered. "Do you know what's going on? The Talons mentioned they're searching for the queen."

Mama scowled. "That murderess." She hurriedly explained about the Keep-wide search for the missing queen. "Your sister ordered the Talons to arrest her unharmed, but I'll bet anything Rozalind killed him."

"Do you know how Father . . . ?" Ren couldn't bring herself to finish the question.

"The menders are saying it was a curse. A powerful one— whoever cast it is strong, with a lot of experience in the Vulgar Arts."

I'll say. Ren tasted a sour tang at the back of her throat. Who knew the Vulgar Arts better than the heir, after all?

She pressed her lips together. "I need to get out of here."

A frown creased her mother's forehead. "The Keep is on lockdown. Talons are scouring every corner for Rozalind. You'll be safer here, with the guards."

"You mean here, right where Rozalind wants me to be?" Ren waved at the room. "I'm done playing by her rules, Mama. I need to stop her. Zofi found the shield tithe we've been using. Maybe

192

there's another tithe we can fight back with, something in the library—"

Mama cut her off. "The library is too exposed. Besides, if you want unusual tithes, the University is your best bet. Plus, you know the court leaves the acolytes to their own devices."

Ren knew. It was why you never saw acolytes at the Great Hall for meals. "If I found some old acolyte robes to wear..."

"I'll see what I can rustle up. In the meantime, when did you last shield yourself?"

"This morning," Ren said. "I do it each day before breakfast."

"I'm afraid you'll need to tithe for this." Mama searched her face. "Get some rest. I'll tell the Talons I'm fetching you medicine; I'll be back in a few hours with what we need."

Ren sank back against her pillows, heart in her throat. The moment the door shut, all she could think about was Father. Did he see Rozalind's face when she cursed him?

She was still awake, staring at the ceiling, when Mama returned with a yellow acolyte's robe. She took one look at Ren's face and murmured, "Scoot over."

She slid into bed next to Ren and began to talk.

She told Ren how she first met Andros. He'd left his crown behind, walked to town in disguise. "When he was younger he did that often," Mama said, "to try and understand his people from within rather than above."

Mama had been on an errand for Madam Oruna's predecessor, haggling for cotton. She caught Andros watching her, and pinned him for a new noble, green to the market. Mama spent half the day showing him around, giving him tips on how to bargain. It wasn't until the end of the day, when he offered to walk her back to the Keep, arm-in-arm, that she finally noticed the ununiformed Talon tailing him.

Only then did she realize who she'd been flirting with.

The story warmed Ren's heart, just a little. Enough for her to catch a few winks of sleep before dawn came.

As the sun rose, Mama slipped Ren a sharp-backed pin from her gown to use for a bloodletter. Ren arranged the bed while Mama dug through her closet. Between several pillows and some rolled-up gowns, they managed to re-create an impressive imitation of a sleeping Lady Florencia, buried under the covers.

"You won't have long." Mama strewed a few crumpled handkerchiefs around the bed, to give the impression Ren had been up all night crying. "They'll send a mender once I leave."

Ren bobbed her head. "I'll be quick. You'll tell Akeylah where I am?"

"I'll go straight to her chambers from here."

Ren noted with approval that Mama had finally stopped harping on about trusting her sisters. "Ready?" Ren crouched by the entrance, Mama's pin poised in the crook of her elbow.

Mama reached for the door.

Ren wore an outfit worthy of Zofi—trousers, a loose top, and silk slippers, soundless on the hard floor. Over it, she draped the hooded acolyte's cloak.

Mama knocked on the wooden panel. "She's asleep," Mama told the Talon who barked in response. "I need to retire to my own chambers now."

A bolt threw, and Ren dug her mother's pin into the soft skin under her arm. Just a pinprick, but enough to let the Arts flood her veins, sharper and stronger after days of shielding.

Heart racing, she performed a tithe she'd only tried once before, and poorly. But she still remembered Yasmin's instructions during their first lesson. Moreover, she remembered the way Zofi had used this tithe in battle, about two minutes after learning it.

She's my sister. The same blood runs in my veins. If she can do it, so can I.

Ren concentrated hard, pictured her surroundings. She lightened and grayed her skin until it took on the pallor of the ash stonewood behind her. She'd spent so long trapped in these four walls that the tithe actually came easier than she expected.

She looked down just as the door opened, and had the disorienting sensation of looking straight through her body at the bedroom behind her.

The Talons were chatting with Mama, who stepped out into the hall to answer their questions—how Ren seemed, whether she'd need a mender.

Ren took advantage of their distraction—and of Mama holding the door wide open, casually leaning one hip against it—to slip out into the hall. She had to move slower than she'd like, making sure to shift the color of her skin with each step, so it blended into the walls she passed.

For a second, her concentration faltered, and Mama glanced at her, panicked, then grabbed the nearest Talon's arm.

"Are you all right, ma'am?" he asked.

"Just tired." Mama turned her full sun-bright smile on, and even at her age, with this much-younger Talon, Ren stifled a smirk to see her charm working. "Are you going to escort me back to my bed, safe and sound?"

The Talon shot an amused glance at his fellow. "Of course, my lady."

Mama perked up even more at the *my lady*, and Ren left them behind, creeping along the ash-colored hallway to the nearest servants' corridor. An itch started in her veins just as she slipped into the passage. There, she let the tithe fade, drew the hood of her acolyte's cloak up, and scurried toward the University, head bowed.

⚹ 20 ⚹

Zofi

The first stormwing Zofi spotted, she mistook for Vidal's bird. The creature had already returned to the band once, bearing a message from Akeylah saying she'd received the cure. The next day, a macaw had come from the aerie bearing even better news—it worked.

It had been a bittersweet realization. Father survived; the kingdom would carry on. Her sisters still had time to uncover and defeat the heir.

Even so, Father would never see Zofi again. Her banishment would continue. She'd never get the chance to prove she was more than the murderer he thought.

But when the stormwing carried on past their camp, and when she spotted a second and a third, Zofi realized something was happening.

"Mother?" She interrupted Deena's lunch with some locals to point at the sky.

By then, a few others in the band had begun to gaze upward, as well. A fourth stormwing passed, and on its tail raced a flurry of other birds, flying much lower. Macaws and pigeons and the tiny songbirds popular out here in the marshlands for short-distance messages. She even caught the brilliant red flash of a scarlet—a royal messenger.

A minute later, a deafening screech had the entire band on its feet. Vidal, who'd been eating by himself, leaped upright. "Birdy!" He raised his arm, fingers splayed to summon the massive creature.

Zofi stifled a smirk. Only Vidal would name his stormwing, the largest and most fearsome raptor in the world ... *Birdy*.

The creature landed in a tornado of wingbeats, which sent cups and plates flying. Zofi held on to the scarf wrapped around her poor hair. Mother had spent the better part of last night browbeating it back into semidecent shape. This would likely ruin it again.

A few curious Travelers crowded the stormwing. More strayed to the edge of the gathering area warily. Zofi followed Vidal to its side. The creature still gave her the chills, but she was getting used to it. "More news from Akeylah?"

Vidal unscrewed something from its leg, and shook his head. "It's from my commander. The higher-ups carry special horns so they can summon their troops' stormwings in case of..." Vidal's words faltered as he unrolled the letter.

Unease fluttered in her stomach. "What is it?"

Slowly, he raised his eyes to hers. "I'm so sorry, Zofi."

The pit of her stomach dropped. Her mind raced to the worst possibilities. "My sisters."

"They're safe." Vidal glanced over his shoulder at the other band members, who'd crept closer now, curiousity overriding their fear. "It's your father. He...he's gone."

Zofi's mouth went dry. "Akeylah said he was better." Her head shook, side-to-side. "No. No. I did everything right. Found Mother, sent the cure in time. It was supposed to work."

"I think it did," Vidal murmured. "This reads like something else."

"What does it say?" Mother stepped in, her voice steady, posture straight. She was always impossible to shake.

Zofi wished she could channel some of that strength. Right now, she felt weak. Weak, useless, and worlds away from the sisters who needed her.

"It's in code," Vidal explained as he showed Mother the letter. "It says a curse killed him, and the whole Keep is on lockdown while they hunt for the perpetrator. But I must be misunderstanding the code. This can't be right...."

"Why?" Zofi managed through a tightened throat. It hurt just to speak. In the back of her mind, she kept reliving the last time she saw Andros. The fury and hurt in his eyes as he shouted for the Talons to take her away. That was the last time she'd ever see her father.

"It sounds like Queen Rozalind is the primary suspect."

"That's impossible." Zofi frowned at her mother. "Rozalind isn't a blood relative; she couldn't curse Father."

But Mother only looked thoughtful. "Unless she's pregnant. If she's carrying Andros's child . . ."

Zofi swore under her breath. *Rozalind could be the heir.*

✳

"Are you sure about this?" Vidal watched her saddle the stallion.

"If I go now, I can make the merchants' road by tomorrow. From there, Mother's contacts will let me swap mounts. With new horses along the way, it should only take me two, three days." She paused to pat the silver stallion's neck. "Mother's friends will take good care of the prince's horse until I return."

"That's not what I mean." Vidal picked up her saddlebag, but held it just out of reach. "Are you sure it's a good idea to go back to Kolonya City right now? My commander ordered me home because she wants her best troops in the Keep. She's expecting trouble." He lowered his voice. "You've already been banished. If anyone catches you, you'll look guilty."

"I am." She jumped to snatch her saddlebag from his hand. "If you're worried we'll attract trouble, we can ride separately. I know how to take care of myself."

"It's not me I'm worried about, Zo."

She tensed at the sound of Elex's nickname. "Don't call me that."

Vidal paused, thrown. "I apologize."

"Don't treat me like I'm ignorant either. I understand I'm painting a target on my back." She finished securing the bags and wiped her hands on her breeches. "I have to do this, Vidal."

"But *why?*" In the midday sun, the green in Vidal's hazel eyes stood out.

"Because my sisters need me." A terrible sense of helplessness had enveloped her ever since she learned about Father's death. She should have been there; she should be in the thick of the fight with Akeylah and Ren, not safe out here in the marshlands. If Rozalind was the heir, and she'd escalated to attacking Andros directly, her sisters would need more help than ever.

But that wasn't the only reason. Her conversation with Elex still rang in her ears. *You're never going to truly be home. Not until you decide to be.*

He was right. Her band couldn't be home until she came here of her own free will. Until she finished what she'd set out to do in Kolonya—changed this world for the better.

She couldn't stay here and pretend nothing was wrong, let the heir triumph. Zofi would never forgive herself. She'd spend the rest of her life without any home, either with her band or back in Kolonya, because she'd been unwilling to decide her own fate.

Vidal ran a hand over his close-cropped hair. "I just hope you don't fall right into a trap alongside your sisters, that's all."

She'd thought about that. The heir would be focused on cornering Akeylah and Ren. Zofi? They thought they'd gotten rid of her. They wouldn't see her coming.

Her hand drifted to the longknife at her waist. The same blade she'd driven into Nicolen's heart. She killed her half brother to save Elex. If it came to it, she could do that again to save her sisters. Just like Elex, Akeylah and Ren were the family she chose. And like Elex, she'd do anything to protect them.

"What did you tell me? Crown or no crown, I can make the Reaches better."

Mother strode into the makeshift horse paddy, arms crossed.

"How will you getting arrested for breaking your banishment make anything better?"

"I know how to blend into a crowd, Mother. There's nowhere more crowded than the merchants' road."

"And what about beyond the merchants' road, when you have to fool your way into Kolonya City?" Mother's eyes narrowed.

"She'll be with me for that," Vidal pointed out. "With a bit of a disguise, I can bring her through as a merchant, or even just claim I've arrested her for pickpocketing."

"We've got two days on the road to plan. We'll figure it out." Zofi reached for a waterskin and began to fill it at the nearby well pump.

"So you're just going to charge off with no supplies—"

"I have supplies." She gestured to her saddlebags.

In response, Mother held up a leather sack. It clinked faintly. "From your old emergency stash. I kept held of it while you were away."

Zofi crossed back to her side and peeled the leather open, just far enough to glimpse the round glass balls inside. *Boosts.*

"What's that?" Vidal asked, curious. They both ignored him.

"Mother..."

"I won't stop you, Zofi. You're grown enough to make your own decisions. But don't ride into this headstrong the way you normally do. Be smart. Learn everything you can in advance of this fight." With that, she tossed something in Zofi's direction.

Zofi caught it one-handed, the other still gripping her boosts. When she turned it over, she found a small leather-bound book, unlabeled.

"Can we have a moment?" Mother said. Vidal bowed at once

and strode back toward camp. Only after he'd passed out of ear-shot did Mother murmur, "That's everything."

Zofi frowned in confusion.

"Everything I've learned over the years. Curses, tithes, all of it."

Zofi's eyes widened. "You've had this sitting around for anyone to find?"

Mother laughed. "Not at all. Take a look."

She undid the leather ties and opened the first page, only to find a blank sheet of velum. "I don't understand."

"The book itself is another trick I picked up." Mother turned it over and showed Zofi a thin strip of metal along the back, narrow as her fingertip. "It's bound to my blood. I have to tithe a drop along its spine to reveal the words. But it will work for you, too, daughter." She smiled. "I'd always meant to pass it down to you one day. That day just came sooner than I thought."

Zofi hugged the book to her chest. "Thank you, Mother."

For an instant, Mother just looked at her, like she was drinking Zofi in. Then, all business again, she finished filling Zofi's water-skin for her. "Stop at the Hook and Barber for fresh horses. Tell them Deena will owe them, if they let you borrow one of the stal-lions." She paused to pat the silver sand-stepper's flank. "Though I doubt you'll have any trouble trading *him*. More trouble getting him back once all this is done."

Zofi flashed a half grin. "I'll just have to channel you when I come back."

"You'll just have to be sure to come back," Mother replied sternly. "From what you've told me this 'true heir' has done already..." She nodded toward the book. "It sounds to me like you'll need every advantage in there. Vulgar Arts included."

Zofi didn't want to think about what it would mean if she failed. If she couldn't stop the heir, couldn't rescue Ren and Akeylah . . . she might be sacrificing herself for nothing.

Or it might be for the good of all the Reaches.

"I'll come back." She didn't say it like a promise. Just a statement of fact. Over Mother's shoulder, she spotted Vidal on his way back, and waved.

"Think he can keep up?" Mother smiled over her shoulder at Vidal.

"If he can't, I'll leave him behind," Zofi replied, loud enough for Vidal to hear, though she flashed him a grin, too. "No offense."

"None taken." Vidal grinned back. "Besides, Zofi, I'm a Talon of Kolonya. If I can't keep up, I don't deserve my wings."

⊰ 21 ⊱

Akeylah

All Akeylah could think about was the relief she'd felt when Andros smiled down at her, just two days ago now. The countercurse had worked. He was fine. Better than fine, up and about, acting like his old self.

She thought she'd done it. Fixed him. Saved the Reaches. Defeated the heir.

Really, the heir had been at her side all along. Snaking her way into Akeylah's heart. She closed her eyes, and behind the lids, she saw the tableau again. Rozalind with the bloodletter in her fist. Kneeling in a pool of cursed blood next to her father's blackened body.

It's not what it looks like, Rozalind had sputtered. Right before she fled the scene.

Ever since that moment, Akeylah had drifted in a haze. She issued orders in a listless, numb tone. First the body—she'd asked the menders to take care of it. Then Rozalind—she'd ordered the Talons to find her. When they asked why, she told them in a voice deadened by anger, by sorrow, by too many in-between emotions to name. "Rozalind knows what happened. She was with him at the end."

It should have worried her, how easily everyone accepted her word. She watched Talons nod to each other, menders gaze down at Father's body with fresh suspicions in their eyes. It proved to Akeylah what she'd known deep down all along—nobody here really trusted the foreign queen.

Akeylah had wanted so desperately for the prejudiced, judgmental courtiers to be wrong. For Rozalind to be the girl she'd fallen for, the girl she'd come to trust, *to love*. Rozalind was more than just some Genalese infiltrator—she was kind, caring, supportive. The one person Akeylah had felt she could rely upon.

But it seemed the Keep's vipers were right, after all. Rozalind had been against them, *against Akeylah* from the very start.

It's not what it looks like ... .That's what Rozalind had said when Akeylah found her crouched over her father, knife in hand.

She balled her fists. *No, Rozalind. It's never what it looks like with you, is it?*

After deploying the Talons, there had been the other tasks. Akeylah had ordered the death knell for Father's passing, bells tolled all across the city. Then she'd called an emergency session of the council of lords and the regional council, jointly.

"We need a temporary regent," Danton began the meeting, first thing.

"What we need is to find the former queen," Lord Rueno interrupted. "Are these Talons even *trying*? How could one lone woman evade them so long?"

Akeylah watched them speak from the head of the room, struggling to keep her mind focused on the here and now. But her thoughts kept chasing after Rozalind. Wondering where the queen was, how she was evading the Talons' grasp. *Whether she regrets it. Whether anything we had was real.*

Captain Lindle, head of the Talons, bristled. "My men are doing their best."

"Why are we searching for the queen, when it was a curse that killed him?" asked another nobleman. "Shouldn't we be investigating his daughters—the Traveler one could be out there doing anything, for Sun's sake. Or the Burnt Bay traitor may have gotten her hands on a bloodletter, despite being locked away."

"There is no evidence to suggest Florencia has anything to do with any of this," Danton interrupted.

"Yet," Ambassador Ghoush said. "But I do agree with you, Ambassador Danton. We need an acting leader. Someone to guide this investigation."

"There seems an obvious choice." Ambassador Perry raised a hand. "All those in favor of Lady Akeylah's appointment?"

Akeylah started at the sound of her name. Raised her head and watched numbly as hand after hand went up around the table. Every ambassador, every noble. Even Lord Rueno lifted his arm, after a pause. The room fell silent. Looking to her to solve this.

She swallowed a hysterical laugh. They wanted *her* to lead? She'd fallen in love with the enemy. Allowed her own father to die.

But they were waiting, expectant. And someone needed to tell them.

She met Rueno's gaze. "I agree with you, Lord Rueno." In another lifetime, she might have been amused at the way he nearly fell off his chair in shock. "Our first priority must be finding Rozalind." Akeylah shut her eyes for a moment. "And since she is most likely carrying the rightful heir, we will need to decide upon a regency until the child comes of age."

A hush fell over the room. She could already see Ambassador Ghoush and Lord Rueno trading stares as they realized what this meant.

"My lady." Captain Lindle frowned. "If Her Majesty is with child, then—"

"Then you understand why I wish you to find her, and quickly," Akeylah interrupted. Whispers broke out, faces lit up, eager at this new gossip, this terrible tale to spread. A queen who murdered her own husband.

Suddenly, Akeylah couldn't do this. She didn't have the energy for these people, these pampered nobles who needed servants to tie their shoes, wipe their rears. What did they understand of suffering? Had they ever watched their lover kneel in a pool of their father's blood? She rose, one hand at her temple. "Excuse me. The stress of the day..."

Danton leaped to her side at once. "We can decide these matters later," he said, and she felt a surge of gratitude. "Get some rest," he murmured to her, before he spun back to the room. "For now, Lady Akeylah is right. Our primary focus must be on locating the queen."

He continued to speak, but Akeylah lost track as she ducked from the solarium. She only just reached her chambers, however, when a noblewoman stopped her.

"Lady Akeylah."

She wrenched open her door.

"My lady, please, it's about your sister."

Akeylah froze. Only then did she recognize the woman, who she'd met just once before. Ren's mother, Martina, as she'd introduced herself last time. After the baths, while they all waited around for Ren to awaken. "I'm so sorry." Akeylah inwardly cursed her fatigue. She couldn't take her pain out on innocent bystanders. "What's the matter?"

Martina glanced around the corridor, pointed.

Akeylah took the hint and led her inside.

"Ren's left her chambers," Martina blurted the moment they were alone. "She felt it wasn't safe to remain where Rozalind expected her to be."

Akeylah thought about the Talons patrolling the Keep, already on high alert for the queen. Her heart leaped. "Where did she go?"

Martina explained, in a low whisper, about the University. How Ren hoped to find some new method to fight Rozalind. "I'm just worried, if somebody finds her...She's already hated by so many people."

"I'll meet her." Akeylah was already reaching for the plainest dress she owned, her previous exhaustion washed away in a flood of adrenaline. She couldn't save Father, but she could ensure no harm befell Ren. "We'll find somewhere safe for her to lay low."

Akeylah understood why Ren wanted to go somewhere Rozalind wouldn't expect. But Rozalind could be anywhere in the Keep right now. And if the queen was bent on finishing the job she'd started when she nearly drowned Ren in the baths...

"Thank you." Martina gripped Akeylah's hands once, tight. "Be careful, please."

Akeylah's hopes climbed, just a little, at the thought of seeing her sister. Perhaps Ren would find something helpful in the University. At the very least, together, they could decide what to do. How to stop Rozalind before she clawed and cursed her way onto the throne.

Akeylah had seen how easy it was to turn the Talons' suspicions to Rozalind. Surely the queen, who lied so well she'd convinced Akeylah she loved her, could turn things back in her favor. All it would take were a few carefully placed suggestions. *Check Lady Akeylah's leg; you'll find the scar where she cursed her father. You already know what Lady Florencia has done, how she betrayed this whole kingdom....*

Once Martina left, Akeylah finished donning a dull dress designed to deflect attention. She turned to go, then froze where she stood.

I didn't shield today, she realized in panic.

Her father's blackened, bloodstained body smiled at her from the doorway.

"Go away," she whispered.

"Akeylah." Her father—*no, not him, the heir again, Rozalind*—tsked and shook his head. "Is that any way to greet your dear departed daddy?"

She forced herself to hold the hallucination's bloodshot gaze. "I know what you did to him, Rozalind."

"Do you?" False-Andros tilted his head at an impossible, sickening angle. She heard bones snapping in his neck, and flinched. "Do you know everything now, little puppet? Who I am, why I was forced to do this?" He stepped off the bed on legs that moved *wrong*. Knock-kneed and bent inward, as though he were collapsing before her eyes.

She stumbled backward and bumped into her desk. Frozen, pinned between a nightmare and the hard wood.

"You made me kill him, Akeylah." He bent closer. Close enough for her to smell the rot on his breath, the same stench that had filled her senses when she'd ripped the curse from his veins. "I gave you a simple order, puppet. Put your sister on trial. You didn't."

"You didn't have to *kill my father*," she growled.

He snapped his fingers, shook his head sadly. "I keep my bargains, puppet. What did I say? *Ignore me, and I'll make those you love suffer.* You ignored me."

"You're a monster." Her voice hardened.

"Perhaps. Perhaps you have to become a monster to get what you want in this world." His eyes narrowed. "Forget trials. I want your sister out of my way once and for all. Make Ren publicly rescind her claim on the throne by tonight, or someone else dies."

"It won't matter." Akeylah straightened her spine. "Even if she does, even if you ruin me next, nobody will crown you. I'll make sure all the Reaches know what you've done."

Father clicked his tongue, with a sound like insect wings

fluttering. "Oh, we'll discuss my coronation soon, puppet. For now, you have your orders. See to it they're completed." With that, the apparition vanished.

Akeylah continued to stare at the spot where the vision had been, long after it faded. So Rozalind wanted Akeylah to pave her way onto the throne?

Over my seas-cursed body.

❋ 22 ❋

Florencia

Right. Here we go. Ren stared up at the University entrance, and pricked her fingertip on the slim needle that served for a knob. The doors clanked, whirred, and began to open on their own.

She tugged her acolyte's cloak tighter and slipped through the widening gap. She walked with her head down, purposefully, as though she knew where she was headed. In truth, she hadn't the faintest clue. But as long as she *looked* like she belonged, hopefully no one would notice.

Ren needed to understand the types of Vulgar Arts curses Rozalind had been using. If that sort of information resided anywhere in the Keep, it would be here.

But Ren couldn't exactly walk up to the headmaster and inquire about illegal cursework. So she moved slowly, canvassing one room at a time. The first floor consisted of studies filled with acolytes, noses buried in their work. She stole peeks at covers, but soon drew too many curious glances. She was forced to hurry past, feigning some other errand.

Finally, on the second story of the University, she came across a library. It was smaller than the library in the main Keep, and the books looked older, dustier. She scanned the shelves. Half the titles she couldn't even comprehend. She started picking and skimming at random.

She found one book on shield tithes, which told her nothing new. Another described curseworkers and the various execution methods used for such "witches." She shuddered at the descriptions, often illustrated. She wouldn't wish that fate on anyone, even Rozalind.

When researching curses and tithes proved unfruitful, Ren turned her attention to a different section of the library. The acolytes were responsible for all the pomp and circumstance of royalty—Blood Ceremonies to recognize relatives, coronation ceremonies for new rulers. Figuring she might be able to at least delay Rozalind's installment as regent once her child was born, Ren delved into that stack.

She was deep into one such tome when she heard footsteps. *Just another acolyte*, she told herself. *Pretend you don't notice.* Her heart pounded against her eardrums.

A pair of silk slippers stopped before her reading chair. A moment later, someone cleared their throat.

She didn't look up. Panic rushed through her. *Go away*, she thought, desperate.

But then. "Your mother told me I'd find you in here."

Ren's head jerked up to find Akeylah standing over her. She opened her mouth to reply, but Akeylah shook her head.

"Not here," she murmured, and strode from the room.

Ren trailed after her. Past several occupied rooms. Inside, acolytes swiveled in their seats to watch them. Then Ren caught the sound of other footsteps, behind them but closing in fast. Someone was in a hurry.

Akeylah paused at a corner office, and gently pushed Ren inside, before she continued down the hall alone. A moment later, the jogging person caught up to her.

"Lady Akeylah," said someone with a deep baritone voice. "One of my men said he saw you enter here unescorted. It is not safe for you to move about the Keep without a guard."

"I have a meeting with Acolyte Ultrea, Captain." Akeylah's voice was even, unharried. "It is my decision whether I require a guard. In this case, I do not. Though I wouldn't need such protection at all if your Talons would do their job and apprehend Rozalind."

Ren suppressed a smile. Not long ago, she couldn't have imagined Akeylah speaking to anyone like that, let alone a Talon captain. The past few weeks had changed them all, perhaps Akeylah most of anyone.

"You are right, my lady, and I apologize for my guards' continued failure. I'm afraid on that point, I bear worse news."

"About Rozalind?" Akeylah's tone sharpened.

"About your sister. It seems Lady Florencia slipped from her rooms sometime this morning. We have notified the Talons to search for her, as well as Queen Rozalind. But it's all the more reason you should not be wandering without protection."

"Very well. I will send for you the moment my business with Acolyte Ultrea is concluded, and you may escort me wherever you like. Until then, however, I don't expect to see you trailing me again."

Silence rang in the hall. Ren held her breath and stared at the study door.

After a long pause, the Talon's footsteps retreated. Another beat passed, and then Akeylah ducked into the office with her. "Ren? We can talk now."

Only then did Ren think to check the name on the desk behind her. *Ultrea.* She couldn't help but smile. "Was this your plan all along?" Ren reached out to embrace her sister, and Akeylah wrapped her arms around Ren tightly. It surprised Ren just how reassuring it felt.

"A little bit of improvisation." Akeylah glanced at the nameplate. "I inquired at the headmaster's, learned Acolyte Ultrea is out of the city on business. Listen, Ren, have you shielded yourself yet today? I had another vision just now."

Ren swore softly. "Not yet. I needed to wait after I tithed this morning."

Akeylah passed her a bloodletter. Ren took it and tithed quickly. Only after the now-familiar shield enveloped her once more, did she think to reach out and catch her sister's hand. "Akeylah, I'm so sorry about Rozalind. I have only a small idea what that kind of betrayal feels like, and still." She thought about Danton, when he and Lexana announced their engagement. How much worse must it be to know the person you cared about was hunting your family?

Akeylah pulled away. "No, I'm sorry. You warned me about trusting her. I just didn't believe she'd be capable of...." Akeylah pressed a hand to her mouth.

Ren winced. She almost didn't want to know. Yet the expression on Akeylah's face, one of mingled pain and horror, made her ask. "Did he...did you see it? When Father..."

The full story tumbled from Akeylah in fits and spurts, and made Ren's stomach turn. Finally, Akeylah stammered to a halt, and Ren thought about what she'd said earlier. "You had another vision, too?"

Her sister nodded shakily. "Rozalind told me she killed Father because I didn't listen to her. Back when she ordered me to put you on trial."

"Sun curse her." Ren clenched her teeth.

"There's more." Akeylah swallowed audibly. "She wants you to rescind your claim on the throne. In public, by tonight. Or she says she'll kill again."

Ren ran a hand through her hair. Hesitated, but only for a moment. "Okay."

Akeylah bristled. "What? No. Ren, we are not giving in to her demands."

"Why not?" Ren spread her hands. "My reputation is ruined, Akeylah. I'm a fugitive within my own home. Even if by some miracle I'm acquitted in a trial, nobody is going to respect or follow a queen with an accusation of treason on her record."

"But it puts Rozalind one step closer to the throne."

"If it prevents her from attacking anyone else today, it's worth it."

"What about tomorrow?" Akeylah stepped toward her. "What about when she demands I step down next, or when she orders us to crown her, will we dance like puppets on her string?"

"Of course not." Ren hefted the book she'd been carrying under one arm, *Coronation Ceremonies and Traditions*. "But she can't claim the crown, anyway. Not by Kolonyan law. She'd only be vying for a regency in the child's stead, and there are ways to block such claims. First of all, she'll need to perform a Blood Ceremony like the one Father did for the three of us, to prove the child's heritage. Even then, if we prove Rozalind is unfit for leadership, the councils will install a temporary regent until the child comes of age. We have ways to fight her, Akeylah, but we need more time. Rescinding my claim buys us that time."

Akeylah frowned at the book. "If you make a public statement, the Talons will just lock you right back in your chambers afterward. You heard the captain just now; they're scouring the Keep for you. It was difficult enough to convince the councils to delay your trial; now that you've proven a flight risk…."

"Did the heir say I had to make such a statement in person?" Ren pursed her mouth, thoughtful. "I could write a letter renouncing the crown. We can say I mailed it to you, maybe even from somewhere outside Kolonya City, so the Talons will focus on Rozalind and not me."

"Where will you really go?" Akeylah's brow contracted with worry. "Perhaps leaving Kolonya isn't the worst idea…."

Ren shook her head. "I'm not abandoning my home. Or leaving you to fight Rozalind alone."

Relief and worry warred on her sister's face. "For that, I'm grateful. But you need somewhere safer than this." She gestured at the office.

"There's a place I can go. A cavern underneath the Keep, where Danton and I used to meet." In another life. Before Danton carried battle plans she stole to his Eastern rebel friends and sank Ren's chance at the throne before she even knew it existed. "Do you have a quill?" Ren crossed the study and unearthed some parchment. "I'll write it now."

Akeylah plucked a fountain pen from the desk, held it out. "You have to be certain."

Ren studied her sister's uneasy expression and forced a smile. "I am. Even if Rozalind weren't strong-arming us, Akeylah, I heard you talking to that Talon captain. You're better at this than I ever would have been."

Akeylah grimaced. "I don't *feel* good at this. I'm only doing what's necessary, because there's nobody else to turn to. I'm not ready to run a country, Ren. It's too much."

Ren took the pen from her sister's hand and squeezed her fingers in the process. "You've held the Keep together during what has to be one of the worst times in the history of the Reaches. Yasmin died, Father was murdered, his queen is on the run.... The fact that there isn't a mob of panicked nobles storming through the halls is testimony enough. You're ready to rule." She held Akeylah's gaze. "And you have your sisters behind you, no matter what."

Akeylah sighed and rested her hand on top of Ren's. "I wish Zofi were here."

"So do I," she murmured, surprised by how much she meant

it. Zofi would know what to do. How to hit Rozalind where she hurt, how to strike first instead of just reacting to the queen's every move.

They'd just have to channel her as best they could. Ren bent over the parchment.

"Read it at dinner, would you?" Ren asked, once she'd signed the testimonial with a flourish. "If the whole Great Hall hears, that should be public enough for Rozalind."

"I will," Akeylah promised. "You just stay safe." Akeylah hugged her one more time, tight and fast, before she went to distract the Talons long enough for Ren to slip by unnoticed. On her way out, Ren grabbed a few more tithing books from the library. Couldn't hurt.

Ren didn't know what she should be feeling. Sorrow, perhaps, at signing away her claim. Or defeat. The heir was one step closer to winning. Yet somehow, with Akeylah on her side and a semblance of a plan, what she felt instead almost resembled hope.

✸ 23 ✸

Zofi

By midday the next day, Zofi and Vidal reached the Hook and Barber. There, Vidal, who had donned his armor just in case they ran into any trouble, proved a source of great amusement.

"Deena's daughter has got herself a trained Talon, fancy that," one woman commented with a guffaw.

"You're surprised?" her friend joked. "I'm just shocked Deena never had one of her own."

They led Zofi and Vidal into a sprawling stable complex. Zofi nuzzled her stallion's nose in apology before she left him in the innkeepers' care and picked out a new horse, another sand-stepper, this one dull gray. At least he'd blend into the crowd better.

"We're serving full Southern luncheon in the lodge." The

woman eyed the sweat sheened across Zofi's and Vidal's foreheads and the dust that coated their boots. "You should stop, rest a while. Food's on us."

"Thank you," Zofi said, and meant it. There weren't many merchants along this road who would open their businesses to Travelers, let alone invite them to dine for free. "But we really need to be on our way." As she spoke, though, her stomach growled in protest.

The woman laughed. "All right, but at least let me fix you a little something for the road. Your mother would kill me if I let you ride away hungry."

Zofi almost protested, but Vidal elbowed her side. One glance told her his stomach was giving him the same pangs. They'd eaten spiced gruel with dried berries last night, and half a sack of dried meats this morning, a diet Zofi was accustomed to living on at times when the band needed to move fast. But even she could do with something more filling.

So they led their new mounts to the front of the inn, and waited until the woman bustled back with a pair of sackcloths bursting at the seams. "It's not much." She offered them up with an apologetic grimace, even though the weight nearly made Zofi topple forward. "Just some hard cheese and pickled veg, fresh-baked flatbread, some jams to go on top...Careful with the red jam, it's hawkclaw pepper. Burn your tongue right off."

"It's more than enough, really." Zofi hugged her one-armed. "Thank you again, for everything."

"Anything for Deena's brat. Her family is mine." The woman smiled with a fondness around the edges Zofi recognized. *Ah.* Definitely another of Mother's conquests.

"I'll give her your best," Zofi promised as they remounted. Only once they were back on the road did Vidal lean across his saddle.

"Isn't hawkclaw pepper...?"

"Ridiculously expensive? Yes." She stifled a grin. "I have a feeling she's very fond of my mother."

"I can see why," Vidal replied, and she spun around to glare at him. His eyes went wide and his hands shot up in surrender. "I didn't—I just meant, because she's got a really, er...commanding presence."

Zofi snorted, and he relaxed, though only a little. It endeared her, really, how easy he was to rile up. "Go on, eat your lunch, my pet Talon."

Now it was his turn to glare, but only until he dug into the food. The flatbread alone was to die for, warm and fluffy. The woman hadn't lied—a single dollop of the hawkclaw jam was enough to make her eyes water. She loved it.

They devoured half the sackcloths' contents before they really settled in to ride. Zofi figured they could make their next trading post by nightfall, as long as they kept a hard pace. But fatigue from the previous day's ride and their now-full bellies had them lagging by the time the sun set. The merchants' road went darker than ever under its thick jungle canopy.

Here and there, lamps illuminated the road, though not brightly enough for them to ride any faster than a trot. Zofi couldn't see the holes or wagon ruts in which a horse might twist its hoof.

Finally, near a signpost for the Dawn Mountains' low road, which cut east through the jungle, Zofi called to Vidal. He'd been riding a few paces ahead, since his uniform served to deter anyone who might be tempted to pick a fight with Zofi. She'd bound her telltale curls in a scarf, and wore a shift to conceal her leather armor, but her short stature and narrow features still stood out, marks of her heritage.

Vidal wheeled around to meet her.

"We're still a couple hours' ride from our next stop," she said. "By then it'll be midnight; the inn will be shut. We should just camp here."

It was a mark of his exhaustion that, despite the fact that he'd been talking all day about having a nice warm bed for a change, Vidal nodded.

They pitched the tent in silence. Almost before she'd finished rolling out the bed mats, he was sound asleep, snores rocking the tent. Zofi felt just as exhausted, but when she laid down at last, sleep wouldn't come. She stared at the tarp overhead and pictured every way this could go wrong.

The heir could already have taken control of the throne. Ren could be dead. Akeylah could be, too.

Finally, mind still churning, Zofi rolled over and slid Mother's journal from her saddlebag. She crept outside, careful not to wake Vidal—though she doubted a whole stampede could do that right now—and lit the lantern they'd hung near the horses.

By its flickering candlelight, she drew her longknife. Pricked her fingertip and traced the small well of blood down the spine of the book.

As far as she could tell, it didn't do anything. The book just sat in her lap, looking like a book. But when she peeled apart the pages this time, instead of blank velum, spidery handwriting greeted her, inked in a dull brown color that reminded her suspiciously of blood.

More of Mother's secrets.

She leaned against a nearby tree trunk, wider than she was tall, and settled in to read.

The first few pages covered things she knew. Boosts, simple tithes. From there it delved into the Vulgar Arts. Some she'd experienced herself—curses to project images into a relative's mind, curses to spy on a relative's thoughts temporarily. Zofi couldn't help thinking the latter might explain how the heir uncovered her, Ren's, and Akeylah's most closely guarded secrets. It made her wonder, too, how often the heir had done that. Had they watched Zofi rock back and forth in her mother's tent, shaking with memories of Prince Nicolen's blood on her hands?

Sands, had they been watching the night she did it? Did the heir know what Zofi was right from the moment she drove the blade through Nicolen's heart?

She turned the page. Read on.

She found curses to sicken a relative, curses to age or kill a relative, in all manner of ways. It turned her stomach to imagine working any of these.

But there were other things, too. Curses to heal a relative's illness. Curses to lend your tithing ability to a relative, something Zofi had never even dreamed of. She wasn't sure what to call these things, these in-between Arts. Vulgar Arts were curses, Blood Arts were tithes, everyone knew that.

Yet, could you really call it a curse if you used the Vulgar Arts to *help* a family member?

Her head swam.

Then again...she remembered the story she'd told Vidal about Traveler Queen Claera. About how the Arts were different back then. When the Arts first came to the Reaches, there was no distinction between the Vulgar and the Blood Arts. *Is this why?* she wondered. Was it because some tithes blurred the lines?

But then she came to a page that made her stop and draw the book closer.

Written across the top, in her mother's cramped handwriting, were the words *Tithe for a Mental Bond.*

Just like the one Yasmin and Andros had performed, so many years ago.

The most vulgar of Vulgar Arts, Mother wrote. *Anyone who performs it must either be blind to the true consequences or utterly careless of who they wound in pursuit of their goals. For the sake of keeping a complete record, I include it here, but with this warning.*

As Zofi continued to read, her lips parted in shock. The book trembled in her hands, until she was forced to set it on the ground, rereading the final paragraph over and over to be sure she'd understood correctly.

The first half explained what she already knew. The tithe bound two people's minds forever. Whatever Andros had thought, Yasmin had heard, and vice versa. It allowed them to communicate instantly, across any distance. It also meant that when Yasmin was pushed from the sky gardens, Andros had felt her death as though it were his own.

But the second half, which detailed how to create the bond... that Zofi hadn't understood until now.

There is only one way to unite two people. To make two people into one, Mother wrote, and in those words, Zofi heard the echo of what Mother always told her, growing up. Any time Zofi asked why she didn't have any siblings, like the other Traveler children.

"Because," Mother had said, "you need to be careful who you share your blood with. It's a powerful bond, a tether that can never be cut. I've only met one man who I trusted to share that with." She'd usually pinched Zofi's cheek at that point. "Who I trusted *you* with."

In a child, the book continued, *two separate people become a single bloodstream.*

If two people wish to bind their minds, they must tithe for this purpose while they produce a child together.

A child.

Bile rose in the back of Zofi's throat. She sat back against the tree and stared at the night forest. Tried desperately to breathe in the fresh air, the scent of the earth beneath her.

It didn't help. The trees went blurry, seemed to spin around her, dizzy with disgust.

Andros and Yasmin had a child together.

A child born of incest. From a brother and sister...Zofi thought about her sisters and felt sick. She couldn't imagine crossing that line. Perverting familial bonds like that.

She knew royalty did things differently than normal people. She'd heard of distant cousins marrying, in cases where no other "noble enough" matches could be found. But a union like this wouldn't just go against custom. This went against the law, too.

In the Reaches, where bloodlines determined who you could trust, incest among close relations was seen as a perversion of the gods' gifts. Children born from such unions were often sickly, or mad, or died young of minor diseases.

Zofi thought she'd begun to know her father. But the fact that he would do this...

I have another half sibling out there.

A shiver ran along her spine. She understood all too well now what her mother meant about being careful who you shared blood with. Yet, careful as she claimed to have been, Mother had tied her bloodline to the worst possible option.

Zofi thought about Nicolen's viciousness. She thought about the bloodthirsty heir. Sands, even Zofi's crime and her sisters'. Were they any better?

Now Yasmin and Andros, too. The twins were willing to flout every law in the land, and for what? To bind their minds. How could that possibly be worth bringing such a child into the world, a child whose origins they'd need to disguise, a child who might be ill or suffer greatly.

It wasn't just dangerous. It was *selfish.*

Head throbbing, Zofi continued to read with difficulty.

While the child is yet unborn, both parents must reach into the child's blood, and tithe for a mental union, much like one would do to temporarily see a family member's thoughts. They must repeat this daily until the child is born—they will feel the effects lasting longer and longer as the child grows with the bond.

Once the child is born, the link becomes permanent.

But the side effect many theoretical texts gloss over is the effect on the child. A child born through this tithe will also be able to hear their parents. The child's is the mind the parents' thoughts pass through; they are the echo of the tithe. The child will hear every thought their parents share, even before they are old enough to comprehend the meanings.

Zofi swallowed hard. She thought about how strange, how painful that must be. To hear everything your parents believed, even before you could walk or talk...

There are few historical records of this tithe being performed. Those we do have indicate that the children created in this way are strong in the Arts; often impossibly so, perhaps due to the Arts that linger from their parents' tithes in the womb.

This effect was doubled in one instance when two cousins produced such a child (see p. 320 for the story of the Ananses Hexchild).

Zofi set the book down.

She'd heard Mother tell that story before. The tale of a girl who, furious at her parents for forbidding her to marry the boy she wanted, cursed her entire lineage in one fell swoop. She died, but so did her parents and sister. Only her cousins survived to tell the tale, and even they bore lifelong scars from the curse.

Zofi always thought the story was a myth. A fairy tale to scare children away from practicing the Vulgar Arts.

Now...

Zofi snapped the book shut and stared at its cover, mind racing. A child impossibly strong in the Arts. A child of a king, who grew up with every piece of knowledge that king carried within their own mind. A child Andros could never, *would* never acknowledge, because how could he admit he'd disregarded his own laws, bedded his sister, and for what? A mental connection that, to Zofi, didn't sound so important.

But a child like that sounded an awful lot like the sort of person who would curse their half sisters. Murder their father. Dub themselves *the true heir.*

To judge by Vidal's commander's message, the Keep was hunting for Rozalind. But maybe they had it all wrong.

⊰ **24** ⊱

Akeylah

This is Rozalind's fault, Akeylah thought as she stood at the head of the Great Hall, Ren's letter in her hand. *She forced us into doing this.*

"I ask everyone here to bear witness to my sister's testimony," Akeylah began, "which she had delivered to me this morning." Nobles at the back of the hall elbowed forward to hear while Akeylah unfolded the parchment. "She writes: 'I, Lady D'Andros Florencia, daughter of King Andros, being of sound mind and body, do hereby renounce my claim on the throne, and all rights, inheritance, and positions that come with it. I beg the forgiveness and understanding of my fellow courtiers. I do this not for pride or for protection, but because I believe it to be the best decision for Kolonya and the Reaches...'"

As she read, Akeylah noticed motion from the corner of her

eye. She glanced up to see Danton storming out of the hall, his expression thunderous.

Inwardly, she winced in sympathy, though she couldn't do anything to help. Could only keep reading the speech Ren had penned. It was well written—it offered apology without admitting to any charges. She walked a thin line between placating the heir and avoiding knotting her own noose.

Akeylah prayed this would be enough to stay Rozalind's hand, at least for now. After all, Ren had given her what she wanted. One less person between Rozalind and the throne.

When Akeylah finished, she didn't stay for the evening meal. She retreated to bed, exhausted from the day, emotions taking their toll.

How could you do this to me? she wanted to shout, to scream at Rozalind. *How could you kiss me so sweetly while holding a knife to my back?*

So far, no word from any of the Talons. Somehow, that didn't surprise Akeylah. Given everything else Rozalind had done, of course she'd be adept at hiding, too. Akeylah just prayed she and Ren could stop Rozalind before it was too late. Before more people met her father's and Countess Yasmin's fates.

Back in her father's chambers, where Akeylah had taken up temporary residence at Captain Lindle's insistence—"it's the easiest suite to secure, my lady"—she collapsed straight into bed, too tired even to pick at the dinner tray some servant or another had brought.

She woke somewhere in the wee hours of the morning, staring up at her ceiling, unsure why she suddenly felt wide awake, heart racing.

Then she heard it again. A faint patter against her window.

Or, well. Father's window. The one that opened onto the back fields. The room was on the third story, at least twenty or thirty feet above the grass, and yet...

Tap.

Her muscles tensed. She rolled out of bed into a crouch and glanced from the window to the doors. Should she alert the guards?

Then again, if it was Ren, she didn't want to inadvertently trap her sister.

Tap.

Instead of guards, Akeylah reached for the bloodletter she kept on the bedside table. She hadn't tried to shield yet today. She wasn't sure if she had enough Arts in her system yet, or if she was still run dry from healing the king. Just in case, she gripped the blade tight and crossed to the windowpane. Holding her breath, she flicked the gauzy curtain aside, just enough to peer outside.

At first she saw nothing except the sky, a small smattering of bright stars set against the purple-pink predawn glow. Closer at hand, a few lights glimmered here and there in neighboring towers, but otherwise, the Keep was dark. Silent.

Tap. Another pebble reflected off the pane.

Akeylah leaned forward until her forehead touched the window. Like that, peering straight down, she was able to see the figure on the grass. A familiar figure, dressed in men's pants and a formal shirt rather than the dress Akeylah had last seen, yet unmistakable. She'd recognize her anywhere.

Rozalind stood on the lawns, haloed by the rising sun as she raised her arm to toss another pebble.

Heart turning over, Akeylah unlatched the window. Opened it just far enough to make Rozalind stop, midthrow.

She shouldn't do this. She should call the Talons right now. Have the queen arrested.

But Akeylah wanted to hear Rozalind's confession from her own lips. She wanted to demand an explanation. And now, with a bloodletter glinting in her fist, unshielded . . . Suddenly, Akeylah felt stronger than Rozalind. Strong enough to confront her enemy head-on.

So she extended an arm through the window and waved once.

Rozalind waved, too, a *come here* gesture broad enough for Akeylah to see even from this height.

This is a bad idea, cried half her mind.

End this, screamed the other half. The stronger half.

Akeylah dressed in pants and a shirt that left her free to move. She may not know how to fight like Zofi, but she'd bring backup. She wasn't a complete moron.

"I'm going for a walk," Akeylah announced to the Talons posted outside her door. "One of you with me."

Unlike the captain, who undoubtedly would have questioned her motives, these low-ranking Talons didn't try to dispute her orders. One fell in behind her, and the other remained at his post, obedient.

Akeylah spiraled down to the first floor, and at the exterior doors, she told the Talon to wait. "I'll call you in a few moments," she said. "If you don't hear from me by the time the sun has fully risen, come outside."

Her contingency plan settled, Akeylah stepped out onto the lawns. Her slippered feet rustled in the grass. The cool air of the dying night kissed her cheeks, sank damp tendrils into her plaits.

She hesitated a second, just beyond the exit, for her eyes to adjust to the lightening sky.

Once they did, she picked out a silhouette against the cherry tower. Rozalind turned toward her, and the dawn light brushed over her face, made Akeylah's breath catch in her lungs.

The queen looked more beautiful than ever, even despite her frightened eyes, the harried, hunted look to her. For a split second, Akeylah's heart wrenched in sympathy. Until she remembered everything the queen had put her through.

She hoped the Talons who'd been stalking her for two days made Rozalind feel even half the suffering she'd put Akeylah and her sisters through.

Her grip tightened on the bloodletter. She stalked toward the queen. Paused a couple paces away, near enough to see the whites around Rozalind's eyes. "Give me one good reason why I shouldn't chain you where you stand," Akeylah said softly.

"I didn't kill your father, Akeylah." Rozalind held her gaze, voice low and pleading.

"I saw you curse him," Akeylah hissed.

"I was trying to save him." Rozalind raised her hands, palms empty. No weapons. Not yet, anyway. "I wanted to heal him, stop the curse, the way you did. But I was too late; I couldn't...I didn't know what to do..."

"Then why did you run? If you were so innocent." Akeylah loaded the word *innocent* with sarcasm.

Rozalind laughed, an unhappy sound. "Think about it, Akeylah. You were calling for menders, who'd bring Talons with them. If I was found next to him like that, covered in blood, a Vulgar

Arts scar on my thigh? People already hate me here." Her voice dropped lower, so low Akeylah had to lean in to hear. "Even you thought I did it. I saw it in your eyes the moment you entered that room. If even *you* could think me capable..."

Akeylah stepped back, expression hard. She wouldn't fall for this. Not again. "You were arguing with him before he collapsed. Half the Great Hall servers heard you."

"He asked me about the child." Rozalind ducked her head. "He...wasn't happy I hid it from him. I can understand that. But we were only talking, I swear. And suddenly his face went slack. He started shouting, as though there were someone else in the room. I begged him to call a mender, but he acted like I wasn't even there." She closed her eyes, grimacing with what seemed like genuine regret. "I should have summoned the menders myself. But I didn't understand what was happening...."

Akeylah stared.

She wanted to believe this story. She wanted to believe it *so badly*, and yet, given what Rozalind had already hidden from her, a secret as huge as her pregnancy...how could she?

"What was he saying?" Akeylah asked, voice carefully neutral.

Rozalind scrunched her eyes shut, as if trying to remember. "First he was shouting that he wouldn't give his sister's murderer anything. Then he said, 'You're no daughter of mine. You'll take the throne over my dead body.' Right after that, he collapsed and started to convulse. The black webs appeared a few seconds later...." Rozalind's voice broke. She pressed a hand to her mouth for a breath before she could continue. "You saw him. I couldn't counter it; I couldn't save him...."

Akeylah stood frozen for what felt like an eternity. Finally, she let out a slow sigh. "Why should I believe you? After all the other lies you've told me, Rozalind. After what you hid from me."

The queen ran a hand over her eyes. Took a deep, shuddering breath. Then she reached for her waist, where Akeylah spotted the dull flash of a bloodletter.

Akeylah raised hers, quicker. "Don't."

Rozalind's hand froze. Hurt and surprise flashed across her features. "I was only..." She hesitated. Swallowed her protest. "I'll take a blood oath, Akeylah. Will that satisfy you?"

A lump rose in Akeylah's throat. She didn't dare to hope.

It's a trick. Rozalind would just curse Akeylah the moment she tithed. Akeylah wasn't shielded. In a few minutes, the sun would finish rising and the Talon she'd left on guard would come outside, but until then, she was alone. Vulnerable.

For a long while, they stood stock still, Akeylah with her bloodletter in hand, Rozalind with her palm hovering above hers. Their gazes locked across a chasm that suddenly felt impossibly huge.

Then Rozalind shivered, hard enough that Akeylah could see it.

"What is it?" Akeylah asked, trying and failing to keep her voice emotionless.

"I don't... I don't quite feel..." Rozalind lifted her hand to her chest.

Akeylah's jaw dropped. Black spiderwebs unfurled along the queen's hands. Crawled up her arms. "Rozalind."

The whole world slowed. One moment the queen was upright. The next her legs went one direction and her head the other. Akeylah didn't remember telling herself to move, but she must have, reacting on sheer instinct. In a heartbeat, her arms were around Rozalind's waist, and she caught the queen halfway to the ground.

She sank to her knees with Rozalind in her arms, pressed her own bloodletter into Rozalind's hand. "Tithe," she ordered. "You have to shield yourself, Rozalind. I'll talk you through it."

But Rozalind didn't seem to hear her. The queen's breath turned to gasps, constricted in her throat. Tears burned Akeylah's eyes. Tracked down her cheeks.

What was happening?

Not her. Not Rozalind, Mother Ocean, please.

Someone else was there. Beside her, a hand on her shoulder.

She looked up into her father's eyes. He smiled, teeth blackened with the curse that had killed him. The faint rays of the sun's rising light reflected off his curse-darkened eyes.

The heir.

Not Rozalind after all.

"Let her go," Akeylah growled.

"All in good time. She's my collateral, don't you see?" His laugh was deep, echoing. It rattled her bones to the core. "You saw what I did to our father the last time you disobeyed me."

Our?

Akeylah tightened her grip on Rozalind. "I did what you asked me to. Ren rescinded her claim. Didn't you hear me in the Great Hall?"

Not-Andros's grin went sharp as talons. "Yes, and for that, I thank you. But that was only your first task, puppet. Now comes your next. Plan a Blood Ceremony for me. The kind fit for a

238

queen." The sick imitation of her father reached out, as though to cup Akeylah's cheek. She flinched away.

"Who are you?" Akeylah spat. "Why are you doing this?"

"Because, puppet. You have something I want. My legacy. It's been denied to me long enough."

Her mind raced. She glanced down at Rozalind, still breathing, though each inhale sounded labored. What was it Rozalind overheard Father saying, before he died? *You're no daughter of mine.* "Are you my sister?" Akeylah studied the apparition's expression.

If she struck a nerve, it didn't show. The vision only smiled wider. "I have no real family. I'm the daughter of the moons, and they taught me everything I need to know."

"Like how to murder your father?" Akeylah replied darkly.

The apparition only laughed. "Like how to clean up Kolonya's messes. Do you really think Andros was a good king? A good *father?*"

The vision reached for Akeylah again, and this time, she did not flinch away. She held her ground, body trembling, as ghostly fingers brushed through her hair.

"Hold the Blood Ceremony by tomorrow night. Or Rozalind dies."

In Akeylah's arms, the queen inhaled once more, a terrifying rattle in her throat. Her pulse felt far too slow, her body heavy and unresponsive.

"Anything," Akeylah blurted. "I'll do whatever you want. Just let her go."

In her arms, Rozalind went still. Her breathing stopped.

Akeylah's world shrank to a pinpoint. To Rozalind, her parted lips, her frozen expression.

"Good." Not-Andros smirked. "I'll see you soon, puppet." In a blink, he vanished.

At the same instant, Rozalind gasped, and her whole body shuddered back to life. Akeylah clutched her tight. The queen curled against her, and Akeylah pushed damp curls back from her forehead, bent to kiss her cheek, her forehead, her lips. "I'm sorry," she whispered, over and over. "I'm so sorry. I should have believed you; I should have listened...."

Behind her came a crash, as the Talon she'd left behind burst from the tower. "Summon a mender," Akeylah barked, before he could recover from his shock at seeing the queen in her arms, prone on the ground.

As he sprinted away, Akeylah rocked back on her heels.

Our father, the vision said.

You're no daughter of mine, Father had shouted before he died.

Either Ren or Zofi were behind this nightmare all along... or they had another sister out there.

❋ 25 ❋

Zofi

Kolonya City had turned green.

Chartreuse drapes shrouded the windows of every building. Jungle-green garlands hung from every railing on the streets leading to Ilian Keep. The few passersby Zofi spotted wore every shade from lime to emerald, and the Keep itself flew dark green flags from each tower.

The grounds around the Keep were silent, the only movement from a handful of merchants in the market square, much quieter than it would normally be. Anyone who strayed too close to Ilian Keep, Zofi noticed, held up their fingers in warding symbols, as though to fend off the curse that had struck down the king.

Rumors flew among the few people who braved the markets. They whispered that the king's family was cursed. First Yasmin, then Andros, and now, that very morning, as rumor would have it, Queen Rozalind had been attacked, as well.

Zofi couldn't help but think about what she'd learned from her mother's notes. About the child Yasmin and Andros had conceived together, her hidden half sibling. Child of a Vulgar Arts curse. Stronger than anyone in the Arts...

Zofi and Vidal crouched under the awning of an empty market stall, half a block from Ilian Keep. After switching their mounts a second time and riding all morning, they'd arrived in the early afternoon, and found a bevy of Talons at every door of the Keep.

"We need to get in there," Zofi whispered.

Vidal frowned. "They're not going to let you just waltz inside, Zofi. Let me go ahead, bring a message to your sisters."

"While I do what? Hide out in the city, praying I find some Traveler-friendly merchant to camp with, one who won't recognize the king's banished daughter?" She shook her head. Already, afternoon sun lit the exterior of the Keep, made it appear to glow, each of the ten towers a different color of shining stone-wood.

Every minute that ticked past was another minute the heir had to prepare. Who knew what was happening within those walls already? She thought about the rumored attack on Rozalind, and an empty pit yawned in her gut.

It was only a matter of time before the heir went after Ren or Akeylah next.

"You'll have to tithe just to get inside," Vidal was arguing. "You'll be defenseless in there."

She grinned and touched the concealed blade at the small of her back. "Hardly." Plus, she could feel the weight of the boosts her mother had saved for her. Five boosts, concealed within different pockets along her thighs. Six tithes she could work today in total. It would be a shame to spend one before she was even through the door, but if she must, she must.

She'd left herself unshielded today, the way she'd been doing ever since she left Kolonya City almost two weeks ago. Only now, standing in the shadow of the Keep, knowing that somewhere within its walls lurked the heir, did Zofi's skin crawl. She was all too aware of how strong the heir was. How vulnerable she and her sisters were.

But she couldn't shield herself. She'd need the Arts just to get inside, as Vidal pointed out.

Besides, with a shield raised, she couldn't fight back.

On their way through the city gate, while Zofi had played the part of an injured local Vidal was escorting to a medic, he'd asked about the state of things. The guards told him Akeylah was planning a Blood Ceremony tomorrow night.

Why, none of them could fathom. "She's the only viable heir left," one guard commented. "She's already been acknowledged. Why all the fuss?"

"Disrespectful, if you ask me," another had piped up. "She should be focused on her father's death, not her own crowning."

Now, however, Zofi wondered if there was more going on than just an unnecessary ceremony. "What are they doing?" Zofi murmured to Vidal. She watched a pair of Talons stop a man who trundled up to the Keep with kitchen supplies. They tapped their arms, and after a moment, the wagon driver withdrew a thin blade from beneath his shirt.

Vidal cursed. "Sun above. They're doing tithe checks." In response to her blank stare, he explained. "Anyone who enters the Keep needs to perform a basic tithe." As they watched, the driver's skin began to shine, brilliant silver with an impervious tithe. "It's to ensure nobody is tithing for camouflage, making themselves appear like someone else while they enter."

"I've never heard of tithe checks." Zofi ran her tongue along the inside of her teeth.

He sighed. "Yes, well, I've never actually seen it done before either. I think the last time Talons were ordered to do this was back when my father was still serving. Genalese forces invaded far enough up the River Leath to come within striking distance of the Keep. Back then the tithe checks also served to make sure everyone entering the Keep was actually from the Reaches and not a Genalese soldier in disguise."

Zofi frowned. "I never heard about an invasion in Kolonya City."

"It was about eighteen, nineteen years ago?" Vidal guessed. He squinted at the towers. "It failed, anyway, which is why it doesn't get mentioned much. Well, that and Yasmin didn't like to publicize it widely. But among the Talons, the way she stopped the invasion made her a legend."

Zofi flashed him a curious glance. "Why? How did she do it?"

"A group of Genalese-led insurgents had recruited hired blades. Mostly disgruntled Eastern and Southern soldiers, but a few Kolonyans, too," Vidal explained. "Their plan was to sneak up the River Leath posing as migrant performers, and break into the Keep. Attack us from within." He shook his head. "It would've worked if Yasmin hadn't believed the rumors everyone else dismissed. Stories about Genalese offering payment for seasonal work down on the coasts. She went herself, located and infiltrated the group alone. Somehow she communicated their every action back to Andros without being detected."

Zofi had a pretty good idea how she'd done that. Her mother's notes about the mental bond tithe flashed through her mind.

"On the last day," Vidal went on, "the group was meant to cross the Living Wall into the city. But Yasmin attacked them from within. Even before the Talons' reinforcements arrived, she'd already carved her way through a dozen of the several hundred attackers."

Zofi whistled under her breath. "No wonder she still gave me a run for my money in training if that's how she battled in her heyday."

"You remind me of her, you know," Vidal said as they both turned to study the Keep once more. The Talons searched the shining silver driver's wagon thoroughly, while they waited for his tithe to fade.

She scowled. "Am I *that* unpleasant?"

He laughed. "No, I just mean…You left everything, your whole band, to ride back here and protect this country. Even though you claim to despise Kolonya."

"I don't despise it," she said after a pause. "I just think it can be so much *more* than it is now. What use is having the kind of strength and power Kolonya does if you don't improve the world with it?"

When she glanced at him again, Vidal was smiling. "Sounds like someone's becoming a patriot, if you ask me."

"I didn't." But she grinned, too.

Across the lawns, the driver's tithe faded and the Talons waved him on past. "Come on," Zofi whispered.

"This isn't going to work." Vidal held out an arm to stop her. "They'll make me perform a tithe, which means you'd need to remain unseen for longer than is humanly possible."

"Longer than possible for you, maybe." Her boosts weighed heavy against her skin. "Remember the time I fought you in training? I can stay invisible for far longer than it takes to walk through a set of doors."

He almost smiled at the memory, before he caught himself. "I beat you that day."

"But I kept tithing longer than you," she pointed out.

"This won't be like training, Zofi. If they catch you sneaking in, we'll both hang for it."

"Just trust me, Vidal. I know what I'm doing." She said the latter with more certainty than she felt. All she knew right now was that she needed to speak to her sisters. Hear from them what exactly had happened, and make a plan to fix it.

Finally, with a sigh of defeat, Vidal strode toward the Keep. Zofi kept pace with him until they reached the broad lawn that led up to the base of the towers. Then she drew her longknife and dragged the edge across the back of her arm.

After the panicked thoughts that had been chasing through her head all day—every day since she learned of her father's death, in truth—it was a relief to focus all her senses on a tithe, and nothing more. She absorbed the world around her, shifted herself to match it with every step she took, until her body went invisible against the empty streets, the warm sunlit grass.

She had no space in her brain left to worry or plot. She just followed Vidal, one step after another, and stayed invisible.

They made it halfway across the front lawn before a guard stepped down from her post to wave at Vidal. "Back at last?" the Talon joked, pushing her helm back to reveal a plump, friendly face. "What kept you, enjoying some Traveler hospitality?"

Zofi clenched her fists at the girl's mocking tone, though she didn't let annoyance break her concentration. She continued to tithe, making sure all the girl saw beside Vidal was an empty street. Not Zofi at his elbow, one hand hovering over the boost she'd need soon.

"Just being thorough," Vidal replied. Zofi hoped this girl didn't know him well. Hoped she couldn't hear the tremor in his voice. "If you'll excuse me, Ulie, I'm not feeling my best, and I still need to report to the captain...." He moved to pass, but the girl, Ulie, apparently, barred his path.

"Just a second." Ulie tapped her forearm. "Sorry. Can't let you pass until you tithe. Regulations, you know."

Her partner had stepped forward, as well, and greeted Vidal with a grin.

Vidal drew a bloodletter. "Anything in particular?"

"Any tithe you like," she said. "Just make it a long one."

Zofi noticed Vidal's shoulders tense with worry. Still, to his credit, he didn't protest. Only flicked the bloodletter across his arm and began a speed tithe. The effect was like watching a person turn into a fly—suddenly his arms moved too quickly to keep track of, and when he stepped to the side, he seemed to blur across the grass at an impossible pace.

Zofi realized why he chose it—to focus the Talons' attention on his movements, in case her own tithe faltered. Not that either of these Talons could fail to notice if a Traveler materialized out of thin air in front of them, but still. She appreciated it.

Her skin itched with the end of her initial tithe.

"Why the tithe checks?" Vidal asked. Or tried to. But his voice sped up, too, so the words all blended together into one quick phrase that left Ulie blinking for a moment while she worked out what he said.

Zofi used the distraction to slap the first boost on her thigh. Fresh energy flooded her veins and allowed her to hold her focus, remain unseen.

"Precaution. Nobody's allowed out without a check either. Not since the queen was attacked."

"Genal?" Vidal's voice still sounded too quick, higher-pitched than usual. It would have been funny if not for the situation.

"Doubtful." Ulie stepped closer—nearly on top of Zofi, who had to skip backward out of the Talon's way. "We've reason to suspect Lady Florencia. She managed to slip out of her chambers, probably by tithing. Hence all this."

Zofi felt an odd surge of pride.

She reached for another boost at her thigh, and cracked it just as Vidal's speed tithe began to fade. Ulie's partner glanced in her direction, brow furrowed, as though he'd heard something. Silently, Zofi cursed herself for getting too cocky.

"If there's been an attack, why are we holding a Blood Ceremony tomorrow?" Vidal's speech slowed to normal as his tithe petered out. "Shouldn't we minimize the royal family's exposure?"

Ulie shrugged. "Above my pay grade. All I know is Lady Akeylah insists. Going to need all hands on security at the event, though."

"I suppose I'll see you tomorrow, then." Vidal affected a deep sigh, and the Talons parted with sympathetic grimaces to let him pass.

Zofi leaped forward, practically on top of Vidal. She tiptoed so close she could feel the heat radiate from his skin, and her toes nudged his heels every couple of steps until they reached the tower entrance. Vidal held it open a second longer than strictly necessary, enough for her to nip through the gap after him.

Only then did they both let out matching sighs of relief.

"How in Sun's name did you manage to hold that tithe so long?" Vidal whispered a few moments later when she reappeared at his elbow.

"A girl needs to keep *some* secrets." She grinned, and bobbed her head toward the nearest stairwell. "Shall we?"

Just then, footsteps sounded. Vidal stepped in front of her just in time to block the view as a pair of Talons strode past, in marching formation. He saluted, and Zofi shut her eyes and pressed her face against his back, praying nobody stopped long enough to notice two pairs of legs where there should've been one.

She was just about to reach for another boost when the Talons called a greeting and continued to march. When they rounded the far corner, she and Vidal exchanged worried glances and hurried in the opposite direction.

"We won't last long with this many patrols around," Vidal murmured.

"There." Zofi pointed at a plain wooden door. A storage closet of some kind. Vidal yanked it open, and they both stared at the space within. It contained several buckets, some cleaning cloths, and a stack of soap bars almost as tall as Zofi.

"You won't fit," Vidal was saying, just as they heard more footsteps, from a different corridor this time, perpendicular to the one in which they stood.

"Find Akeylah," Zofi murmured, climbing over the buckets into the closet. She had to stand with a foot in each bucket and lean behind the tower of soap to squeeze inside. "Tell her where I am."

He hesitated, but the footfalls left him with no choice. Vidal wedged the door shut, and Zofi held her breath against the astringent soap smell, waiting.

❈

By the time Vidal returned, Zofi's legs had cramped and she'd lost feeling in the arm she was balancing on the soap shelf.

"Quick," Vidal said as he yanked open the door. "We're between patrols."

Zofi nearly tripped out of the closet in relief and scurried after him to a narrow passage, which led down a series of stone steps. They curved under the alder tower, and eventually turned into a muddy tunnel. Finally, Vidal pointed her toward what looked like a solid rock wall. "Akeylah's in there," he said. "I'll wait out here, guard your backs."

Zofi approached the wall. Stared at it for a while, until she noticed the cool breeze drifting through hairline cracks around the edges. She gripped one of the protruding rocks, hanging on by her fingernails, and tugged.

A hidden door swung outward, and she crossed inside, heart in her throat.

In the center of the room stood Akeylah and Ren. Alive. Unharmed.

"Zofi..." Akeylah couldn't even finish her sentence.

Zofi raced forward and flung her arms around her sister. An instant later, Ren wrapped her arms around them both, and Zofi shut her eyes, let herself savor the embrace, just for an instant.

"You're both safe," Zofi said, throat tight.

"Safe is a relative term," Ren replied, voice muffled where her face was pressed against the scarf Zofi still wore around her curls.

"But compared to Father and Rozalind..." Akeylah broke from the embrace first, pain scrawled across her face.

Zofi kept a hand on Akeylah's shoulder for support. "The guards out front said she was attacked?"

"We were wrong." Akeylah looked back and forth from Zofi to Ren. To judge by the bags under her eyes, Zofi wondered if Akeylah had gotten any sleep at all in the past couple of weeks. "About everything. About Rozalind. She's not the heir; she's the heir's latest victim." In a breathless voice, Akeylah recounted the morning's events. Everything Rozalind had told her, and the heir's subsequent attack.

When Akeylah got to the part where she asked if the heir was their sister, Ren looked shocked. But Zofi found herself nodding.

"That makes sense," she said, "given what I learned about Andros and our aunt Yasmin."

If Zofi thought Ren was surprised at learning they had another sibling, it was nothing compared to the expression on her sister's face when Zofi explained where she came from.

"*Incest?*" Ren hissed.

"They must have been desperate," Akeylah murmured. "To perform a tithe like that, one with such dire consequences."

"I have some idea why they did it." Zofi recounted the story Vidal had told her about Yasmin single-handedly stopping a Genalese attack on Kolonya City.

"Still." Ren rubbed at her temple. "There are laws against incest. Ever since Queen Aumelline's time, when a few mad nobles tried to breed children stronger in the Arts. It left the children with horrible diseases, health problems. Nowadays acolytes even require a tithe that proves no blood relation during Kolonyan wedding ceremonies."

Zofi bobbed her head. "Now imagine you've grown up your entire life hearing your parents' every thought—how they govern the realm, every decision they make. But you've got no chance of inheriting their position, simply because of who you are. Because of how they created you."

"The heir does seem to resent her parents," Akeylah murmured. "From how she talked about Father."

"What makes you so you sure the heir is a girl?" Zofi asked.

"Just a comment she made." Akeylah furrowed her brow. "She said she had no real family, that she was 'the daughter of the moons,' and she knew how to clean up Kolonya's messes. Then she asked me if I really thought Andros was a good father...."

Zofi shrugged. "Makes no sense to me."

But a funny look had come over Ren's face. Halfway between realization and denial. "How long ago was this Genalese attack Yasmin stopped?"

"Vidal said eighteen or nineteen years ago." Zofi considered Ren. Her sister had her plotting face on. "What is it?"

Ren ignored her, spoke faster, almost to herself. "So we're looking for a girl who knows the Keep well, is about my age, hates her parents..." She raised her voice. "Akeylah, when was Rozalind attacked?"

"This morning, around dawn."

"So whoever did it would still be tired from the curse, do you think?" Ren took a step toward the cavern exit.

Akeylah's frown deepened. "I'd be flat on my back for weeks if I did what she did—cursing Rozalind *and* making me hallucinate at the same time? But the heir is a lot stronger than me. Or any of us."

"But if I went looking for her now, do you think she'd still be visibly weakened?" Ren pressed.

"You'd have to know who you were looking for," Zofi broke in. "We can't exactly canvass the entire Keep trying to guess which distant relation looks the sleepiest. Any more than we can order them all to strip and show us if they've got Vulgar Arts scars."

Ren glanced to Akeylah. "How visible are the scars? I mean, do they show through fabric?"

In response, Akeylah drew her skirts up. The faint blue glow on her thigh pulsed with her heartbeat. "You have to wear dark colors or very thick fabric, I've found."

Ren shut her eyes. Squared her shoulders, as though deciding something. When she opened her eyes again, they locked on Zofi. "Would you do me a favor?"

"Anything."

Ren's gaze drifted toward Zofi's hip. To her knife. "I think I know where to look. But I've a feeling I might need some backup...."

* 26 *

Florencia

The maids' quarters were empty at this hour. Ren's footsteps echoed across the familiar floors as she crossed to the large chalkboard where Oruna marked the girls on duty and their current assignments.

How did I not see it sooner?

But how could she have? How could she have guessed about Andros and Yasmin, how far they'd go to bind themselves, all the havoc they'd wreak in doing so?

A girl about her own age. A girl ostracized by her parents, who longed for their approval, their recognition. A girl who grew up with their voices inside her head, believing she deserved the throne. A girl who had to watch it offered to others on a gilded platter while she remained in the shadows.

The last ugly skeleton hidden in the family closet.

The daughter of the moons. Who knew how to clean up Kolonya's messes.

It's the moons who favor girls like us, they always said when they snuck around the Keep. After they'd finished cleaning up the nobles' messes. *This is madness,* part of her whispered. And yet...

Ren had always felt like the heir hated her more than her sisters. Maybe it was just the drowning in the baths, or the way the heir kept insisting Akeylah put her on trial, but to Ren, it felt personal.

What if it was? What if the heir hated Ren because they'd known all along who she was? Because they were in the exact same situation, until only Ren was raised out of the shadows.

Ren stopped dead before the schedule. She'd hoped, prayed she might be mistaken. But there it was scrawled in chalk. A white stroke through her name, to indicate she'd begged off sick today.

This is wrong. It's impossible, she thought. Yet with every step she took toward her best friend's door, her certainty grew.

Somewhere, deep down, part of her had known.

The new gowns, all in dark colors, long-sleeved. The offers of information on Lexana, the insistence on helping research Rozalind.

Things are actually better with my mother now, she'd said. Ren's gorge rose as she realized what that meant.

Things were better now that her mother was dead.

But my father...I just want him to say he's proud of me, just once. Because he'd refused to acknowledge her? Or because she was a product of incest, the child he wanted to hide from the world?

Ren rapped on Audrina's door. No reply. But the knob turned easily in her hand. She pushed the door inward just as her friend sat up in bed.

"Who's—oh. Ren. Hi." Audrina bore deep bags under her eyes, and her face had a sunken look to it. Still, she forced a polite smile, strained at the edges. "Can I help you?"

"No, Aud, this time I thought I should help you." Ren stepped into the room, only a single pace. She leaned her back against the wall and surveyed the narrow space, a mirror image of the one in which Ren had spent so many years. Just a twin bed, with slim shelves built into the wall next to it, and a foot of space between to dress in.

Ren squinted at Audrina's shelves. Among the darning needles and piles of yarn, she spotted a bloodletter, blood still caked on its blade.

"I figured you'd be exhausted right about now," Ren said. "After what you did to Rozalind." She tore her gaze from the shelf to meet her friend's once more.

For a split second, the span of a heartbeat, she thought she was wrong. She wanted to be wrong. Desperately. Audrina was her oldest friend, her best friend, her one true ally in the Keep.

Or so she'd believed.

But Audrina dropped the polite smile. It bloomed into a grin, broad and feral, and it was like watching a mask crack and peel. The girl Ren thought she knew crumbled away to reveal the monster underneath.

"What gave me away?" Audrina asked.

"You told Akeylah you were the daughter of the moons. Because the moons favored us, right? And you clean up Kolonya's messes—did you think I'd forget how we spent our lives down here?"

"You forgot a lot of things about our friendship." Aud's hand crept toward the bloodletter.

"Don't." Ren drew her own blade from beneath her skirts.

257

She'd shielded that morning, but Audrina might not know that. Besides, it never hurt to have a blade in her fist. A blade she could use for more than just bloodletting if the need arose.

She clenched the hilt tight and prayed Audrina wouldn't be able to see the tremor in her fingertips.

"Going to curse me, sister?" Aud tilted her head. "I wouldn't blame you. You must want revenge for what I've done. To you, to those bastards you chose over me, your supposed best friend. You preferred them, too, just like Father. You three are the acceptable daughters."

"Let me help you, Audrina. You're sick." She dared a step forward.

"Sick?" Audrina flung back the covers and launched to her knees. Quick as a blink, she grabbed the bloodletter from her shelf, but she didn't tithe. Not yet.

Ren held her breath, shaking inside.

"Yes, Ren, you're right. I am sick. Sick to death of watching you be handed everything *I* deserve."

Ren's heart cracked. "Audrina, I didn't know—"

"How are you any better than me? You've killed hundreds of Kolonyans. You committed treason, for Sun's sake. Everything I've done, I did to protect Kolonya." The bloodletter trembled in her fist. "My entire life, I've been a weapon. Forged by my parents so Yasmin could go hunt some Genalese. They used my brain like their playground, shared every plot, every dark thought, and they didn't even care that *I heard everything.*"

"It's not fair, Aud. You shouldn't have been put through that," Ren whispered.

To her surprise, her friend laughed. "Put through it? It made

258

me who I am. They made me stronger, smarter. Willing to sacrifice anything for the throne. They created the perfect weapon, in the end."

"Is that why you killed them?" Ren said it to remind herself who this was, what she'd done. Because right now, she was tempted to believe in the old Audrina. Her best friend, the girl who was always willing to help her. To lend a hand, be a shoulder to cry on, even a spy when Ren had needed one.

But Ren knew better now. *She is my enemy. She always has been.*

Audrina rolled her eyes. "You're just like them. So shortsighted. I didn't hate my parents for creating me; I hated them for not trusting what they made. Even after I was old enough to explain I'd heard everything they planned over the years, every council decision, every concern and triumph. They still didn't understand. They were worried that blubbering Acolyte Casca might tell someone who I was, so I killed him. Did they thank me? No, they hated me more, feared me for it. I could hear it in their minds."

Audrina turned the bloodletter over in her palm. Considered its edge. "No matter how hard I worked, they only ever looked at me with disgust, because I reminded them of what they'd done. How they'd created me." She bared her teeth. "I tried to tell Mother about the crimes you and your bastard sisters committed, that night in the sky gardens. She wouldn't listen; she just went on and on about *my* sins. Yelled at me for threatening you all, for ruining Father's plans."

"That's when you pushed her," Ren murmured. It wasn't a question.

Aud wiped at her cheek with one fist. "I didn't mean to. I was just so angry...." She scowled. "But when she fell, a weight lifted. One less voice in my head calling me a monster."

"So you decided to kill me next," Ren guessed. "What's a little bit more murder, once you've offed your own mother?"

"You're traitors," Audrina replied simply. "You deserve to be punished."

"I deserved to drown in a bathtub?" Ren raised her bloodletter.

So did Audrina. "You're just as bad as Father. You used me the same way he did. 'Oh, Audrina, my best friend, you mean so much to me...Now could you please spy on Sarella? Run these errands? Follow Lexana around, because I think that bumbling idiot is blackmailing me. Oh, are you upset, Aud? Let me bribe you with a fancy dinner and we'll call it even.'"

Ren flinched.

For a second, real pain flickered across Audrina's face. "I thought you were my friend, Ren, but you're just like the rest of my family. I'm nothing but a tool to you." She tugged up her sleeve. "Unfortunately for you, this tool has a mind of her own."

Ren's heart lurched at the sight of Audrina's arm. Bright blue scars crisscrossed her skin. They glowed even brighter where they intersected, nearly blinding. No wonder she needed the long sleeves, the dark gowns.

Ren raised her bloodletter, too, but she pointed it at Audrina instead. *What am I going to do, stab my best friend?* But what else could she do now, except bluff?

"Killing your way to the throne will only prove your parents right about you, Aud."

Aud's smile twisted, went vicious. "I never said they were wrong." She rested her bloodletter against her forearm. "This country needs someone like me. Someone who does what's necessary." Then her blade flashed, and Ren stumbled backward on instinct.

She'd shielded that morning. She shouldn't feel any effect from Audrina's efforts. But her breath came shorter, harder. Panic, perhaps?

She looked down at her hands and dropped the knife in shock. *Impossible.*

She was shielded. She should be impervious to curses. And yet, tendrils of black appeared under her fingernails. Inched toward her knuckles. Small thin spiderwebs at first, but growing by the second.

Across the room, Audrina laughed, eyes glazed with the tithe. "I...told you. I'm...strong," she gasped.

The webs crawled to Ren's wrists. Surged up her arms.

"Zofi," Ren shouted.

Her sister sprang from the main room where she'd been hiding, crouched just out of sight, listening to the conversation. Zofi took one glance at Ren and slapped a hand against her leg. Ren watched in confusion, not sure what Zofi was doing—it didn't look like any tithe she'd ever seen. Yet a dark trickle of red appeared against the brown fabric of Zofi's breeches.

A second later, Ren felt as though a warm, thick blanket had enveloped her. The spidering curse began to fade from her hands, shriveling against her skin even as she watched.

Zofi. Fighting back Audrina's curse.

"Stop. Her," Zofi muttered through gritted teeth, and Ren jarred herself back to reality.

Ren snatched the bloodletter she'd dropped and leaped for the bed. She grabbed Aud's hair in a fist, wrenched the girl's head to the side, and pressed the blade against her throat.

In response, Audrina screamed.

It was a deafening, window-shattering sound. Footsteps thundered from all directions, and Ren staggered backward, releasing her.

"Help!" Audrina shouted at the top of her lungs. "The traitors are here." She smiled as she said it. At the same time, Aud dragged the bloodletter across her arm once more. Ren flinched, expecting an attack. Then she stared in horror as Audrina's glowing Vulgar Arts scars winked out of sight.

A *camouflage tithe*. Hiding the evidence of her crimes. So if anyone burst into this room now, they wouldn't see the monster under their noses.

Zofi grabbed Ren's arm and yanked her into motion. "We have to go."

"But—"

"Call the Talons!" Audrina lurched after them into the maid's chambers. She dove for a bellpull on the wall. Too late, Ren realized which one it was. She grabbed Aud's wrist to stop her, but she was too slow. A deafening clamor rang through her skull, echoed through the room.

The emergency alert. Every Talon and mender in the Keep would be racing toward the maids' chambers now.

"Run!" Zofi shouted in her ear, and together they took off at a sprint.

"This way." Ren took the lead, bolting for the passage into the boys' dormitory. They sprinted along it. But then, at the far end, shadows appeared, racing their way. Uniformed shadows.

Talons.

"Right," Ren barked, and nearly shoved Zofi through a wall. The side passage led past the dungeons, out into the practice fields. If they could get outside, they could make for the city, lose the Talons in the cobbled streets. They just needed to—

Crash.

Ren collided headlong with a pair of stocky figures that seemed to materialize out of nowhere. Talons from an adjoining corridor.

Zofi drove her fist into one Talon's throat, and kicked at the other's legs. But her movements were sluggish, tired after her tithe. The first Talon choked on her blow, but the second dodged her kick. A split second later, something pricked Ren's neck. She looked at Zofi, saw a feathered dart protruding from her sister's shoulder.

The world went dark.

·⊰ 27 ⊱·

Akeylah

"R oz." Akeylah hovered on the threshold.

The queen rolled over to squint through sleep-blurred eyes. "Akeylah. What happened?"

Akeylah crossed to her bedside. Rozalind had been moved to the general nursing wing today, so menders could care for her in rotation.

The curse had taken a toll.

Akeylah had just finished speaking to the mender in charge. They hadn't told Rozalind about the baby yet. They thought Akeylah would be better equipped to break the news.

Her stomach knotted with a million different fears. Not least of which was Ren and Zofi, who'd gone off half an hour ago to follow Ren's hunch. Ren had insisted Akeylah stay behind, in case it went badly. Zofi was the warrior, anyway.

But Akeylah couldn't help feeling like she should have gone. Like her sisters were walking into the viper's den while she sat up here, safe and sound. So she'd come to the infirmary to distract herself, hoping for good news.

She should have known better.

She perched on a visitor's chair next to the sterile, narrow bed, and gripped the queen's hand. "You're safe," Akeylah murmured. "That's what matters." The backs of her eyes stung. "Rozalind, I should have listened to you—"

"Don't you dare apologize." Rozalind tightened her fingers around Akeylah's. Tugged her forward, until Akeylah slid off her chair and onto the bed instead. Rozalind lifted their clasped hands. Kissed Akeylah's fingertips, one by one. "I would have suspected me, too, in your shoes. After all, I tried to make you lock up your own sisters."

"You were trying to protect me. I realize that now." *I protect you, first and foremost.* Rozalind was trying to keep that promise.

"I knew someone was threatening you. Your sisters seemed the most likely culprits. They were both in line for the throne, same as you. But I should have trusted them. Should have trusted *you*, when it came to your own family."

Yes, well. The heir was her family, too. "Being family doesn't make people trustworthy," Akeylah replied. "It's the choices they make. The promises they keep or break." She traced her thumb across the back of Rozalind's hand. "You kept your promise to me. I'm the one who broke it. I let the blackmailer make me think..." Her voice cracked.

"No." Rozalind reached up with her other hand. Tucked a plait behind Akeylah's ear. "I'm the one who should have been honest with you from the beginning. Told you about everything, no matter how much I worried it would change things between us."

Akeylah couldn't help it. She glanced at Rozalind's stomach.

The menders had tried their hardest. Used every medicine available. But in the end, the curse had taken too great a toll on the queen's body.

Rozalind caught Akeylah's look. Her free hand drifted to her belly. "The baby?" she whispered.

Akeylah shook her head, just once. "I'm so sorry, Rozalind."

The queen closed her eyes. A tear leaked. Then another. When she opened them once more, she stared woodenly at the drapes strung around the bed. Her gaze fixed on something Akeylah couldn't see. "You know, I…" She swallowed hard. Cleared her throat. "It was a duty. To bear heirs. I was aware of what would be expected of me when I agreed to come here, to wed a king. But I didn't expect to feel…" Her hand tightened into a fist over her stomach. "I just thought maybe this time the child would survive," she continued in a whisper. "They seemed strong…And innocent, in all this."

Akeylah laid down alongside Rozalind. She reached out, and Rozalind buried her face in Akeylah's neck. Akeylah held her tight. Felt warm tears trickle across her bare skin, and traced Rozalind's back in small circles. "It's not fair," she whispered into the queen's mess of curls. "It's not right."

So much loss. Andros. Yasmin. The baby. When would it end? With Akeylah or her sisters in the Necropolis next?

She held on to Rozalind until the tears dried. Until the queen sank back into the sheets, exhausted.

"You should rest." Akeylah kissed her temple. "You've been through a lot."

"What about you?" Rozalind's gaze sharpened, as though she'd only just remembered the rest of the story. "Is the black-mailer still demanding something from you?"

"Trying to," Akeylah said. "But Ren thinks she knows who it might be. Something the blackmailer said to me when she cursed you, reminded Ren of—"

As if in response, a deafening crash of bells interrupted her.

Akeylah startled upright. So did Rozalind, though the latter groaned and leaned back against her sheets, a hand pressed to her stomach. "The emergency alarm," Rozalind spat through gritted teeth. "You should—"

Akeylah was already on her feet, racing toward the entrance. Halfway out of it, she collided with the head mender, his brown robes a whirlwind around his feet. "It's coming from the maids' chamber," he called to the room in general. A few other menders leaped up. "Someone needs help."

Akeylah's stomach turned to rock. The maids' chamber.

Ren didn't share details about her hunch. She said she wanted to wait until she was sure. But she'd mentioned she was heading to the servants' quarters...

"Rozalind, I'll be back soon," Akeylah called over her shoulder. Then she joined the flood of menders who raced from the nursing wing. Together they hurried through the halls, past curious onlookers and Talons sprinting in the same direction.

By the time they reached the maids' chambers, the doors had been secured. The menders parted for Akeylah, whispers preceding her as they recognized the acting regent and sank into curtsies. At the entrance, Akeylah found a pair of Talons at attention.

"Good news, my lady," one Talon said in a voice like gravel. "We've apprehended the traitors."

"Who?" she asked, head swimming, still thinking about Ren's hunch. About the heir.

The Talon frowned. "Lady Florencia, of course. As well as Lady Zofi, who it seems has disobeyed your late father's wishes and returned despite her banishment."

"We believe they may have been colluding," another Talon spoke up. "In the attacks on your father and Queen Rozalind."

"We have this maid to thank for her quick, heroic actions." The first Talon stepped aside, and Akeylah locked eyes with a girl she recognized.

Audrina. The girl she'd found in Ren's chambers. Who had walked with Akeylah to the baths that fateful day, when Ren nearly died. When the heir attacked.

Suddenly, the pieces clicked.

She could still hear the heir's voice. Saying she knew *how to clean up Kolonya's messes.* What if she meant that literally? She'd been stuck down here like Ren, acting the servant, when really...

Akeylah replayed the day Ren nearly drowned in her mind. She'd knocked on Ren's door, startled Audrina out of bed. She thought she'd interrupted Audrina's nap. Instead, she realized, she must have walked in on Audrina in the middle of her curse...

Today, Audrina looked even more tired than she had that morning. Unlike that day, however, a tiny smile played at the edges of the girl's mouth. Barely noticeable. Gone the longer she held Akeylah's eye.

"I saw them creeping through the corridor," Audrina said to the Talons, though she kept her gaze on Akeylah. "I recognized Ren—excuse me, Lady Florencia. She used to be my friend; I never thought she'd do something like this." Audrina's voice trembled, frighteningly convincing. "I told her she should turn herself in. That's when she and Lady Zofi attacked me. I didn't know what to do—I just grabbed the bellpull..."

"You did the right thing," the second Talon reassured her in a friendly tone.

"Where are my sisters now?" Akeylah asked. It took every ounce of self-control she had to maintain an even-keeled tone.

"In the dungeon, my lady. Sleeping off the effects of the low-dose phantasm venom we used to capture them."

"Notify me the moment they wake." Akeylah held Audrina's eye. "In the meantime, I'd like a moment with this girl. Alone."

The Talons exchanged glances. But when Akeylah strode forward, into the maids' chambers, they filed out obediently. The instant the doors shut, Audrina broke into a wide smile. "Wise decision, puppet. I would've hated to jail you, too."

Akeylah balled her fists. "If you think I'm still dancing on your strings—"

"You'd be wise to," Audrina interrupted.

"Rozalind lost the baby. You can't curse her anymore." Akeylah glared at the girl.

"Perhaps. But I've got two new sisters to experiment on now. Did you know that I've grown strong enough to eke my way through your little shield tithes?" Audrina raised a hand and wiggled her fingers in Akeylah's face.

"I don't believe you," Akeylah snapped.

She shrugged, utterly unconcerned. "Then test me, and we'll see which one dies first. Ren or Zofi, hmm. I despise Ren, but Zofi's the more dangerous of the pair...."

"What do you expect me to do, just hand you the throne? Offer up all of the Reaches as collateral?"

"That's exactly what I expect, puppet. The throne is mine, and I'll take it one way or another. If I have to perform the Blood Ceremony with you in chains, I will. And my first act as queen will be to execute you for cursing our father." She tapped her chin. "On the other hand, you could be smart. Pass the mantle peacefully, and I'll let you live. You could even remain at court. We'll need a new Eastern ambassador, since our current one is a traitor."

Akeylah swallowed hard. Her mind raced. *Play this right.* "My sisters live, too," she finally said in a low voice. "If I do this for you."

"I knew you were the smart one." Audrina's grin widened. "Your sisters can't stay in Kolonya, but Zofi can return to her people—provided she stays there this time. And Ren can head east. We'll blame her treason on Danton, since it *was* his fault to begin with, really. As long as she stays somewhere I never have to lay eyes on her again, I can be reasonable."

"How do I know you'll keep your word?" Akeylah crossed her arms. "What's to stop you from cursing all of us the second you have the throne?"

"Nothing." Audrina spread her hands, palms up in a gesture of peace. "But then again, there's nothing to stop you from cursing me either. Mutually assured destruction is the only insurance I can offer you." She shrugged, still smiling. "It's the way of the Reaches, isn't it? The irony of the gods' gift. The Arts made bloodlines both our greatest strength and deepest weakness."

Akeylah studied her opponent. Then she extended a hand, slowly. "Once I perform the Blood Ceremony, you let Ren and Zofi walk free."

"And you, Akeylah. You forgot yourself." Audrina clasped her hand. "Agreed. I get the throne, you get your family."

Akeylah tightened her grip, hard enough to hurt. "We have a deal."

❊ 28 ❊

Zofi

She woke to the rattling of chains. It echoed through her skull, pounded against her temples. Zofi groaned and rolled over, only to find herself squinting through iron slats at a puddle of her own sick beneath her. Her hand went immediately to her waist. Found her belt empty, her blades missing. Even the last two boosts she'd stored in her pockets were gone. She felt the empty pockets where they used to be, and panic clawed at her throat.

She was unarmed. Helpless.

"Welcome back to the land of the living," Ren called from somewhere in the distance, and Zofi forced herself to forget self-pity.

She squinted at the familiar surroundings instead. Dank, moist walls, a hard-packed earth floor, the wrought-iron bench on which she lay. And on the far side of the narrow enclosure, metal bars, floor to ceiling.

The dungeons.

"What happened?" Her voice came out in a croak. She cleared her throat, hard, and the cough nearly made her retch again.

"Phantasm darts." Ren's voice drifted over again, near at hand, though she couldn't see her sister through the gloom. She squinted at the bars, and spotted a thin hand gesturing at her.

Ren was in the next cell over.

Zofi rolled off the bench, hit the floor hard on hands and knees, and sucked a breath through gritted teeth. When she tried to move, she found herself dragging a chain, connected to her left ankle, bound to cast-iron hook in the wall. "I feel like I've been run over by a truck."

"That's generally the point of phantasm venom, I think," Ren replied.

Zofi squinted. The only light source flickered, which meant it must be a lantern or a torch, not natural sunlight. "How long have we been down here?" Last time, when the Talons darted her and dragged her to Kolonya City, this stuff knocked her out for three days solid.

"About a day, as far as I can tell. The guards don't talk much, but I've got a fast metabolism. I woke up in time for dinner last night." Ren's voice soured. "Trust me, you didn't miss much."

Zofi crawled to the bars and wrapped her hands around them. The chain on the bed extended just far enough to let her lean against the cell door. She bent forward as far as she could to peer around. The hall outside the cells looked empty. Somewhere in the distance, she caught the low hum of conversation. Guards, chatting away. "So the Blood Ceremony..."

"Should be tonight," Ren agreed. "Probably in a few hours, since they just brought lunch about an hour ago."

"No word from Akeylah?"

Ren made a negative sound in the back of her throat.

Zofi rested her forehead against the bars. The cool metal did little to alleviate the pounding in her head. "That's it, then," she murmured. "Audrina wins."

"Barring a miracle, I'd say so." Ren sounded resigned. Defeated, in a way Zofi had never heard from her sister.

"You know her best," Zofi said after a while. "How will it really be with her on the throne?"

Ren laughed without humor. "She murdered her own parents, then tried to drown me, her only real friend." She sighed. "Honestly, I don't know. She had her moments, when she seemed kind and caring, but now... How much of that was just her calculating the best way onto the throne, and how much was real?"

Zofi stared at the ceiling. Watched a single drip of water gather and inch its way down her cell wall. "Maybe even Audrina isn't sure. I mean, she knew who you were all along. She knew you were her sister, the daughter her father *didn't* despise. Even if you were her friend, even if she cared for you, I'm sure those emotions all tangled up together."

"Hatred is not the opposite of love," Ren whispered, and sounded as though she were quoting someone.

"That would probably be apathy," Zofi said. "Hating someone takes so much energy, so much—"

"Care," Ren finished with a sigh.

Zofi nodded to herself. She watched another drip inch down the wall.

She wondered where Akeylah was. How the Blood Ceremony would go. How long it would be before Audrina returned, this time with a crown on her head, to have Ren and Zofi executed.

She prayed for a quick death.

She had a feeling they wouldn't be so lucky.

"Zofi?" Ren's voice sounded closer now, as though she'd crawled to the nearest part of her cage. "When Aud tried to curse me, through the shield tithe...What happened? I thought I felt you fighting her, but I don't understand how."

Zofi closed her eyes. She remembered leaping into Audrina's room, seeing the curse on Ren's hands. She'd reacted on instinct. Slapped a boost to tithe. Except instead of performing a normal tithe, she'd pushed her mind outside her own body.

"I don't know how I did it exactly. I just remember I saw..." She searched for a way to describe it. "You know how normally in a tithe you see your own veins? I saw mine, but I saw yours, too, beside me, and Akeylah beside you...even Audrina, I think, this big black cloud." Zofi shook herself. "I threw a shield around you, the same way I would've done to myself. I didn't even know if it would work, but it seemed like the only way to help."

"Did it..." Ren cleared her throat. "Did it leave a mark?"

Zofi blinked. She hadn't even thought to check. She tugged her breeches down far enough to squint at her thigh, where she'd cracked the boost. Sure enough, a pale blue glow shone in a jagged X where the glass had broken her skin. "Yes." Zofi's voice shook.

She'd worked the Vulgar Arts. Just like her mother the curse-worker.

It stunned her, how easy it had been. Instinctive. So similar to a normal tithe, to one she'd work on herself. It raised all over again the questions she'd had while reading her mother's journal. Should there be some exceptions? Should Vulgar Arts that worked in someone else's favor, to help or save them, really be called curses?

"Thank you," Ren whispered. Zofi could see Ren's hands wrapped around the bars of the neighboring cell, if she tilted forward far enough.

Zofi slid over to join her. "You'd have done the same for me."

That's what got her thinking.

Shield tithes guarded the tither from being attacked, but also made it impossible for them to use any other tithes or curses for a whole day. It was like a dam, blocking a person from the Arts.

If Zofi could shield another person as easily as she could shield herself, she could also use the shield for more than just protection...

"Ren." Her voice went sharp, urgent. "If all three of us shielded Audrina at once, I think we might be able to bind her, stop her from being able to curse anyone. At least for a day."

Ren fell silent, thinking. "Maybe," she replied at last. "But what good would it do?"

"Akeylah said the heir was threatening Rozalind. It's why Akeylah agreed to hold the Blood Ceremony in the first place. I'd bet anything Audrina is threatening us, too, now. But if we could bind Audrina, she'd have no bargaining power."

"Aud was strong enough to break through my shield tithe." Ren tapped a fingernail on the metal bar. "And you said yourself the way her parents conceived her, the tithe they did, makes her stronger than anyone when it comes to the Arts."

276

"Stronger than you and me and Akeylah combined?" Zofi watched the condensation along the ceiling. Three droplets intersected, joined together in a wide trickle down the wall.

"Even if we could bind her, which would require us somehow getting out of this dungeon, finding bloodletters, and getting Akeylah on board...What then? We tell the whole court that Akeylah called a Blood Ceremony to recognize the child of Andros and Yasmin's incestuous relationship?"

Zofi shrugged, her shoulder digging into the cold iron bar. "It's what Audrina wants. Recognition for exactly who and what she is. So we bind her, prevent her from harming us, then give her what she wants. We tell the whole court exactly what she's done. Our secrets are already out there, yours and mine. She can't hold them over us anymore. And her body is covered in Vulgar Arts scars."

"But she camouflaged them, didn't you see?" Then Ren hummed a little, seeing her own mistake. "Ah. She wouldn't be able to do that either, if she was shielded..."

Zofi nodded. "All we need to do is convince the court to arrest her. Even if they imprison you and me, too, at least Audrina won't win the throne. It'd fall to Akeylah."

Ren's fingernails tapped against her bars again, faster now. "We'd still have to get out of the dungeons somehow. Not to mention steal a moment alone with Akeylah to fill her in. *And* find some way all of us can tithe and shield Audrina at once. Besides, even if we managed all that, Audrina has convincing enough proof of what I did. I'm sure she has something up her sleeve for you, too, to ensure you can't walk away from this."

Zofi studied the cell. This was the best future she could hope for. This, or a hangman's noose. But at least if she went down for Nicolen's murder now, there'd be a reason. She'd leave the world behind her a better place.

"It would be worth it," she murmured. "Even if we're both executed, we'd put the Reaches in the hands of someone who will better them, someone we trust."

Because she couldn't only think about her own fate. She had to think about her family, too. Her band, all the Travelers. Everyone in the outer Reaches who had suffered under the Kolonya-first rule of the past several centuries.

Somewhere in the dark, Ren cleared her throat. "I agree. Though this is all a moot point. We're trapped down here. The guards aren't exactly going to run messages for us prisoners."

"Maybe." Zofi craned her neck to peer up the corridor toward where the guards were stationed. She knew it was too much to hope that Vidal or one of his friends might be stationed down here. But she'd spent enough time in Vidal's company to understand how Talons worked. By the rule book, as much as possible.

Ren was right. The Talons wouldn't exactly deliver mail for prisoners. But they *would* tell the queen if an inmate said something important. And there was one thing royals usually wanted to hear from people they'd arrested.

Zofi took a deep breath. "Guards!"

In the distance, the faint sounds of chatter stopped.

"This is Lady D'Andros Zofi speaking," she shouted.

One of the guards grumbled and stomped up the corridor. "Quit the bloody racket," he growled.

Clanking, Zofi rose to her feet, the irons still clapped around her wrists. She lifted them to bang on the cell door. "My sister and I have discussed the situation," Zofi said, trying her best to channel her inner Ren. The prim and proper sister. "Please notify Her Highness Lady Akeylah that Lady Florencia and I are ready to confess."

⤗ 29 ⤖

Akeylah

This isn't going to work.

"How do I look?"

Akeylah nearly started out of her skin when Audrina appeared at her side, to take a turn in her shining gold gown. The dress was long-sleeved and floor-length by necessity. Gold, the color of the Sun Throne. Gold, to position herself in opposition to Nicolen, the Silver Prince, the last acknowledged heir.

"Perfect," Akeylah told her. It was the truth, after all. Akeylah had to admit, Audrina understood this political game better than her. Better even than Ren, who lived and breathed Kolonyan traditions.

Audrina had planned today's event meticulously, from her clothes down to the arrangement of the seating, placing the courtiers who'd protested Akeylah's, Ren's, and Zofi's initial acknowledgments nearest to the dais. Audrina anticipated the most support from them, since they'd already expressed dislike for the other available options.

She'd even invented a fake mother for herself, a noblewoman who'd passed away a few years ago, who Audrina had apparently researched obsessively. Akeylah heard her gushing about "dearest mummy" to the tailors' assistants that morning, as they prepared for the ceremony.

She waxed so poetic about her imaginary mother and the tragic way she'd died that halfway through the story, even Akeylah was tempted to believe it.

But Audrina's darker side also showed. She shrieked and threw one tailor from the Keep after he accidentally pricked her during her fitting, ignoring his desperate pleas about how long he'd worked there. After that, the other attendants pinned and sewed in nervous silence, while Audrina rattled off lists of nobles to Akeylah—which ones she bore grudges against, and how she planned to make their families repay those grudges.

"You don't think it harsh, to begin your new reign doling out punishments?" Akeylah had asked quietly, while Audrina turned this way and that, admiring her gown.

"Oh, I'll show mercy eventually." Audrina had smiled at herself in the mirror. "Once I'm sure they've fallen in line."

Akeylah had done just that. Fallen in line, ordered the Great Hall staff to follow Audrina's whims, paid the tailors for Audrina's gown. Even went so far as to visit the University herself to requisition the acolytes and the ceremonial equipment they'd need.

But the more time she spent with Audrina, the stronger her fears grew. This girl would prove a terror if she took the throne. Audrina would sacrifice anyone, even Kolonya itself, in service of her own desires.

"Just about ready now." Audrina peered through a slim opening in the doorway, a little offshoot fitting room of the Great Hall. The same room where Andros had died just a few days ago. Akeylah couldn't stop glancing at the far corner where he'd fallen.

To distract herself, Akeylah stole a glimpse over Audrina's shoulder at the Great Hall. It had been completely rearranged. In place of the usual dining room setup, the servants had lined up rows of chairs facing front, so it almost resembled a wedding hall, with a processional aisle in the center. That was the aisle Audrina would walk down, once Akeylah summoned her.

It was a different style than the last Blood Ceremony Akeylah had seen, in the sky gardens where she and her sisters had been confirmed as Andros's daughters. But then, Audrina seemed to take pleasure in the difference.

"I'm doing this my way," she'd said whenever anybody questioned the changes. "A new ceremony for a new queen."

Now, servers escorted nobles to their assigned seats. Up on the dais, a bevy of acolytes arranged the stage. The deep silver bowl that Akeylah, Zofi, Ren, and their father had bled into at their own Blood Ceremony stood front and center, on a raised pedestal. The symbols carved around its edges flashed in the bright lamplight of the hall, and the acolytes who flanked it matched Audrina in their gold ceremonial robes.

Behind the bowl stood the throne. At its right hand, on a

cushion, rested Father's crown. Even from here, all the way at the back of the Great Hall, Akeylah caught the glint of the talons that curved down either side of it, wickedly sharp.

Usually a Blood Ceremony would be performed separately from a coronation. One was meant to acknowledge the lineage of a future heir, the other meant to crown said heir. Today, however, Audrina had elected to combine the events.

"This will be a celebration fit for a queen," Akeylah murmured now, eyes downcast.

Audrina's expression sobered. "You'd better be able to keep your sisters in line, the way you claim."

"Of course, Your Highness," Akeylah answered without missing a beat.

About an hour ago, a Talon had visited from the dungeons to inform Akeylah that her sisters wanted to confess. Audrina had tried to dismiss him, but Akeylah understood what the message really meant.

Ren and Zofi needed to talk.

She'd managed to sneak away when she returned to her own chambers to dress. She'd stolen into the dungeons with only a few minutes to spare, and the moment Zofi explained her plan, Akeylah had formulated one of her own.

A way for all three of them to bind Audrina at once.

A way to ensure Audrina took responsibility for her crimes. Crimes that could only have been committed by a member of the royal family. Half the menders in the Keep had seen Father cursed, after all. There was only one way to be certain they all recognized the true culprit now.

So Akeylah had returned to Audrina's side, freshly dressed,

and in her meekest voice yet, had made a suggestion. "I've been thinking," she'd said, face averted, head bowed, in the manner she'd learned Audrina preferred. "If only you and I perform the Blood Ceremony, won't it just prove *we* are related?"

Audrina had stared. "Of course, puppet. That's the whole point."

"But, I mean, who's to say you couldn't be a relation on my mother's side, like my brother Siraaj or my sister Polla?"

Audrina had hesitated.

"It's just, I thought about my sisters' request to confess," Akeylah had pressed on. "Perhaps this might be a way to accomplish two things at once. Hear their testimony before court, and prove your relation to our father. If all three of us perform the Blood Ceremony with you, there can be no doubt as to your parentage."

"It would speed things up," Audrina had finally admitted, after a long pause. "If they confess to their crimes, we can proceed with their banishments straight away." She'd looked at Akeylah then, gaze sharp. "But if this is some sort of trick on their part..."

"I can ensure they'll do as they're told," Akeylah had answered, head still bowed. "I told you what I want, Your Highness. Myself and my sisters free of all this. Alive."

"Then see to it they obey me, and we'll all get what we deserve today."

I hope so, Akeylah thought now. Her gaze swept the crowd at the side of the dais. *There.* In a far corner, she watched a bevy of Talons lead Zofi and Ren into the room, still in chains. Murmurs swept through the gathered courtiers.

This would be tricky. They'd need to time their tithes perfectly with the proofs they offered in the Blood Ceremony. Only after Audrina's relationship was proven before the court, yet before Audrina took the throne, could they speak.

Speak, and pray the court believed them over her. Three liars against one.

Akeylah drew a deep breath. "Ready?"

"I've been ready for this my entire life." Audrina stepped aside so Akeylah could enter first. "See you on the other side, puppet." Audrina flashed one last wink. "And don't forget that ambassadorship waiting for you." Her expression sobered. "Or the reunion with our dear father if you screw this up."

Akeylah suppressed a shudder. But, "I look forward to putting this unpleasantness behind us, Your Highness," was all she said, voice smooth as silk. Dimly, Akeylah wondered when she'd gotten so adept at lying.

Rozalind was right. Time in this Keep changed a person.

Then she swept up the Great Hall toward the dais.

Heads turned. Every noble in the room looked her direction. Even Rozalind, who Audrina had insisted on moving up from the nursing wing, was in attendance. She sat in a wheeled chair, similar to the one Akeylah's father had used toward the end, but she looked healthy enough otherwise, her skin returning to its usual dark, Sun-blessed glow.

Her eyes tracked Akeylah all the way up to the dais, bright with concern. Akeylah flashed her the tiniest, quickest smile she dared.

For the occasion, Akeylah wore dark green, accented with

emerald. The color of mourning, ostensibly because of her father's recent death. In Akeylah's heart, however, she wore this color for a myriad of reasons. To mourn her sisters' lost reputations. Her own ruined innocence, as she collaborated with this megalomaniac.

She wore it as a cry for all of Kolonya if they failed today. If Audrina won.

When she reached the dais and climbed the steps to stand beside the acolytes, a hush fell. Akeylah surveyed the courtiers with a pang deep in her heart. She counted more than a few whose lives Audrina already planned to make a living nightmare. Who could say how many more the girl would take a disliking to, or how cruel her punishments might become?

Akeylah wet her parched lips. *Mother Ocean, guide our path today.* Then she spread her arms wide in greeting.

"Nobles, lords, and ladies, I thank you all for gathering here today." She forced a smile. "I am sure you all have questions." A nervous chuckle passed through the crowd. "I can only imagine your confusion when you received your invitations to this event. After all, my father, Sun guide his soul, only just held a Blood Ceremony, to recognize my sisters and me."

She cleared her throat. "But my father neglected to invite one person to the last ceremony. A person who rightfully should have been included. My lost sister, now found and ready to be recognized at last."

Murmurs started up. Heads turned as nobles asked one another if they had any idea who she meant.

"Lady D'Andros Audrina, please join us." Akeylah watched

every head in the room swivel as Audrina strode through the double doors at the far end of the Great Hall. The whispers grew louder, especially among the ladies. Akeylah guessed at least some of them must recognize the girl who, until recently, served them. The same way Ren once had.

Audrina looked nothing like a servant now.

She moved with a sedate, calm grace Akeylah envied. Head high, shoulders back, dressed in her skin-hugging golden gown, she looked every inch a queen. She peered down her nose at every row of people she passed, and the faintest hint of a sneer touched her lips when she locked eyes with some of those noblewomen in particular.

Finally, she reached the stage and ascended to take her place beside Akeylah.

Akeylah cleared her throat. "I have brought my other sisters Lady Florencia and Lady Zofi here as well, in order to properly confirm our fourth sister's heritage. Captain Lindle, please bring them to the stage."

Unlike Audrina's graceful processional, Zofi and Ren shuffled up the steps, manacled at the wrists and feet. Their clothing was rumpled and stained from their night in the dungeon, and they both had deep bags below their bloodshot eyes.

Audrina's tiny smirk widened when Ren tripped on the top-most stair. Zofi caught her just before she fell. Akeylah clenched her fists at her side to stop herself from reaching out, too.

She needed to play her part. Had to remain Audrina's faithful puppet until the last possible instant.

Audrina followed her gaze and leaned close to Akeylah.

"Remember our bargain," she murmured. At the same time, she tilted her wrist to show Akeylah the slim blade fitted along the underside of her sleeve. A bloodletter sewn into the very fabric, poised so she could dig it into her forearm at any moment. "One wrong move and none of you leave this hall alive."

Akeylah plastered on a broad smile for the onlookers. "Of course, Your Highness."

Then the acolytes took over. "Lady D'Andros Zofi," the lead acolyte said. "Step forward and make your proof."

The words stirred Akeylah's memory. Reminded her of the first time they'd all done this, when Father was still alive. When he set all this chaos into motion.

Part of her wished she could go back to that time. Back before she knew the dark secrets her family was keeping, even—or perhaps especially—Father. If she could, Akeylah would tell her past self to flee while she still had the chance.

Zofi shuffled forward, chains clanking. An acolyte passed her a bloodletter, and Zofi added a prick of her blood to the bowl. At the same time, Akeylah noticed her sister's brow crease, her eyes go sharp with concentration. After a few seconds, she shuffled backward, fell into line once more, with only the barest hint of a glance at Akeylah.

Yet Akeylah caught the trace of a smile curling one edge of Zofi's mouth.

"Lady D'Andros Florencia, make your proof," the acolyte continued.

Ren mimicked Zofi, stepping forward and tithing into the bowl. Her blood hit the basin and the whole bowl lit up bright silver and hummed faintly. Just like Zofi, Ren's gaze went hard and focused, but not on the Great Hall. On something else, something internal.

It happened fast enough that Akeylah hoped Audrina didn't catch it. The bowl still ringing faintly, Ren stepped back into line with a nod at Akeylah.

"Lady D'Andros Akeylah," the acolyte said. "Make your proof."

Akeylah approached. She drew back her sleeve, and an acolyte handed her a fresh bloodletter, silver-handled and gold-plated. Made especially for ceremonial occasions.

She tithed. A single drop of blood fell into the bowl, traced down the silver basin. As it glowed and hummed, louder this time, Akeylah forced her mind away from the Great Hall, into the tithe instead.

She was getting used to working the Vulgar Arts. In a split second, she saw her sisters' outlines beside her. Zofi, Ren, and Audrina, the latter a black thunderstorm on the horizon, although she sensed layers around Audrina's power this time.

Her sisters' shields, already in place.

Akeylah harnessed the Arts in her system and cast them out over Audrina. It felt the same as shielding herself, a tithe she had plenty of practice with this week. She gathered the Arts like a warm woolen blanket and wrapped them around Audrina instead of herself.

It took more concentration to shield another person. But a few beats, and Akeylah had secured the shield around Audrina's form, knotted it tight.

Akeylah stepped back into line. Time for the finale.

"Lady D'Andros Audrina." The acolyte extended a hand toward her. "Prove your relation, before all the Reaches."

"Gladly." Audrina accepted the final bloodletter. She tithed across the back of her hand, too wary of her scars to roll back her sleeves, Akeylah realized.

The bowl glowed and sang, louder than ever, and the whispers that had circulated the hall since Audrina's entrance burst into full-blown shouts of surprise.

"Before we continue with this ceremony," Akeylah spoke again, raising her voice over the hubbub, "many of you are aware that the past few weeks have been a trying time for our family. My father would like his throne to pass to his rightful heir, the heir best suited to leadership. To that end, we have some confessions to hear, from those who are not worthy of the title."

Audrina grinned at Ren in particular, triumphant.

Ren stared back, impassive. She always did have the best hunting face.

Akeylah did her best to remain sober, too. She didn't enjoy this task. But it needed to be done. "The first event I'd like to address," she said, "is my father's murder at the hands of Lady Audrina."

A beat passed in dead silence.

Then the hall erupted. Nobles leaped to their feet. Captain Lindle dropped the chain attached to Ren's and Zofi's manacles and stared at Akeylah in almost comical confusion.

Audrina, on the other hand, reached for her wrist with a scowl. "Traitorous bitch," she snarled. Her bloodletter sprang into her fist. "She's the one who cursed him," Audrina howled, though the shouts in the hall nearly drowned out her voice. "Akeylah killed Andros. She's the murderer."

"Arrest her," Akeylah told Captain Lindle calmly.

He started forward.

Audrina leaped backward out of his reach. "Florencia caused Burnt Bay. Zofi murdered Prince Nicolen. These girls are murderers and traitors, all of them!"

"Lady Audrina, please." The captain stalked after her. Cornered her on the far end of the stage. "Don't make this any more difficult than it needs to be."

Most of the Great Hall stood now, craned their necks and stepped out into the aisles for the best view of what was happening on the dais.

"You'll pay for this," Audrina growled in Akeylah's direction. Quick as a flash, she sliced her arm through the fabric of her gown.

Akeylah held her breath.

Her hands tingled. She looked down and her heart skipped in fear—tiny curls of black had started under her fingernails. As she watched the tendrils inched up her fingertips.

But then the black retreated. Her fingers went gray, then returned to their normal golden brown. She glanced up and saw Audrina's eyes widen with fury.

We did it, Akeylah thought. *We bound her.*

Captain Lindle grabbed Aud's arm. Other Talons had stormed the platform, and a pair caught Ren and Zofi each. Audrina glared death in Akeylah's direction, practically spitting. "Akeylah is the one you need to arrest," she shouted. "She killed our father, not me."

"It's over, Audrina," Akeylah said, voice pitched soft enough that only those on the dais could hear. "You can't hurt anybody now. Please, let's end this without any more bloodshed."

She held Audrina's eye until the other girl broke. Akeylah

291

watched her take stock. Look from Akeylah to Zofi and finally settle on Ren, gaze still narrowed. Suddenly, without warning, Audrina tore an arm from the Talons' grip. She reached down to drive a fist into her own leg. Akeylah didn't understand, not until Zofi shouted and she noticed a red stain begin to pool through Audrina's gown....

❋ 30 ❋

Florencia

Everything was going according to plan. Their shield worked—Audrina couldn't beat all three of them combined.

But then Audrina did something else, hit her leg the way Ren had seen Zofi do, down in Audrina's chambers. Blood pooled along Aud's skirts, and everything changed.

Ren's stomach sank as Audrina lurched from the captain's arms. The bloody stain on her gown spread. So much blood, more than a simple tithe should produce. And Audrina didn't look right either. Her back arched, and her eyes went glassy, unfocused. Ren didn't understand—Aud didn't have a knife in her hand, so how...?

Zofi cursed loudly.

"What is it?" Ren asked her. "What did she just do?"

"It's...a Traveler thing," Zofi muttered. "Boosts. They let you store the Arts for later use. But Mother always told me boosting with a shield tithe was dangerous—whatever tithe you try to work will hit the shield and rebound...."

Audrina moaned. That's when Ren saw it. The black spreading along her fingertips. Up over the backs of her hands.

"What about a curse?" Akeylah appeared at their elbows, voice tight.

"Even worse," Zofi murmured.

Ren's chest ached.

Audrina was a monster. A terror. She'd cursed Ren and her sisters, killed their father, their aunt.

But Audrina had also lived the kind of life Ren couldn't even imagine. She'd grown up with the horror of her parents' voices in her head, every day hearing how they disapproved, judged her, despised her.

She was a monster, but what else could she have been, raised like that? Trained from too young an age in statecraft, in war, in the price of running a kingdom and the terrible decisions it required.

Ren couldn't help but remember the other Audrina. Her friend. The girl who stayed up late to console her the first time Danton left. Who helped her darn extra socks to avoid Sarella's wrath. Who snuck out of the maids' chambers with Ren to dance in the fields behind the Keep in the light of the triple moons, stolen bottles of strongwine tucked under their arms as they howled at the sky.

The moons favor girls like us. Girls who didn't follow the rules. Girls who wanted more than the servants' lives they'd been forced into.

Ren had so much in common with Aud. More than she ever knew.

Unable to help herself, Ren strained forward. Tried to wrench free from the Talon holding her. "Let me help her," Ren begged. "Please. She's dying."

The Talon glanced around the stage, finally settling on Akeylah, who nodded. Then he seemed to give up trying to figure out who he should and shouldn't be restraining. He released Ren, who dropped to her knees beside Audrina, chains and all.

Somewhere in the background, she heard Akeylah loudly order the crowding nobles to make way for the menders.

"Aud." Ren fumbled for her friend's hands. Audrina's fingers were fully blackened now, curled like claws. "Aud, hang in there, please." She glanced over her shoulder at Zofi. "What can we do? Can she tithe, heal herself?"

Zofi caught Ren's eye. Shook her head. "The only thing…" Zofi hesitated. Looked at the Talon gripping her arm.

With a sigh, he let her go as well, and Zofi knelt beside Ren.

"She might be able to heal herself if she has another boost on her. I don't know that it would work; even a positive boost is dangerous to use with a shield tithe, but…" Zofi explained what to look for. A round glass phial somewhere on Audrina's body.

Ren reached for Aud's waist. Felt through the fabric of her dress, up to her rib cage.

Audrina's eyes fluttered. Focused on Ren, even as black tendrils clawed their way up her throat. "Ren?" she whispered, and in that single, quivering word, Ren heard her friend. The girl beneath the villain's mask.

Ren raised Audrina's hand to her chest, and bent down into Aud's view. In her peripheral vision, she saw Zofi continue to search up and down Aud's legs, failing to find whatever it was she needed.

"I'm right here," Ren murmured. She ignored the burn in the back of her eyes.

"They never...wanted me." Audrina's gaze flickered to the ceiling, back to Ren. The black webs of her own curse had reached her jaw, and unfurled across her cheeks. Darkened her lips like a strongwine stain.

Ren swallowed around a knot in her throat. She knew who Aud meant. The parents she'd spent her whole life trying so desperately to please.

"You don't need them." Ren dropped her voice to a whisper and clenched Audrina's hand so hard she worried it might hurt. If Aud could feel anything in her blackened fingers, that was. "You've got a friend who loves you like family. Who *is* family. You're my sister, Aud."

A ghost of a smile touched Audrina's blackened lips. "Sister," she breathed, eyes locked on Ren's. "I wish...we could've been." Then the curse's web reached the whites of her eyes, swallowed them, and any light left in her faded. Her hand went limp in Ren's.

"Audrina." She shook her arm. Touched her cheek. *"Audrina."*

She forced herself to remember the girl her friend had been. A girl full of secrets, more than Ren could have guessed. But also a girl who'd danced with her under the moons, who'd let Ren cry on her shoulder a hundred times.

For all Audrina had done to her, Ren realized she'd still been holding out hope. Hope that her friend was in there, deep down. Hope they could mend this, fix the mistakes their parents had made, somehow.

Menders thundered onto the dais. Late. Too late.

Ren fell backward, into someone else. Zofi, she realized, crouched at her left. Then Akeylah knelt on her right, and they both caught her hands. Ren shut her eyes. Clung to the sisters she had left.

※

"How bad is it out there?" Zofi craned her neck to peer through the doors toward the Great Hall.

Akeylah looked as though she'd just been to war and back. Then again, Ren supposed, they all had. She roused herself from her stupor enough to focus on Akeylah's report.

After the menders carried Audrina's body from the hall, the Talons had tried to reclaim some semblance of order. They'd gathered Ren's and Zofi's chains once more, marched them to a back room that Captain Lindle deemed securable, which apparently meant they could post enough guards on every entrance to block any escape routes.

"I called an emergency council meeting," Akeylah said. "The council of lords and the regional council will both be in attendance. Convenes in fifteen minutes, which should be enough time to..." She nodded at Ren.

Ren looked down at her skirts. It was a mark of her mental state that she only just now realized they were stained in Audrina's blood. "I still don't understand what that was," Ren said to Zofi as she touched the stains. "The boost, or whatever you called it."

Zofi glanced at her, away. "It's not my secret to share. But...do you remember the thing Danton found that serving boy trying to plant in your room?"

Ren thought back to the time when Danton caught an errand boy hiding an object in Ren's shoes. A mysterious round glass ornament with dark red liquid inside. "How did Audrina know how to make something like that, though, if it's such a secret Traveler device?"

Zofi shrugged. "Same way she knew anything the three of us tried to keep secret, I'm guessing." Her sister's mouth twisted into a grimace. "But Audrina's knowledge wasn't perfect. The boost she sent that boy to use against you, for example, would never have worked. You can only make boosts for yourself, not another person. And if she'd grown up a Traveler, she would have known better than to do what she did today. Mother's warned me about shield tithes ever since I was a child. If you're shielded and you use a boost, even for something positive like to heal yourself, the Arts can't get out of your system. They rebound on you. Curses are even more dangerous, obviously, but it would've been terrible no matter what tithe she tried."

Ren shut her eyes. Swallowed hard. "So, what happened to her..."

"Was what she tried to do to us." Akeylah grimaced. "Ren, I'm so sorry. I know she was your friend."

Ren kept her eyes shut tight. "I just can't believe I didn't see it. All this time..."

A hand came to rest on her shoulder. Akeylah's. "You couldn't have known."

Ren shook her head. "I knew she despised her parents. I knew she resented my rise in station—and the way I treated her. Just like her parents. I used her."

"You asked her for help," Akeylah countered. "That's what friends do."

"But if I'd realized sooner..."

"It's no one's fault but Audrina's," Zofi spoke up, voice hard. "Don't you dare shoulder her crimes. She made the decision to attack us. She could have trusted you, Ren, the way you did her. She could have explained who she was, could've asked us to help her confront her parents. She had other options. She ignored them."

Akeylah's hand left Ren's shoulder in a rustle of skirts.

Finally, Ren looked up and found Akeylah eyeing the narrow window, the only one in the room the Talons had selected for them. "We need to go soon," Akeylah said. "To meet with the council." She turned her arm over, and only then did Ren notice.

"Sun above." Ren lifted her own wrist, too. Studied the faint glow along the underside, which matched the mark on Akeylah's arm, and Zofi's. It was narrow, thin as a paper cut, but still obvious in color and shine. "How are we going to explain this?"

All three sisters had matching Vulgar Arts scars. Marks from where they'd worked together to shield Audrina.

"Father made an exception for me when I cured him," Akeylah murmured. "We might be able to argue this was one of those cases. After all, we didn't hurt her. We were just trying to protect ourselves."

"So we should be forgiven for performing Vulgar Arts that led to a girl accidentally killing herself in front of half the kingdom?" Ren massaged her scar with a forefinger.

"We could just hide them." Zofi traced her own scar.

"How long could we conceal something like this?" Ren protested.

"Audrina managed for years." Zofi ran her tongue across her teeth. "So did my mother. So did Yasmin."

Ren sighed. "Well, then, how do we explain everything else that just happened?"

"I've been thinking about that." Zofi finally looked up from her wrist. "Audrina never revealed your secret, Akeylah. And how many people know what our father accused me of doing, really?"

Akeylah tucked a plait behind her ear. "Captain Lindle, maybe. A few Talons. Rozalind and us. Why?"

"Not like me." Ren laughed once, bitter. "The whole court— Sun above, the whole of the Reaches know what I've done."

"What you're *accused* of doing," Zofi corrected. "If you ask me, the evidence sounds pretty thin on the ground. Is there actual proof?"

Ren pursed her mouth. "Some forged notes between me and a supposed rebel commander. Audrina wrote them herself."

"Which should be easy enough to prove, if we can find a sample of her handwriting anywhere else," Akeylah broke in, catching on.

"The maids have to keep weekly logs of their chores." Ren ran a hand through her hair. "There would be samples there. But I still don't see what you're getting at, Zofi."

"Well." Zofi's fingertips danced to the hilt of her knife. "The entire court just watched us confront a secret sister nobody knew we had, who tried to curse us in front of everyone. She's covered in Vulgar Arts scars. And you can prove she forged your correspondence with the rebellion."

Ren's forehead creased. "You want us to blame everything on her? Even my crimes, or yours?"

"Why not?" Zofi spread her hands. "She's guilty of most of it, anyway."

"It gives us a simple explanation." Akeylah began to nod. "One that will play well with the councils."

The thought didn't sit right with Ren. "Audrina did terrible things, but so did I. So did all of us, in one way or another."

"Speak for yourself," Zofi muttered. "I'd choose Elex over Nicolen any day."

"Still." Ren glanced toward the doorway. On the far side of the stonewood, she heard a murmur swell, from the crowd still gathered out there. Likely watching the servers clean the dais, wondering if there would be any more action to this show. "I don't like pinning it *all* on her."

"What would you rather do, confess?" Akeylah asked. "The court would demand your head, Ren." Her sister shuffled closer, until her skirts brushed Ren's arm. Akeylah knelt so their gazes were level. "There are better ways to do penance than offering yourself up as a sacrifice. You can't make up for what you did if you're dead. Alive, you may not be able to undo your mistake, but you can help put things right."

Ren blinked, taken aback. When she glanced to Zofi, she found her smiling, too.

"Listen to our smartest sister, Ren." Zofi nudged Akeylah's shoulder. "That's the future queen of the Reaches, after all."

Akeylah's face flushed, and she rose to her feet once more. "We haven't discussed anything of the sort."

"You're already doing the job," Ren pointed out.

"Only out of necessity. You were both gone, so—"

"So you held the entire kingdom together. Not everyone could've done that." Ren stood, too. "All while managing a blackmailer and curing our father's curse."

"I don't know what I'm doing," Akeylah protested. "This whole time, I've been faking it. Just trying to get through one day at a time."

"Sounds like leadership to me." Zofi grinned. "Besides, Ren and I already took a vote, down in the dungeons. You missed it while you were up here preparing a party for our nemesis, but we decided you're the best choice."

Akeylah narrowed her eyes. "I was up here making a deal with our enemy to give up the throne in order to keep the two of you safe. That hardly sounds like the decision a future queen should make."

"On the contrary, it sounds exactly like what a queen would do." Ren smiled. "Stall long enough to find a way to defeat your opponent."

"And above all, protect your people," Zofi added. "Family included."

Akeylah glanced back and forth between them. Finally, she exhaled, shoulders sagging. "Well, I guess that covers at least one thing we need to speak to the council about."

Zofi cast her a sideways glance. "Mm. Well, while we're setting topics for this meeting, I have another one to bring up . . . ."

❊ 31 ❊

Zofi

This is an outrage," Lord Rueno shouted when Zofi, Akeylah, and Ren entered the solarium. The council of lords and the regional council had already crammed around the map table, too many bodies squeezed into the tight space. Ambassadors Ghoush, Perry, and Kiril looked by turns infuriated, worried, and annoyed. Danton, on the other hand, had eyes only for Ren. He nearly collapsed from relief the second she crossed the threshold, and Zofi had to stifle a smile.

Whatever else he might've done, Danton was loyal to her sister. Zofi liked him for that.

Rozalind was there, too, still in the wheeled chair, though she flashed all three girls a reassuring smile when they entered.

Akeylah turned toward Rueno, poised as ever. "The attacks upon my family?" she asked. "I quite agree, Lord Rueno, it is outrageous."

"What are *they* doing here?" he spat, gesturing wildly between Zofi and Ren.

"I presume you have a reason for allowing your sisters, one of whom was recently under house arrest and the other of whom was banished by your father, to walk in here free of restraints?" Ambassador Ghoush added, a little more politely than her brother.

"I do." Akeylah swept a look around the crowded room and strode sedately to her seat next to Rozalind's chair.

Danton rose while Akeylah sat, and then he offered his own seat to Ren. A few other lords and ladies peered at one another, embarrassed they hadn't remembered to rise for the king's daughters.

Zofi ignored them all and perched on the windowsill, one leg swinging beneath her.

"For the past several weeks, our family has been dealing with crisis after crisis, beginning with my aunt's tragic death," Akeylah began, the way they'd rehearsed. "Afterward, my father fell ill, we believed from grief. But when he died, the truth came out." Akeylah laid her palms flat on the table. Half the audience leaned in with her, breaths held. "My father was not ill—he had been cursed. Cursed by the same daughter you met today, who tried to force my sisters and me to take responsibility for her crimes."

Zofi noticed Ren flinch, just for a second, before her face smoothed.

She understood. Ren felt guilty staining her friend's name any more than it already had been. But what else could they do? Akeylah was right—none of them could change the past. The only way to fix things was to move forward. To work toward a better future.

"Audrina was a troubled girl." Ren took up the thread. "She

hated our father for a number of reasons—some understandable, I must admit."

Understatement of the year, Zofi thought with a grimace.

"But Audrina reacted with violence, by sabotaging our family and this country. That we cannot forgive." Ren locked eyes with Lord Rueno. "Her plots included those documents your daughter found, which she planted in a room she brought Lady Lexana to. Audrina forged the letters. You'll find that if you look at Aud's handwriting in Madam Oruna's record books, it matches my supposed rebel correspondent's exactly."

"As I brought up to you privately, Lord Rueno," Danton interrupted. "The seal on those messages you found, when compared to a legitimate rebellion seal the Talons located, is not an exact match. Rather, a convincing copy."

Rueno gritted his teeth and shifted his glare to Zofi. "That still doesn't explain her return."

"My father banished Lady Zofi based on more lies Audrina fed him," Akeylah said. That much, at least, was entirely true. "She is back at court with my knowledge and blessing."

"Don't worry." Zofi grinned at Rueno. "You'll be seeing plenty more of me soon."

Akeylah cleared her throat. "In good time, sister. Right now, the menders are investigating evidence of Audrina's behavior—"

"With all due respect, Your Highness, what could menders ascertain about her behavior?" Ambassador Ghoush frowned.

"The menders discovered evidence that Audrina used the Vulgar Arts," Akeylah said. "In the form of several marks on her body."

A few nobles sucked in sharp breaths.

Unconsciously, Zofi's fingertips drifted toward the bracelet she wore on her wrist. A copper cuff, wide enough to conceal her new scar. It matched the gold cuff on Ren's arm and the silver on Akeylah's. Jewelry Rozalind had scrounged up earlier for them from her personal collection.

"When you say marks..." Ambassador Ghoush seemed a little slow on the uptake today.

"We mean Audrina has more scars than a professional curseworker," Zofi replied. *I should know.*

"She used the Vulgar Arts against all three of us," Ren spoke up. "As well as against my father and our aunt Yasmin. We suspected it was her, but now, well...the scars are proof."

"But *why*?" Ambassador Perry leaned forward in his seat. "Do you have any idea why your sister went to such lengths, what her aim was?"

"She wanted the throne," Zofi said.

"We were in her way." Akeylah pressed her lips into a thin line.

"And she was angry with our father for not recognizing her," Ren added, more softly. "For not offering her the same opportunity he afforded the rest of us."

"Why didn't he acknowledge her when he acknowledged the rest of you?" Ambassador Ghoush asked. "Why not recognize all his bastards at once?"

Akeylah cleared her throat. "I believe he chose not to because he was ashamed of her origins, ambassador."

"Who was her mother?" Rueno frowned, catching on immediately.

The girls traded glances. Finally, Akeylah answered. "Yasmin."

The solarium broke out in gasps. Zofi caught more than a few scowls of disgust, and others gaped in shock.

"To judge by this reception, he wasn't wrong to hide that information," Zofi muttered.

Akeylah cleared her throat, almost loud enough to drown out Zofi's words. "With your permission, lords and ladies, ambassadors, I'd like to motion to review Audrina's crimes in more depth at a later meeting. After we've had time to complete a full investigation. Even my sisters and I may not know the full extent of her actions."

A rumble of agreement passed around the table.

"Good." Akeylah dared a small smile. "Now, in the meantime, we have several pressing issues on the table that we need to address."

"The crop blight, for example," Ambassador Kiril spoke up.

"Or the succession of the throne," Ambassador Ghoush suggested, a single brow lifted. "We assumed we had an heir, since the king arrested his other two eligible daughters, but facts appear to have changed."

"Facts have changed," Ren said. "But our regard for Father's decision has not."

Rozalind spoke up for the first time. "Before he passed, my husband indicated that he wished to name Lady Akeylah his successor. It's the announcement he planned to make, the evening he…" She hesitated, winced.

The room fell silent for a moment.

Under the table, Zofi saw Akeylah reach for Rozalind's hand.

"For what it's worth," Ren said, after a pause, "my sisters and I are all in agreement with Father's wishes, Sun guide his soul."

"Akeylah is the best choice for queen," Zofi added. "Do any of you object?"

A few nobles traded stares, but nobody replied. Even Lord Rueno sat quietly in his chair, though Zofi noted the way his gaze darted among the sisters. She could practically read his thought process. *Well, Akeylah is the least of three evils....*

Finally, when no one offered an objection, Akeylah spoke again, her voice softer. "I am humbled by my family's and your belief in me. I will do my best to live up to your expectations." Her gaze drifted to Ambassador Kiril. "Ambassador, you spoke of the crop blight as another pressing concern."

Kiril bobbed his head. "When we last met about this issue, the agricultural guild had developed a cure for the blight. But two weeks have gone by now, and none of my farms in the Western Reach have been able to lay their hands on this so-called cure."

"Nor have any Eastern farmers," Danton said. "We were already low on provisions before this blight; now I fear famine is imminent."

"To that end, I've several announcements to make." Akeylah gestured at Zofi, who rose from the windowsill. "My sister, Lady Zofi, will be taking up a permanent position on the regional council."

Rueno and a few of the other nobles, heretofore silent, opened their mouths to protest. Ambassador Ghoush beat them to it. "Seats on the regional council are reserved for representatives of the outer Reaches, Your Highness." Ghoush squinted at Zofi. "Unless you would like to install her in Countess Yasmin's old seat."

Akeylah raised a palm to halt the ambassador. "Actually, she'll be joining us as the official representative of a group who should have had a seat at this table all along. Lady Zofi?"

A smirk played on Zofi's lips as she casually leaned on the

back of Akeylah's chair and surveyed the room. Lords and ladies, ambassadors and queens. People accustomed to wielding power. People not accustomed to sharing that power with the likes of her.

It made Zofi's smile widen. "Centuries ago, when the Reaches were first born, six ships with six different captains settled this land." In the back of her mind, she thought about Vidal. About the night she told him this story. *You can still help change people's minds. Help change the Reaches—by telling that story.* The Travelers' story. Or at least one of them.

Elex was right. She didn't need to do what others told her. And Vidal was right, too—she didn't need a crown to make a difference. She would make her own title.

Build a better world, queen or not.

"Back then, my people, the inhabitants of the sixth ship, were the lifeblood of the other five Reaches. We carried knowledge throughout this land. We connected you all, until your ancestors grew frightened of our knowledge. They distrusted us simply because we claimed no land for our own. They called us drifters, assumed we had no homes or loyalty."

She straightened. "But land does not make a home. The ground you were born onto is not what makes you an Easterner, Danton, or you a Westerner, Ambassador Kiril."

Both of their heads bobbed in unison, buoying her spirits. At least some people understood where she was coming from.

Maybe this wouldn't be as impossible as it felt.

Akeylah took over once more. "That is why I've decided to reinstate the Travelers as the Sixth Reach, the Traveling Reach."

Dead silence fell.

"And as my first act as the ambassador to the Traveling Reach,"

Zofi said, "I offer our aid with this crop blight. I have sent messages to the leaders of thirteen of the largest Traveler bands. I've received agreements from six already, but I anticipate all of us will come together in this time of need."

"Agreements to do what, exactly?" Lord Rueno interrupted.

"To distribute the cure to the outer Reaches," Zofi answered. "The agricultural guild has already produced enough curative potions to cover half the crop fields in Kolonya. My riders will take these existing potions to the outermost Reaches while the guild produces more here in Kolonya. We expect to bring the cure to all the fields in the Reaches within the next month." In reality, Zofi thought they could do it faster, but this was the conservative estimate she'd settled on. Just in case.

Still, all around the table, jaws dropped.

"A month." Ambassador Ghoush fanned herself. "But it takes most trading caravans three weeks just to journey from the Northern Reach to Kolonya, never mind all the way down to the Southern Reach."

"Traders don't travel like we do." Zofi grinned. "Doubt me if you like, but at least give me a chance to prove you wrong." She noticed more than a few others stifle smirks at that.

"I, for one, am eager to work with the Traveling Reach." Danton flashed Zofi a wink. "I have a feeling there's a lot we could learn from our fellow countrymen."

Zofi's chest swelled.

She knew this was only the beginning of what would be a long, difficult road. Neither the regional council nor the rest of Kolonya would like everything she had to say, as the speaker for a group that hadn't had a voice of their own for centuries.

She wouldn't be offering them favors every time they sat down in this solarium.

But for the first time in a long while, hope stirred in Zofi's heart. Hope for change. Hope that her people might reclaim the power they'd once had.

Hope that despite everything she'd just gone through, she might achieve her dream after all.

✳ **32** ✳

Florencia

Ren clutched her sisters' hands as they gazed down at their father's body. Encased in a clear glass casket, dressed in his formal wartime uniform, he looked as though he were merely sleeping. His face seemed years younger than it had in his final days. The lines and creases had melted away, thanks to the menders' exacting care.

Outside, the distant strains of flute music coupled with the roar of excited voices.

The mourning period had ended. And unlike Yasmin's rainy, tearful procession, today they'd planned a parade, in joyful recognition of everything King Andros had accomplished in his lifetime.

He'd made mistakes. Just like the daughters who surrounded him now. Just like the sister who preceded him to the grave.

But his people loved him. And he'd done great things, too, in between those mistakes. So, conflicted as Ren felt now that she knew about Audrina's past, they'd planned him a send-off fit for a beloved ruler.

"He looks so...calm," Zofi ventured. "So at home."

So do you, Ren thought. Then again, they were in the stables, Zofi's home away from home. They stood in the back of a wagon the stablehands had outfitted to bear them and the coffin. Enormous warhorses flanked them, four yoked to their carriage and dozens of others lined up behind, each with a Talon on its back. Somewhere in this procession rode one Talon in particular who Ren guessed would be glad to see Zofi once all this had ended.

"I hope he's in a better place." Ren studied the faint smile on Father's lips.

"I wish I felt that calm." Akeylah wrung her hands together. "Ren, Zofi, are you both certain you don't want to ride in the covered carriage with Rozalind?"

The enclosed carriage stood a few paces ahead. Rozalind, still too weak to stand for very long, rode in that, where she'd be sheltered from the crowds they were about to ride into.

"People are going to have to see Zofi and me eventually," Ren said. "You've announced the lifting of our sentences. Rumors are already spreading about what you told the councils with regard to Audrina. People know we didn't do what they thought." Her voice sounded far more confident than she actually felt.

Deep down, she was terrified. Some Kolonyans might not believe the stories. They might still blame Ren for Burnt Bay, for their families' deaths.

They wouldn't be wrong.

Akeylah's mouth twisted into a wry expression. "Sometimes I

wonder if you're a glutton for punishment. Do you *want* people to throw rotten food at you?"

Zofi's hand drifted to her longknife. "I'd like to see them try."

Sometimes Ren wondered, too. But still. She squared her shoulders. "Like I said, we'll have to go out in public eventually. May as well get it over with now. Besides, I want to say goodbye properly." She rested her hand atop Father's transparent casket, one they'd had specially crafted in the last week.

Akeylah placed her hand over Ren's. After a pause, Zofi added hers, too.

"I'm going to miss you both," Akeylah said.

"I'll be back before you even realize I'm gone." Zofi flashed a smile. "And Ren isn't leaving right away, is she?"

Ren hesitated. Her gaze drifted to the stable doors. Somewhere outside was a certain ambassador she needed to talk to. Because she had an idea. A way to, like Akeylah had suggested, begin to atone for what she'd done.

"Next week, if I can," Ren replied.

Akeylah spun toward her, startled. "So soon?"

"Don't worry." Ren waved a hand. "I won't be away long. Just, I want to get things in motion as soon as possible."

"Of course." Akeylah forced a smile. "As long as you don't leave me alone with the court vipers for too long. I can barely stomach Sarella, let alone handle Rueno without you."

Ren laughed. Then the stable doors creaked open. Somewhere ahead, the first horse in the processional began to move. A few moments later, their wagon lurched. Ren lost her balance, but Zofi grabbed her arm, steadied her. On her other side, Akeylah took her hand. All three girls held on tight.

"When I die," Zofi added in a low murmur, "don't you dare show me off like this."

"You mean you don't want a gold carriage?" Ren's jaw dropped in mock surprise.

"What about just one really fine horse that we strap your body to?" Akeylah smirked.

"Mm, maybe." Zofi turned to peer over her shoulder at the blinding silver sand-stepper, which apparently Vidal, her Talon friend who Ren suspected was more than a friend, retrieved from an outpost along the merchants' road. "Only if it's *that* horse, though."

"What's his name?" Ren squinted at the enormous creature.

"Used to be D'Nicolen, but I don't think it suits him." Zofi's mouth twisted in distaste. "Vidal suggested I rename him Horsey." Her sisters snorted. "I was thinking maybe D'Andros...if that's not strange."

"I don't think it's strange at all." Akeylah rested a hand on Zofi's shoulder.

The carriage burst from the shadows of the stables. The cheers grew deafening. Ren's heart beat against her rib cage.

Here it comes. Kolonya's hatred.

The bright sunlight forced Ren to squint. Through it, she saw rows upon rows of people from every walk of life, lining the streets all the way from the Keep to the distant Necropolis.

Some cheered. Some cried.

Eyes fastened on her. But she didn't see the anger she expected, or hear any chants about Burnt Bay or traitors. Slowly, block by block, as they rolled through the city, her hands still clasped in Akeylah's and Zofi's, she began to relax.

Most people didn't even seem to notice the sisters. They focused on Andros. She heard songs she recognized, snippets of ballads about his exploits in younger years. How much he sacrificed to defend Kolonya against Genal.

How much indeed. *If only they knew.*

Still, it buoyed her spirits to see how they cared for him. It made her feel like, despite her own crimes, she might one day do enough good to tip the scales.

Several blocks from the Necropolis, Ren turned. Behind their carriage—an ornate golden monstrosity—a second vehicle trundled along. Unlike the king's, this one went unremarked. A simple wooden construction, barely as large as the coffin it carried.

"I'm glad," Akeylah whispered, "that we decided to bury her in the same place."

Ren was, too. Audrina never received the recognition or the position she so longed for in life. At least in death, she deserved to lie in her rightful place.

With a jerk, the carriage halted outside the Necropolis, a stone miniature of Kolonya City, made up of tombs. They rode through its wide gates, as far as the wagons would allow. Then they disembarked to continue on foot.

The sisters drew a handcart with the king's coffin between them. Together they rolled him through the narrow corridors of the Necropolis, toward the Keep-shaped tomb where his sister waited.

By Kolonyan tradition, family must carry you to your final resting place in order for your spirit to reach the Blessed Sunlands. When they fit his casket underneath Yasmin's, Ren said a silent prayer he would find her. Reunite with the other half of his mind.

Back outside, Ren alone marched back to the carriages. She had one more burden to bear.

Her best friend. Her worst enemy.

In the end, Audrina was both of those things and neither. Ren knew that in Aud's own way, she'd tried to protect the throne.

Audrina had seen Ren's and Zofi's and Akeylah's sins, and she'd made the same judgment call Ren did. She thought Kolonya would be better in her own hands.

Ren couldn't blame her.

A surge of emotions struck when she accepted the handcart, laden this time with a smaller coffin. Audrina was lighter than their father. In her plywood box, she was easy to lift onto the lowest shelf of the royal tomb.

It was the least Ren could do. Carry her here. Audrina was her sister, after all—in some ways, more a sister than either Akeylah or Zofi. Before Ren had any idea who she was, Audrina had been there. A confidante, a friend.

She betrayed Ren, eventually. But first, she'd helped her.

Outside, beyond the walls of the Necropolis, the crowds sang funeral songs. Blessings to honor the deceased. Ren kissed her fingertips, laid them atop Audrina's coffin, and prayed her sister would find the peace she'd never known in life.

❋

Mama met Ren in the center of the Necropolis. As befitted a member of the royal family, albeit the extended one, Mama wore full mourning greens—a floor-length, wide-skirted gown and a veil nearly as long as the dress itself. It must have cost a fortune.

"I figure I'd best get use out of the tailors while they'll still serve me," Mama explained when Ren reached her side. She kissed Ren's cheeks, one after the other. "Since my daughter has decided to surrender the crown that should rightfully be hers."

"Don't be dramatic, Mama. The tailors will still make any gown you like."

"Not the kind of gowns I'd be owed if I were the mother of the queen." Mama sighed. "Alas, my daughter prefers the company of rebel ambassadors to pursuing her mother's plan."

"I thought you approved of my fling with an ambassador." Ren flashed a wry smile.

"Back when I thought he'd prove a useful ally on your way toward the throne. Now, after the man has already thrown aside one fiancée? Sun above, no."

Danton and Lexana had called off their engagement officially earlier that week. Lexana had wasted no time running off with Josen, and her father had wasted just as little time cutting off her inheritance. But by all accounts, Lexana was happier than ever, selling what remained of her possessions to purchase a tavern in town with Josen.

Ren shook her head at her mother, though she kept smiling. "Was it really that important to you? Me being crowned?" At the same time, Ren scanned the small group that remained around the tomb. She picked out Zofi beside Vidal, his hand resting lightly on the small of her back. Nearby, Akeylah stood next to Rozalind's wheeled chair, hand tangled in the former queen's.

Rozalind looked far better than she had last week. The ashy pallor had left her face, and she moved easily. The menders said she'd be fully recovered within the next week or so. In time for the coronation.

"Of course. I wanted you to be free. To be able to choose a life for yourself. Not like me, chained to noble ladies' whims." Mama arched a brow. "But somehow, you managed to do all that without a crown, daughter. So I suppose I cannot complain too much. Except for the fact that you're leaving home to run far away." She reached up to pinch Ren's cheek.

"Mama, stop." Ren batted her hand away. "I don't leave for another week. And I'll be back soon, I promise."

"Not soon enough. Not that I ever see you while you're *in* the Keep, so I suppose it's no different...." Mama was off again, grumbling, but Ren couldn't suppress her smile.

Across the courtyard, Danton caught her eye.

She tilted her head, a silent question. One they still knew how to ask each other across roomfuls of people. *Can we talk?*

He nodded.

Ren kissed her mother's cheek and sidled through the mourners to reach him.

"Florencia." He caught her hand, pressed his lips to her palm. "I am so very sorry for your loss. Your father was a great king, and a good man."

She raised a brow. "Despite the fact that you argued with him constantly?"

"What good is it to have friends if you can't fight with them when they do something wrong?" Danton grinned.

She smiled, too. Then it dripped from her mouth. "Listen, Danton..."

"I'm not going to ask you," he said. "If that's what you're worried about."

She blinked, confused. "Ask me what?"

"For anything. I won't beg for more chances to prove myself. I won't bother you anymore. If you don't want to be with me romantically, I understand, Florencia. But I hope I can still remain your friend."

She couldn't help it. She laughed. "Actually, that's not what I was going to say." She hesitated. Tilted her head and considered him, playful. "Though, now that you mention it." She caught his eye. Saw there the same fierce desire she always did, when they stood like this. Alone together, the only two people in the world.

Only Danton had ever made her feel that way. And for everything he'd done, she could think of just as many mistakes she'd made.

"I'm not making any promises." Ren's voice softened. He leaned closer, and she breathed in his sharp pine scent like a sigh of relief. "But I'm not saying we're completely off the table."

The hope that flared in his eyes made her heart skip.

"However." She stepped back, just far enough to clear her head. "I have a proposal for you. Unrelated to us."

He crossed his arms. "I'm interested."

"You don't even know what I'm going to say yet."

"No. But I trust you, Florencia. You've always been the smarter one of us."

"Please write that down. I'd like to quote it against you later." She smirked. Then forced the amusement from her face. "We need to make things right, Danton. What we caused in Burnt Bay..."

His smile melted as well. "If there were some way to fix it, seas know I would have by now."

"We may not be able to turn back time," she said. "But I've

been thinking about what you'd planned to do with your dowry money from Lexana. About how you wanted to fund the Eastern Reach, so people there didn't need to rely on violence as the only solution."

He nodded. "But Lexana and I decided we couldn't marry for that reason alone. She wanted to be with Josen, and I didn't want to live a sham either."

"Understandable. It just got me thinking. So I spoke to my sisters, and I got Akeylah's blessing."

"To do what, exactly?"

Ren glanced over at Akeylah, still holding Roz's hand. "She's granted a stipend to the Eastern Reach. To rebuild from the war."

Danton's eyebrows rose. "Andros always said we couldn't afford that."

"Yes, well." Ren watched fondly as Akeylah twined her fingers through Rozalind's without thinking. "Given our current peace with Genal, Akeylah has decided our money will be best spent on ensuring all the Reaches enjoy the same quality of life."

Danton ducked his head close enough that his hair brushed Ren's cheek. "Speaking of our peace with Genal ... Do you think we'll hear new wedding bells soon?" He, too, watched Akeylah's and Rozalind's body language.

Ren lifted a brow, amused. "Give them a minute to enjoy themselves first," she scolded. "Before we turn their relationship into a political gambit."

Danton laughed. "My apologies."

She squinted in mock disapproval. "But speaking of politics. Akeylah would like me to accompany you out east to distribute the money. So we can make sure it goes where it's needed most." In truth, Ren had volunteered. But Akeylah had seen by her expression just how much Ren needed to start righting her wrongs, in whatever way she could.

"A wise move," Danton said. "Monetary support from the crown should help quell any latent rebel support. Though I'll be honest, I wouldn't be surprised if Akeylah's coronation alone quiets the rebellion. She's one of us, after all. At least partly."

"It's a whole new world," Ren murmured.

Danton slipped his hand into hers. Tentative at first, until she squeezed his hand in return. "May we learn from our history." Danton bent to kiss her temple. "So we need never repeat it."

·⇥ 33 ⇤·

Akeylah

The sky gardens looked like they did the night of the first Blood Ceremony, way back when Akeylah had first arrived in Kolonya City.

A platform had been erected in the central courtyard. Acolytes stood in straight-backed rows across it. Between them were the holy instruments of Father Sun. The Sun sword, an immense steel broadsword King Ilian had ridden into battle with, four centuries ago at the birth of Kolonya. And the formal throne, which servants had carried up from the receiving hall where it normally resided.

Akeylah had never seen it in person before. It looked even more intimidating than in the paintings. Its blinding golden surface had been sculpted to look like Father Sun himself, with spurts of flame like the vast tentacles of some sea monster, and diamonds pocking its surface.

Akeylah could not tear her gaze from it.

Only one item was missing—the crown.

All across the gardens, nobles milled. They exclaimed whenever the criers announced a new arrival, pointed and whispered about the new gowns and tuxedos nobles sported. Everyone had worn their finest to meet their new queen.

Akeylah remembered the first night she'd stood on this dais, and she had to bite back a smile. She'd been entirely out of place, dressed in an outdated gown she stole from her mother's dressing trunk.

Now, at least she looked the part.

She, Zofi, and Ren wore the same fabric, gowns commissioned by Rozalind's tailor. They were the same verdant shade of green, a peridot that paid tribute to the end of their mourning period. The tailor had skillfully blended mourning green with accents of gold, for the Sun they were here to celebrate.

The tailor had also tweaked the style to suit each of their body types. Zofi's fit loosely, sleeveless with a short skirt cut to her knees, to allow her easy motion. Ren's was cut to hug her curves from collarbone to ankle, with slits to display her long legs and high heels—bright gold for the occasion.

As for Akeylah, the tailor had given her sheer sleeves, an allusion to a more Eastern style of dress, but with a Kolonyan twist—an asymmetrical skirt and sheer, plunging back. She loved the way it spoke to both parts of her—Kolonyan and Eastern alike.

She'd imitated that style for her hair, as well. Done the front half up in Eastern braids and left the rest loose and wavy down her back. She'd noticed more than a few ladies pointing and whispering at her tonight, but for once, she hadn't felt self-conscious. This time, she knew they were murmurs of approval.

Still, when she, Ren, and Zofi stepped up to the center of the dais, Akeylah's pulse fluttered. *Remember, we all agreed.*

Even after that first regional council meeting, Akeylah couldn't shake her doubt. Part of her wished Ren or Zofi could take her place.

"Either of you would be better at this," she'd told them again and again. "You're both stronger than I am."

"It's not sheer strength Kolonya needs right now," Zofi had replied.

"Besides, what makes you think you aren't strong?" Ren had asked. "You lasted longer against Audrina than either of us."

"Because she saw me as the weak link, the one she could make her puppet."

"And look how wrong she was." Zofi had winked.

Still. All those conversations failed to reassure her as she faced down the weight of this responsibility. *Queen of Kolonya.*

Somewhere in the back of her mind, she heard her father's words. *The best leaders are those who accept the crown as a burden rather than claim it as a prize.*

Akeylah tried to reassure herself with that as she followed her sisters onto the dais.

"Hello, everybody," Zofi's voice boomed across the rooftop. Everyone quieted at once, like a curtain falling across the crowd. "Thanks for having me back, Kolonya. This time I promise to behave." Laughter sounded.

Surprisingly, given the way Kolonya had initially reacted to Zofi, the nobility had warmed to her since Andros's death. Perhaps it was because they'd seen Audrina, seen what a truly terrible ruler could look like. Or maybe it had more to do with the Travelers' new status as the Sixth Reach and Zofi's brand-new title of ambassador.

If you asked Akeylah, however, she'd attribute it to her sister's forthright attitude. Zofi was always unapologetically herself. There was something trustworthy about that. Even if she despised you, at least you knew where you stood.

"I'm excited to be here tonight," Zofi was saying, "Because tonight marks a change. Not just for our family, or for Kolonya, but for all the Reaches. We have an Easterner ascending our throne, and the Sixth Reach has been granted a voice of its own." A smattering of applause dotted the crowd, mostly from the ambassadors and visiting nobles from the north and south.

Akeylah spotted Danton cheering.

Zofi's offer to help distribute the crop blight cures, a process she'd already begun with the help of her mother's well-connected friends, probably helped her popularity, too. In fact, Zofi had become something of a trendsetter—Akeylah spotted more and more young girls in trousers and men's shirts dining in the Great Hall.

"I know the past several weeks have been just as trying for the Reaches as they have been for our family." Ren took over now. "My sisters and I thank you for standing by us, and for being ready to move forward into a new era with a new leader to guide us."

At her signal, acolytes stepped up to the dais. One laid a

cushion before the throne. Another picked up the sword and stood at the ready to present it to Akeylah.

Her stomach knotted around itself, tighter than a sailor's rope.

"Princess D'Andros Akeylah." The lead acolyte took center stage. "Step forward for the blood oath of royal office."

Akeylah stepped forward and extended her right arm. Her left was still wrapped in the silver cuff she'd donned after their showdown with Audrina, hiding her scar.

She accepted a bloodletter from the acolyte. Like the one they'd used during the Blood Ceremony, it was ornate. Golden, and sculpted like a stormwing feather. She held the blade to her forearm.

The blood oath in this case was a formality. A way to add weight to the swearing-in of a new monarch. Still, sweat prickled her brow. She'd never performed this tithe before.

Zofi had reassured her it was a simple process. Tithe, speak only the truth, and you would be fine.

Lie, and the oath would burn you alive. *No pressure.*

But her sisters were right there beside her. Across the rooftop, she saw all the nobles she'd met over the past couple of weeks, whose concerns she'd listened to and handled as best she could. Even the sight of Lord Rueno and Ambassador Ghoush reassured her. She'd faced their ire in council meetings and lived.

She could handle this.

Akeylah drew the bloodletter across her arm. The tithe overwhelmed her, as it always did when the Arts hit her bloodstream, but only for an instant. *Find the truth.* She focused on that command.

When she opened her eyes, a faint steam appeared in the air around her body.

Every eye on the rooftop fixed on her. The whole kingdom held its breath.

"D'Andros Akeylah, daughter of King D'Daryn Andros, in sight of the gods and all those gathered here tonight, make your oath to this kingdom," the acolyte said.

She gritted her teeth against the heat in her veins. Took a slow, steadying breath.

"I, D'Andros Akeylah, do hereby accept this throne, and all the rights and responsibilities that come with doing so. I swear to govern to the best of my abilities, to exercise wisdom, justice, and above all, mercy, in every decision I make."

As she spoke, her nerves faded. Her voice grew steadier. Stronger.

She raised her head high and smiled at everyone in turn, from the servants up to the highest nobles. "I pledge my life to each of you. I am your servant, and I will do everything in my power to create a brighter future for you all."

The heat of the blood oath made sweat prick her brow, but it didn't even bother her now.

"Today, I humbly accept the title of Queen of the Reaches. I pledge to fairly govern the Central Reach, Kolonya, as well as the Eastern Reach, my homeland, Tarik." She noticed a murmur pass across the rooftop at the name. *Tarik* was a forbidden word. Banned ever since the country had been renamed the Eastern Reach.

This was the first line they'd rewritten, a departure from the oaths her father, and his father, and every king and queen before, had spoken.

But she wasn't finished.

"I promise to protect the Southern Reach, once known as

Ananses. I will guard the Northern Reach, formerly the country of Harenae; and the Western Reach, which was founded as Oonkip. So, too, will I nurture and aid the Sixth Reach, the Traveling Reach."

Whispers shot through the crowd. Jaws dropped. None of those country names had been spoken at court in centuries. Most people wouldn't even dare whisper them at home.

Now the queen herself spoke them aloud.

The blood oath petered out of her system, and the acolyte accepted the bloodletter, but Akeylah continued to speak. "My father believed in the power of the unified Reaches. But in order to be united, we must stand together as equals. From this day forward, none of the outer Reaches need deny or disguise their history. Their names will be spoken as freely as they once were. And their representatives will have stronger voices than ever on my council."

She didn't know what she expected. Resistence, perhaps. Or disdain.

Not applause.

It started with Danton. Then a small contingent of Eastern nobles began to clap next. Soon it spread to the other ambassadors, even Ghoush. Akeylah's eyebrows rose as Lord Rueno brought his palms together, and other Northerners cheered.

Then a Southern lady knelt. It swept through the crowd.

Akeylah stood dumbstruck as the entire rooftop took a knee. Even her sisters, Ren first, then Zofi, the latter with a broad grin.

"Father Sun has heard your testimony." The acolyte's voice boomed across the rooftop. "In his sight and in the sight of all the gods, your oath has been accepted. Kneel, for the mark of your office."

Akeylah knelt along with the rest.

On the far side of the dais, she spotted the face she'd longed for all night. Rozalind climbed the steps carefully, a pillow balanced in her hands, atop which rested the crown.

After much debate, they'd decided to retire her father's crown, with its warlike talons. They'd opted for a new design, one to represent an era of peace.

Rozalind crossed the stage at a sedate pace, head high, shoulders back, every inch the regal former queen passing her title along to the next. But when her back turned to the audience, she flashed Akeylah a quick wink.

Rozalind's fingertips brushed her temples, cool as ever, and she laid the crown on Akeylah's brow.

The gold felt cold against her forehead. The crown itself was graceful, slender, with six spires to represent the six Reaches, and set throughout with stones the same blue as the waves Akeylah used to watch from the cliffside where she grew up.

When she opened her eyes once more, everyone on the rooftop, still kneeling, lifted their hands to the sky, palms up in an offer of fidelity.

"Rise," the acolyte said, "Queen Akeylah of the Reaches."

"Have I mentioned that you look positively delicious tonight?" Rozalind's voice was a breath against her cheek, sending a thrill down her spine.

"Funny," Akeylah replied, voice light, "because it's you I'm looking forward to enjoying later." Her fingertips traced Rozalind's curves, came to rest on her hips. "My queen," Akeylah added, soft and sly.

"You're the queen now." Rozalind paused in the middle of their dance—a slow, easy spin, the most Rozalind could handle at present—and touched the crown Akeylah wore.

"Hmm. Two foreign queens, fraternizing in public." Akeylah lifted a brow. "I believe we are many Kolonyans' worst nightmare. An end to safe and traditional life as they knew it."

"Good." Rozalind grinned. "It's about time we shook things up around here." She tucked a finger under Akeylah's chin. Tilted her face until they were cheek to cheek, the corners of their lips brushing. "I'd like to make you one more promise, my queen."

Akeylah caught her breath, felt her eyelids flutter closed. "You've fulfilled yours. You protected me."

"I will never be done protecting you. But going forward, I'm done keeping things from you."

Akeylah drew back, just far enough to meet the queen's gaze. Rozalind's dark eyes twinkled in the bright light of the lanterns dotted around the gardens.

"No more secrets," Rozalind whispered.

A smile curved across Akeylah's mouth. "Deal."

Someone cleared their throat loudly, and both queens leaped apart, startled. Zofi stood at their side, smirking. "Sorry to interrupt, Queenie. Just stopped by to tell you how shocked I am—it almost seems as though people approved of your speech."

"Queenie?" Akeylah snorted. "You're about as creative as that

Talon of yours." Her expression turned thoughtful. "But, we did get a better reaction than I'd dared hope for."

"Time will tell." Zofi surveyed the crowd, gaze sharp as ever. "I've already been told how 'surprisingly cultured' I am three times tonight, by nobles who looked shocked a Traveler could string a basic sentence together. Don't expect to fix everything overnight."

"Good thing we're in this for the long haul." Akeylah slipped her hand into Rozalind's, who squeezed her palm in reassurance.

Ren and Danton swept up, having just finished a dance, arms tangled around each other. "Queen Akeylah." Danton swept into a bow.

Akeylah's face heated. She didn't know if she'd ever grow accustomed to that.

Then again, perhaps it would be better if she didn't. If she ever got used to it, she might forget where she came from. A little Eastern nobody, who'd grown up under the thumb of a cruel step-father. Now she was the most powerful person in the Reaches— arguably in the world. It hurt her head to think it.

It hurt her heart to even consider forgetting the long, hard road she walked to get here.

"Ambassador. Sister." Akeylah smiled. Glanced back and forth between him and Ren. "Are you ready for your journey?" Ren and Danton planned to leave the next morning, to ride out to the Eastern Reach and distribute funds and supplies to villages damaged by the war.

"Ready to start rebuilding Tarik?" Danton's expression sobered. "I've been waiting for this ever since the Seventh War ended. Your Majesty, I can't thank you enough—"

"Please, don't." She held up a palm. "Tarik was my home, too. Besides, as you say, this is long overdue." She glanced at her sister.

Ren smiled. "I couldn't agree more." She stepped away from Danton, and Akeylah unwound her arm from Rozalind's waist to embrace Ren quickly. "I know you'll hold down the fort just fine while I'm gone," Ren murmured against her neck.

"I'll try my best," Akeylah said.

Ren locked eyes with Rozalind over her shoulder and laughed. "Is she always this modest?"

Rozalind sighed. "Infuriatingly so, sometimes."

Zofi slapped both their backs. "Oh, calm down. You're related to me; you can't be that fragile."

Akeylah snorted. "What about you, sister? Are you itching to get back on the road again?" She followed Zofi's gaze across the rooftop, to a familiar figure in uniform. While she watched, Vidal caught Zofi's eye and beckoned her over. In the distance, another song started up, a faster-paced tune. "Or are you going to miss anything back here?" Akeylah added with an innocent flutter of her eyelashes.

"Hmm." Zofi scratched her chin in faux deliberation. "Yes and yes, I'd say." With that, she flashed Akeylah a wink and skipped toward the dance floor, into the arms of her Talon. Danton and Ren joined them, and Akeylah and Rozalind peeled off to the side, hands entwined.

"And you?" Rozalind asked, voice soft. "Are you ready for what comes next?"

Akeylah leaned her head against Rozalind's shoulder. Glanced down at their clasped hands, then out at the dancers spinning through the gardens. "Right now, I feel ready for anything."

✻ 34 ✻

Zofi

Zofi pulled Akeylah into a tight embrace. "I'll be back as soon as the cures are delivered." Her mother's friends had begun distributing the crop potions last week, but the more bands they could recruit to help, the faster this would go. Zofi planned to deliver one round of potions to her band, then ride out to some of the more remote areas of the Western Reach to request assistance from the smaller bands who'd be dotting that region this time of year.

"Be careful." Akeylah released her and stepped back to survey the supplies she'd forced upon Zofi.

More than Zofi needed, if you asked her—a fully stocked saddlebag, complete with a brand-new tent, hunting supplies, fishing tackle, and enough food to last her a month. Not to mention, of course, the crop potions. Phials upon phials of the stuff, encased in blown glass just like boosts.

Zofi had taught the agricultural guild how to blow glass to contain the sensitive liquid, since it preserved the potions most effectively. She also carried instructions on brewing the cure, which she'd distribute to every town she passed on her route. It was a complicated recipe, but there would be some eager young alchemists here and there, she knew, who could take a shot at producing more of the stuff.

"With all this, I'd better be careful," Zofi said. "I'm liable to get robbed the minute I ride out of the city gate."

Akeylah groaned. "I wish you'd let me send a Talon with you. You won't accept any escort? Even just one?" Her grin widened a little too much for Zofi's liking.

"For the last time, I'm doing this alone. Unless you want to *command* me otherwise, sister." Zofi arched a brow, challenging.

Akeylah backed down, though not without a disapproving harrumph. "It's your choice, Ambassador."

That title would take some getting used to. Zofi reached up to tie her personal rucksack onto the saddlebag. The only things in it were the new boosts she'd crafted a few days ago. Just in case.

"I travel faster alone," Zofi replied without turning around.

After a beat, Akeylah sighed. "As you prefer. Thank you again, Zofi. The Reaches owe your people a great debt for all this."

"That's a debt I plan to cash in, next time an issue arises in the regional council meetings that affects my people."

"In that case, I can't wait until your return." Akeylah beamed. "I do love watching Ambassador Ghoush turn purple...."

"I'll do my best," Zofi promised, laughing.

But half an hour later, as she rode across the north gate out of Kolonya City, she wondered if Akeylah might have had a point about Zofi needing an escort. Because behind her came the sound of hooves, the huff of a horse at full gallop. Adrenaline spiked in her veins. She grasped her longknife, drew it, and whipped around just in time to watch Vidal careen across the bridge over the River Leath.

She circled her horse around and watched him ride.

He did look handsome in the early morning sunlight, dressed in a simple cotton shirt, halfway open, and plain trousers. No uniform. His hair was a messy tangle, as though he'd just flung himself out of bed. Only the clawed hilt of the sword at his side gave him away.

"This is familiar," Vidal panted when he reached her. "Me chasing you down."

She grinned, remembering the first time he'd stopped her leaving Kolonya City. "At least I didn't steal the horse this time."

"Zofi, please, let me come with you."

"Like that?" She glanced at his empty saddle. All he'd brought was a sword.

"If I need to, yes."

She sighed. Circled her horse close to his, until their knees touched. "What does your commander say about you riding off like this?"

"It doesn't matter. I'll quit the Talons." He reached for her hand. Drew her in, both leaning in their saddles until their faces hovered a breath apart.

"No, you won't." Gently, she untangled her hand from his. Cupped his cheek instead, and rested her forehead against his. In the back of her mind, she heard his words, the last time they were on the road together. *For as long as I could remember, I wanted to*

337

serve Kolonya. "Your place is here, Vidal. Being one small piece of something greater, remember? I won't let you give that up for me."

"I can do both. Serve the Talons and aid your mission. You're an ambassador now, you'd be entitled to a Talon escort if you asked for one." He slid his hand around the back of her neck, tilted his head. "I could stay with you." Their lips brushed together.

This time, when he kissed her, it was soft. Slow. The fire didn't leap through her, but kindled slowly. Built and built until she'd run her hands through his hair, gripped tight and parted her mouth to kiss him back, burning inside.

Already she missed this. His touch, his scent, his kisses. *Him.*

But when they parted, she forced a smile. "You wouldn't be able to truly commit to either me or the Talons if you split your loyalties like that. I can't do that to you. You're the kind of Talon Kolonya needs, Vidal." Her smile ached at the edges, just like her heart. This was harder than she thought it would be. "Frankly," she added, "I know you'll do a lot more good here than you would gallivanting through the desert with me."

Deep down, she knew this was the right decision. Even if it hurt.

Their horses shifted under them, antsy. Vidal stilled his. Looked away. She pretended not to notice the pain in his eyes. "I love you, Zofi," he told the grass under their feet. Unable to look at her.

Her throat ached. She made herself grin. "Don't be so dramatic." But her eyes must have given her away, because when he met them, he smiled, too.

"I guess we both understand loyalty now, hmm?"

She laughed, remembering their first argument in the streets of Kolonya. Both of them shouting about who understood loyalty best. "I guess we do."

He kissed her, one last time, and it reminded her all over again what she'd be leaving behind. Fire that sizzled along her nerves, crying for *more*. They drew apart, her breath came short, and every part of her body ached with desire.

"Goodbye, Zofi," he murmured.

She shook her head. Grinned. "I'll see you around, Vidal."

❄

Fiddle music swept through the camp. Zofi collapsed against a bench, breathless after her eighth dance in a row. Across the flickering bonfire, she caught sight of Elex and Ora, lips locked in a kiss. She smiled to herself and glanced away. No unpleasant sting of jealousy accompanied the sight. She felt only happiness, for his sake. Elex deserved that kind of joy after everything he'd been through.

Opposite the flames from him, Mother was holding court. She listened to a pair of newer members ask questions about the crop cures. The band planned to divide in the morning—Norren and Rull would lead a group to the far west, Mother would lead another to the towns along the Western and Central border, and Zofi would take the remainder into the swamplands south of here, dotted with tiny secluded towns most Kolonyans didn't even know existed.

Zofi wanted to be sure those encampments got the cure, too, same as any larger settlement.

Tomorrow would begin a long few weeks of travel. Navigating boggy terrain on oft-outdated maps, since villages in this region tended to shift with the tidal marshes they lived on.

Tonight, however, they celebrated. Not only did the band toast Zofi's return, albeit a temporary one. They also reveled in their new status. They were an official Reach now, with an ambassador of their own. A voice.

It wouldn't change everything overnight. It would be a long road to get to the future Zofi imagined, where her people were treated just like any other citizen in the Reaches. But this was the start.

"Ambassador."

She started. Turned to find Norren standing beside the log she was reclining on. Zofi laughed. "You don't need to call me that, Norren."

"I know." He grinned. "But I'd like to speak to you in your official capacity, so I figured I'd use the official title."

Her eyebrows rose. "Of course. What is it?"

"Well." He paused. Then he drew a piece of paper from his back pocket and unfolded it. He'd written a list as long as her arm, she realized, in cramped handwriting that made her eyes ache just to squint at it. "I have some suggestions I'd like to make."

She snorted. "Just a few?"

He plopped onto the log beside her. "This is the preliminary list," he assured her with a wink. "Things you ought to bring to the attention of this council you're on."

Zofi set aside the mug of Heine's moonshine she'd been about to start on. "I'm all ears, Norren."

As the night progressed, more and more people drifted her direction. Eventually, about halfway through Norren's neverending list of suggestions, others joined in, shouting changes to his ideas, adding thoughts of their own.

By the time Zofi looked up to see the fire dying, she realized she'd accumulated as big an audience as her mother normally would. This time, though, Mother knelt with the crowd at Zofi's feet, a broad smile on her face as she watched her daughter lead.

That night, well after Essex set, when they finally called it a night, Mother stopped Zofi on her way to her new tent, the one Akeylah had given her.

"I'm proud of you," Mother said.

"For what?" Zofi asked, joking. "I didn't play my cards right; I didn't win the throne."

"No," Mother admitted. "You didn't win. You did something better." She squeezed Zofi's shoulder. "You changed the whole game."

ACKNOWLEDGMENTS

Readers: If you made it this far, thank you for sticking with Akeylah, Ren, and Zofi to the end of their journeys. Watching so many of you venture into the world of *Rule* and fall in love with these sisters has been an absolute dream come true. As a friend said, "It's like all these readers have visited the inside of your brain now." I hope you enjoyed the trip, because I certainly loved sharing this story with you!

But it takes more than just one writer to bring a book (or two) to life. This series wouldn't exist without my wonderful teams at Alloy and Little, Brown, and I owe a huge debt of gratitude to everyone at both companies.

Thank you to the Alloy crew: Annie Stone for this initial idea; Joelle Hobeika and Joshua Bank for championing it; Eliza Swift and Hayley Wagreich for keeping it moving; Sara Shandler for her assistance all along; Romy Golan for helping it reach foreign markets; and Viana Siniscalchi for expertly taking the helm of this project, and for talking me off the ledge when the sophomore book fears hit hard.

Thank you to everyone at Little, Brown: Hannah Milton for all of her tireless help in every area; Kristina Pisciotta for fielding one million and more publicity questions; everyone at NOVL for getting the word out about *Rule*; the LBYR marketing crew—Jennifer McClelland-Smith, Emilie Polster, and Valerie Wong—for making sure this series found its way into the hands of our readers; Annie McDonnell, Allie Singer, and Brandy Colbert for ensuring every word on the pages is right; Virginia Lawther for making *Rise* a beautiful final book; Marcie Lawrence for her fantastic cover art (I didn't think she could top book one's cover, but I love this one even more); Alvina Ling, Megan Tingley, and Jackie Engel for giving this duology the green light; and Pam Gruber for falling in love with *Rule* in the first place, as well as for her whip-smart edits that made *Rise* a (hopefully!) worthy follow-up.

Thank you to everyone else who helped make *Rule* a success: to the booksellers, librarians, and teachers who championed it; to my fellow Electric Eighteens and the panelists who coaxed me through my first few public appearances; to Zoraida Córdova for her help with my launch party; to my family and friends for spamming *their* families and friends with book news; and to everyone who read and shared this series with others.

As always, a huge thank-you to my agent, Bridget Smith, for being my sounding board and voice of reason, and for championing all my many diverging projects.

For this book in particular, I also need to thank the generous souls who allowed me to crash on/in their various couches/spare rooms/floors/basements while I wrote/edited/panicked about revisions:

Kris and Dale: thank you for opening your home to me, and for giving me a place to relax in between bouncing all over the country. FYI, readers, you have Kris to thank for bribing me with chocolates in order to revive Ren.

Tricia and Shelby: I'm glad I was able to spend time with you in LA. Even through trying circumstances, your respective optimism and pragmatism was inspiring, and our catch-up was long overdue!

Kevin and Melanie: it was great to explore your new city together. Thank you for providing a quiet haven right when I needed one to sort through my second round of edits.

Emily: I owe you for once again being the responsible fur-baby parent. Miss you, and I hope all four of you are enjoying it up there north of the wall.

Eva, Shunan, Allison, and the MerYork peeps: cheers for saving me space on your couches. Someday when I'm a real adult again, I promise to return the favor.

Meraki: especially the Ubud crew who kept me company as I wrote the first draft of *Rise*, and the Dublisbon squad who were there for my final edits—I couldn't do this living-out-of-a-suitcase thing without you all. Thank you for your endless support, and for letting me derail our group chats with book news far too often.